TARGET PART TWO: THE TAKEDOWN

RICKY BLACK

MAILING LIST

If you want more information regarding upcoming releases, or updates about new content on my site, sign up to my mailing list at the end of this book - You'll even receive a novella, absolutely free.

CONTENTS

Prologue	1
Chapter 1	3
Chapter 2	12
Chapter 3	26
Chapter 4	43
Chapter 5	54
Chapter 6	65
Chapter 7	76
Chapter 8	87
Chapter 9	106
Chapter 10	122
Chapter 11	140
Chapter 12	151
Chapter 13	161
Chapter 14	168
Chapter 15	178
Chapter 16	188
Chapter 17	199
Chapter 18	216
Chapter 19	226
Chapter 20	235
Chapter 21	245
Chapter 22	258
Chapter 23	266
Epilogue	275
Did you enjoy the read?	277
Target Part 3 Preview	279
24. Chapter One	280
Also by Ricky Black	289
Read Blood and Business	291
About Ricky Black	293

PROLOGUE
TUESDAY 15 OCTOBER, 2013

THE STREETS OF HULME, Manchester, were deathly quiet, a rattling wind shuffling the sparse tree leaves. Only a few faces were out; kids in parkas and hooded tops mooching around, spitting on the floor and talking in loud voices. They were unaware they were being watched.

A car at the bottom of the street idled with its lights off. The passenger, a brawny dark-skinned man with closely cropped hair and scarred features, turned to the driver.

'Are we gonna have a problem?'

The driver shook his head. He was a dreadlocked killer known as *K-Bar* on the streets of Leeds. He tugged on a pair of weathered leather gloves. Both criminals wore black jackets, combat trousers and plain black trainers. He stifled a yawn, a gun resting on his lap. In the dark car, it was hard to see the livid bags under his eyes.

'The right people know what we're doing.' K-Bar cocked the gun. 'We're gonna go through the back, nice and quiet.'

Grimer nodded. Black balaclavas securing their faces, they moved. The youths glanced at them but didn't speak. In silence, they made their way to the back of a terraced house, Grimer keeping a lookout while K-Bar broke in. They checked their weapons and padded through the living room, silenced guns at the ready.

Grimer approached the stairs, K-Bar covering as he tested the steps for any noise. They ascended, searching each room. Approaching the master bedroom, they saw a flash before gunfire ensued. K-Bar ducked, Grimer following his lead. The gun smoke made it hard to see, but they had been in similar situations before, and their movements were fluid. The shooter's aim was off, but they needed to be quick. Police were likely en route.

'Cover me!' K-Bar yelled, rolling into the bedroom. Grimer rose from his position, firing multiple shots in the shooter's direction. K-Bar spotted the muzzle spray and picked his shots carefully. He hit the shooter, who dropped with a scream. Hurrying towards the prone frame, he kicked the gun away, training his own on the shooter. The shooter wheezed, staring up at the figures, unable to recognise them.

Grimer moved to flick on the bedroom light. They surveyed Brownie, gritting his teeth in obvious pain. They hadn't seen him since he'd fled Leeds after almost killing Lamont. His frame remained stocky, but his face seemed thinner. Living on the run hadn't agreed with him.

'You're lucky we don't have time to get deep,' K-Bar snarled. 'We took out your shit crew. Marrion's gone, and Antonio squealed like a bitch when we put him down. You're the one we wanted, though.'

'I don't give a damn. I ain't a punk,' growled Brownie, eyes watering from pain, blood trickling from his shoulder down to his t-shirt.

'Yeah, you are. You tried getting a kid to do your runnings, and you really thought you and that clown you worked for were gonna run our thing?' K-Bar laughed, Grimer chuckling in his booming voice.

'Fuck you. Go to hell.' Brownie spat on the floor.

'Let's forget the talking then. You can hold this for *Teflon*.' K-Bar fired, shooting Brownie twice in the head.

CHAPTER ONE
MONDAY 12 JANUARY, 2015

IT DIDN'T FEEL real for Shorty. He was being driven towards the Leeds streets he'd always known, yet felt more disconnected than ever. No music played, so he stared out of the window as Akeem drove in silence. He knew nothing about him, other than the fact he worked for Lamont. Akeem was probably around six feet tall, with a sculpted beard, short cropped hair and dark eyes. He'd shaken his hand, asked if he was okay, then said no more. He was in the zone. Shorty knew the type. He'd been around street people all of his life. He was sure there were hidden depths to Akeem; Lamont wouldn't have him around otherwise.

As the buildings and scenery melded into a blur, Shorty thought about Lamont. They hadn't seen one another in over a year, but he knew everything. Lamont's shooting shocked him, but not much. They were at war, and he'd been an unfortunate, near-fatal casualty of events. The streets were temptresses. They lured fools with promises of riches and fame, but Shorty had seen many close to him fall, none more so than Marcus Daniels.

Marcus, Shorty, and Lamont were like brothers. Marcus feared no one and took what he wanted from life. He and Shorty were formidable; they fought and even killed together. When Marcus was gunned down, he'd lost a part of himself. Everything that happened since had only added to that.

Shorty's eyes grew heavy. He tried to force himself to stay awake, but the car started to swim, his eyes drooping.

'We're here.'

A strong hand shook Shorty. He jolted awake, following Akeem up a short driveway. Akeem firmly knocked three times, then walked into the living room of a detached house. The walls were a refreshing cream colour, the furniture smoke-grey. On the sofa staring into space, was the man he'd come to see.

'You need anything?' Akeem asked. Lamont Jones shook his head.

'Not right now. I'll contact you shortly. Your time is yours until then.' Lamont didn't turn. Akeem nodded at Shorty and left. There was an awkward silence. Shorty examined the fixtures in the room. The layout was like Lamont's old house, but more colourful; fresh red and pink flowers, various plants and paintings of sunsets on the walls. He assumed this was down to Jenny's presence.

'Would you like a drink?' Lamont glanced at Shorty, who looked away after a moment. He had a habit of doing that; assessing a person until they confessed their deepest, darkest secrets.

'Brandy, if you've got it.'

Lamont headed to his drinks cabinet. He removed two glasses, then reached for a diamond-shaped bottle. Shorty's eyes were immediately drawn to it. Lamont noticed.

'You don't mind, do you?'

He shook his head. It was the drink they'd shared the night of Marcus's murder.

'That's fine.'

Lamont handed him a glass and sipped his own, closing his eyes.

'Don't tell Jen. I'm not supposed to be drinking.' He motioned to his stomach as he took another deep sip.

'Is she okay?' Shorty asked. It had never been so difficult talking to his friend. They hadn't always agreed, but they'd never struggled to communicate. Now, he felt like he was playing catch-up.

'She works a lot, trying to grow her business.'

Shorty dumbly stood, not knowing how to prolong the conversation. Lamont sat, motioning for him to do the same. He slid into an armchair, wishing he had a spliff, or a line of cocaine to make it all easier. He drank the cognac, savouring the unique taste.

'So . . . You're out then,' said Lamont. Shorty didn't reply. He didn't need to. It was still a surprise. One minute he was facing twenty years in prison for murder, stuck on remand. The next, the charges were dismissed, and he was free. Whatever that meant.

'Good looking out on them solicitors, man. They definitely earned their cash.'

'You don't have to thank me. I wasn't going to leave you languishing in there. I did everything I could to get you out.'

'I know, fam. I'm sorry that I wasn't around. When it happened.'

Another awkward silence engulfed the room. Marrion Bernette, a Manchester gangster with a grudge against Shorty and Lamont, had orchestrated his shooting. He and his team sought to divide them, sending shooters to end their lives. Shorty was forced to kill three people, and Lamont had been shot twice.

'You were running for your life. If you could have been there, I know you would have been. How are you feeling?'

The concern on Lamont's face touched him. He shrugged, noting how fragile Lamont appeared. His arms and shoulders looked thicker, but there was a haunted look in his once powerfully intelligent eyes.

'I feel disconnected, fam. Like I'm in my pad, looking at this shit through someone else's eyes. I thought I was gonna be in that cage for the rest of my life. I was prepared for that . . .'

'Amy's doing well. So is Grace.'

Shorty's heart soared at the mention of his daughter. He hadn't seen her since his arrest.

'Bet she's huge now.'

'Cheeky too. I tried giving Amy money on your behalf, but you know what she's like.'

Shorty did. Amy was wilful. It didn't shock him she hadn't taken his money.

'I'm gonna get myself cleaned up, then see them in a couple days. They still at the same house?'

'We can see them tomorrow.'

Shorty shook his head. 'I need clothes, and my hair's all fucked up—'

'Everything you need is in the spare room upstairs. We can stop at Trinidad's first thing if you wanna get lined up.'

Shorty genuinely smiled for the first time in forever.

'You still always think of everything.'

'That'll never change, Shorty. You're more than welcome to stay until you get yourself sorted. Jen's fine with it.'

Shorty doubted that. He and Jenny had never cared for one another, and in her position, he wouldn't want a murderous thug around.

'It's cool, I'll go lay at one of my older spots. Thanks, though.'

Lamont led him upstairs, pointing to a door.

'Your clothing is on the bed. I guessed at sizes. There's a connecting bathroom, so take your time. You should have everything you need.'

Shorty thanked him. The room had a similar cream decor to downstairs, and a rich, white bedspread. On the bed were two pairs of black jeans, a pair of trainers, shirts, and t-shirts, along with other bits and pieces. There was a thick envelope at the top, resting on the pillow. He opened it, glancing at the stacks of notes. Tossing it back on the bed, he went to take a shower.

Lamont leafed through a book when he re-entered the room.

'You found everything?'

'Yeah, boss. Good looking out for that cash. I'll pay you back when I'm on my feet.'

Lamont waved him off. 'We're brothers. Consider it a portion of your cut. You must be starving. Let's get some food, and I'll bring you up to speed.'

———

JENNY'S FINGERS lingered on the laptop keyboard as she stared into space. The hairs on the back of her neck bristled. She shook her head, trying to shake the visions plaguing her. She needed to concentrate on the email she was sending. It was an opportunity to lift her dwindling business from near closure, and she had to make the most of it.

'Can I get you a drink, Jen?'

Jenny shook her head. Nadia had been with her for years. She'd had more staff, but was forced to let them go when business dried up. She'd built her business from scratch, establishing a name and a certain reliability that her clients respected. That went downhill when her partner, Lamont Jones, was shot outside her house the previous year. She'd cradled his body, sure he was dead. The aftermath was a blur. Jenny recalled K-Bar, one of Lamont's soldiers, telling her everything would be okay, assigning men to guard her. She'd practically lived at the hospital, eating little, watching as the love of her life underwent multiple operations. She had been a quivering wreck; sure someone would come and finish the job.

Jenny had taken an extended leave of absence from her florist business, leaving Nadia in charge. The poor girl had done her best, but too much was going on, and the customers left in droves. By the time she was back on her feet, the business was on its last legs. She assumed control, but it seemed an uphill battle. She needed to bring the clients back, and she was struggling to think what to do.

A company had contacted her yesterday, requesting a large order for a charity benefit. Sensing she was desperate, they weren't offering much money, but it was a good cause, and she needed the positive publicity. Nadia closed her office door. Jenny sighed. Lamont had offered to put money into the business, but she'd turned him down.

After leaving the hospital, it devastated him to learn about the state of her business. Insisting it was all his fault, he begged her to let him be involved, claiming he could get his business partner Martin Fisher to help her. She refused, insisting she could do it herself.

Lamont left her to it and focused on the business of getting stronger. He went to the gym as soon as the doctor allowed it, hiring a personal trainer and pushing himself harder than both Jenny and his doctors had liked. He moved them to a new house and tried to buy her a new car, determined not to let his injuries sideline him, insisting he was okay.

And so, she let him believe it. She pretended she couldn't see him sometimes wincing when he moved too quickly. She pretended she couldn't smell liquor when he would come to bed. They were both trying to find their way back, neither knowing how. For the past few months, they had stumbled through.

Lately, he seemed tenser. He insisted he was stressed with business, but Jenny didn't know if it was that simple. It was dark outside by the time she locked up her premises and climbed into her ride. She wanted nothing more than a long bath when she got home. Lamont's car wasn't in the drive, so she entered the house, running a bath, pouring various oils and soaps into the piping hot water.

When the bath was set, she warmed up some spaghetti from the night before, forcing it down along with two glasses of white wine. She grabbed a book she'd started reading, lit a candle, and sank into the bath with a sigh of relief, distracted from her mounting issues for a short while.

―――――

'BRING ME UP TO SPEED THEN.'

Lamont sipped his wine, weighing up his words. They had gone to a restaurant in Garforth, fancying a longer drive. The place was packed, with low lighting, black leather chairs, and mahogany tables. Lamont was already on his second glass, Shorty sticking to water. They'd ordered steaks, sitting in silence until now.

'We took some hits. When I got shot, everything was up in the air.'

'What about the money side of it? You had Chink running it, so didn't that fall to pieces after he got slotted?' Shorty asked. Years back, he would have been animated, wanting the drama. Now, he was merely curious.

'We had contingencies in place. I moved a lot of things around after we fell out over the Georgia thing.'

'Rapist bastard. I'm glad he's dead. Have you spoken to her?'

Lamont shook his head, his expression hardening.

'Why not?'

Lamont lowered his voice, though it was so loud with all the background conversations that it was impossible to overhear.

'She was grinding him.'

'Who was?' Shorty rubbed his eyebrow.

'Georgia. She was sleeping with Chink. For years.'

Shorty's eyes widened. 'How the hell do you know that?'

Lamont didn't reply. As he waited, comprehension dawned on his face.

'You didn't . . .'

Lamont sighed. 'I caught them kissing years back. I told Chink to end it, or I would. Thought he had, until Georgia told me everything.'

'And you never told Marcus?'

'Do you think Chink would have still been breathing if I had?' Lamont finished his drink, ordering another.

'What about K-Bar? He tried to come see me while I was inside, but I wouldn't let him.'

'I heard. K did well steering the ship. He had everyone watching, waiting for him to fail. He stumbled a few times, but we made it through.'

Shorty sensed from Lamont's expression that there was more unsaid. Certain things seemed off with him. He'd put it down to his accident, but he wasn't sure. His friend seemed on edge, and Shorty wondered why. Their food arrived, and both men ate in silence. Shorty sprinkled extra salt and black pepper on the steak and began to tuck in. He hadn't been hungry until now, but his appetite had returned with a vengeance.

'Maka was worried about you getting out.'

'Why?'

Maka was one of Lamont's lieutenants. He worked with his friend, Manson, making good money for the team. He and Shorty had always been cool.

'The Timmy situation. He was worried that you might have something to say about it.' Lamont was being careful with his words. He watched Shorty sag, the devastation palpable.

Timmy Turner was Shorty's younger cousin. Desperate to walk a mile in his shoes, he'd allowed himself to be manipulated into turning on them. He set up Shorty to be murdered by Marrion's shooters and had held a gun on Lamont. He couldn't pull the trigger, though and had been murdered by Maka in the aftermath.

'Maka did what he had to do. Tim made his choice. I should have shown him a better way,' Shorty mumbled. They continued to eat, listening to the soft lounge music playing in the background. They were primarily surrounded by families enjoying their meals, laughing and joking. Shorty wondered why the atmosphere between them was so strained. They had been friends since they were five-years-old, yet they were making stilted conversation, as if they didn't know how to be around each other anymore.

'Why are you still here?'

Lamont glanced at him.

'Pardon?'

'Why are you still doing this? Why are you still in the life when you said you were walking away?'

Lamont looked at his friend for a long moment before replying.

'Things change.'

'What does that mean?'

TARGET PART TWO: THE TAKEDOWN

Lamont reached for his wallet. 'Let's pay the bill. Stay the night, and we'll sort everything tomorrow.'

Shorty's brow furrowed. He wiped his mouth, watching Lamont hand a black card to the waitress, genially making small talk. He wondered if it was all an act. The waitress giggled, tossing her hair back as he spoke. Shorty needed to work out what was going on. There was something he wasn't being told.

A red Mercedes was parked in the driveway when they arrived home. Lamont parked next to it, and the pair made their way inside. He flicked a switch, and the pitch-black hallway filled with light. Shorty followed him to the living room, watching his friend go straight to the drinks cabinet. He took out the cognac from earlier, pouring some into a glass as Shorty observed.

'You can sleep in the room where you found your clothes. We'll talk in the morning.'

Lamont slapped his hand. As Shorty headed up the stairs, he watched him heading towards another room, clutching the bottle, his shoulders slumped.

CHAPTER TWO

TUESDAY 13 JANUARY, 2015

SHORTY RUBBED his eyes as he clambered from bed the following day. He audibly yawned and stretched, feeling his bones creak. His sleep had been poor. The bed was comfortable, but Shorty's mind refused to shut down. He was nervous about seeing Grace, and about what to do next. The talk with Lamont had been brief, and he'd been vague about what was going on in the streets. He hoped Lamont had a plan.

Shorty had wanted to write to Grace when he was on remand, but shame kept him from putting pen to paper. He couldn't explain where he had been. There was so much to work on, and he needed to be on point.

Lamont's behaviour worried him. He'd always liked a drink, but he couldn't recall seeing him indulge with such abandon. There was a sadness that Shorty couldn't put his finger on, but he would get to the bottom of it.

After a shower, he dressed and headed downstairs, his stomach rumbling. He made his way to the kitchen, pausing when he saw Jenny already sitting at the table, drinking a cup of coffee. She glanced up.

'Hey.'

TARGET PART TWO: THE TAKEDOWN

'Hi. Sorry, didn't mean to disturb you.'

'Don't be silly. L mentioned you might stay a few days.' Jenny appraised him and signalled to her cup. 'Do you want one?'

He nodded.

'Sit down and I'll make it for you.'

He slid into a wooden chair, watching Jenny pouring coffee from a fancy-looking coffee maker. She checked how he took it, adding milk and sugar.

'It must be weird for you, being out and about,' she remarked.

'Yeah, it is.'

'I'm sorry, I didn't mean to pry. L's still sleeping. Guessing you made a night of it?'

'We went for dinner, then came home.'

Jenny's brow furrowed. 'Oh, I just thought . . . He didn't come to bed until . . .' She shrugged. Shorty took the cup with thanks, unsure how to prolong the conversation.

'How is he doing?'

'What do you mean?' She blinked.

'L. Is he okay?'

Jenny smiled.

'It's hard to tell sometimes. He keeps a lot to himself. I don't think he's sleeping well. Ever since.' She paused. 'Ever since the accident, I think he sees things differently. Like he's trying to find his place.'

'I know how that feels,' Shorty admitted. He sipped the coffee, nourishing the spike of energy the caffeine gave him.

'You know it's his birthday tomorrow, right?'

Shorty had forgotten.

'Is he doing anything?'

'I wanted to throw him a party, but he refused. I was going to take him to dinner. You should come.'

'Nah, you two go. You don't need me around.'

'Don't be silly. L will want you there. I'll make the arrangements.' She made to leave the room.

'Jenny?'

13

She turned.

'Are you alright?'

Jenny stared for a moment before nodding.

'I'm fine, Shorty. I'm going to work, so I'll talk to you later. Help yourself to whatever you need.' She lingered for a moment, then left.

―――

LAMONT'S EYES SHIFTED OPEN, and he immediately stifled a groan. Sitting up, he massaged his temples and checked the time. It was after ten. Jenny's side was empty. She would already be at work. Showering, he dressed in a black shirt, jeans and boots. He reached for his phone and headed downstairs to hunt for caffeine. To his surprise, Shorty sat in the kitchen, an empty cup of coffee resting in front of him.

'Hey,' said Lamont, not wanting to disturb him.

'You good?'

'Yeah. Did you find everything alright?'

Shorty nodded. 'Jen went to work.'

'She leaves early. I'm surprised you're up. I thought I'd have to fling water at you to get you up.'

Shorty grinned. 'I didn't sleep well.'

'Wasn't the bed comfortable?'

'Course it was. I just couldn't settle. Guess I'm nervous.'

'It's fine to be nervous.'

'Not for me it isn't.'

Lamont grabbed a cup from a cupboard.

'Nor me.'

He made coffee, Shorty declining a second cup. He remained standing, holding the steaming mug with both hands.

'We need to talk about your future.'

'There's a lot we need to talk about.'

'Like?' Lamont watched him again.

'Like, why you're up drinking at all hours of the night? What

TARGET PART TWO: THE TAKEDOWN

happened to the L that used to wake up at 5 am every morning, rain or shine?'

'You're looking for problems where there aren't any.' Lamont ignored his question.

'Am I?'

'Yes, you are. Think about Grace and Grace only. She needs you.'

Shorty had nothing to say to that. He would re-address it another time.

'Do you think I need to bring her a present?'

Lamont shook his head. 'I think she'll just be glad to see you. You can always take her shopping.'

WHEN THEY WERE READY, Lamont called Akeem, and they piled into a black Mercedes 4x4. Shorty settled into the leather seating, Lamont next to him. Akeem started the engine, and they rumbled towards Chapeltown.

Lamont stared ahead, but Shorty glanced out of the window all the way to Chapeltown like a child on a school trip, taking in all the changes. For the longest time, he had lived and breathed the streets, but now he felt out of touch. As they drove up Chapeltown Road, though, he saw a few old faces, still posted up, doing the same thing.

Akeem parked near the barbers. He stuck close to Lamont, his eyes flitting in all directions. Shorty admired his skills. He stayed sharp.

The door clanged to announce their entrance. A few people sat around waiting for cuts. Loud reggae music blared from the system, a loud argument about football competing with the track. The oldest man in the room broke into a smile when he saw the trio. Turning off the shaver he held, he put it down and wiped his hands, then firmly shook Lamont's hand.

'Good to see you, L.'

'You too, Trinidad.'

'Shorty, it's good to see you out, son.' He shook Shorty's hand next before greeting Akeem.

'Thanks, Trinidad. How's tricks?'

Trinidad scratched the back of his neck. 'Old age, man. Joints are stiff with all that arthritis, and that there settling in. I'm still living, though, so I cannot complain.'

Shorty grinned. He'd known Trinidad since he was a kid. A lot of the youths chilled at his barber shop back in the day. He would give free haircuts if he knew you didn't have the money, more concerned with helping people than making a profit. This generosity led to him nearly losing his shop. Lamont stepped in, lent him the money to pay his debts, then invested money into dragging the barbers into the 21st Century. All of a sudden, he owned the barbers, but kept everything the same and made sure Trinidad felt important, which he was.

They settled into their seats, and Shorty spoke with a few faces he recognised. Their words were friendly, but he saw from their shifty eyes they didn't trust him.

'Oi, Trinidad,' One of them started. 'Any word on the next meeting?'

Trinidad shook his head. 'Should find out in the next few days. Stop by here, and I'll let you know.'

'What meeting?' Shorty asked.

'Ask L. He'll tell you all about it.'

Shorty frowned, unsure why Trinidad was being cagey. He let it go and told the man what he wanted. After Trinidad trimmed his hair, he cleaned himself in the bathroom, then they said their goodbyes. The sky darkened as they packed into the ride. He ran his hands through his shortened hair, clicking his seatbelt into place.

'Does Amy know that I'm out?'

Lamont hesitated. Shorty sighed.

'This is gonna be fun.'

TARGET PART TWO: THE TAKEDOWN

SHORTY TOOK a deep breath as they pulled onto the familiar Oakwood Street. The same cars were parked as if he'd never been away. He climbed from the ride, wishing he'd consumed more liquor. This visit would have been easier if he was drunk.

The last time Shorty had been on this street, he'd clutched a bloody gun. He'd demanded to see Grace, knowing the police were after him for the murders of the Manchester contingent. He'd argued with Amy, his daughter's mother. She'd almost let him in, but her boyfriend called the police. They came for him, but not before he'd clocked her boyfriend in the head with his gun. He'd evaded them long enough to ditch the gun and his gloves. The police caught him, but hadn't found the incriminating weapon. Shorty would make sure they never did.

Lamont hung back, letting him take the lead. Akeem watched from the car as Shorty knocked on the front door.

'Shorty?'

His breath caught in his throat. Many a night in his cell, he'd fantasised about the fiery redhead currently staring open-mouthed. Her misty green eyes still entranced him, her figure as trim as it had always been. He forced himself to meet her gaze.

'Hey, Ames. Is Grace in?'

'When did you get out?' Amy ignored his question.

'The other day. Is she in?'

'You couldn't have given me some warning? You can't just—' Amy spoke to Lamont now. Tutting, Shorty manoeuvred around her and went to the living room. Amy called after him, but he ignored her. The channel was set to the news. The heating was on, and the room had a toasty feel. In the corner, writing at a desk, sat Grace Turner.

Shorty stared at his little girl, his heart about to explode. Feeling eyes on her, Grace looked up, gazing at her father. For the longest moment, they both stared. Amy and Lamont paused in the doorway, tentatively watching the moment. Shorty's eyes blurred, but he didn't wipe the tears away. Grace's lip trembled. Then, she ran out of the room.

'Grace!' Amy hurried after her. Lamont watched as Shorty stood, shoulders slumping.

'Give her time, bro. It'll still be raw.'

Shorty nodded dumbly, wanting to burst into tears. He yearned to hold Grace and tell her everything would be okay. She didn't even want to be around him, though, and that was tough to stomach.

After a few minutes, Amy came back into the living room.

'Is she okay?'

'She will be,' Amy's voice was ice cold. 'You're out then? For good?'

'They dropped The charges. Can I see her?'

'She needs to adjust.'

'I just wanna see her. Please, Ames.' Shorty hated the pleading tone in his voice.

'Shorty, she needs time. You have to understand that she hasn't seen you in over a year. Do you know what she has seen? The papers calling you a murderer. Police searching the house; for drugs, for guns. You need to give her time.'

He swallowed, his posture stooped, arms slack by his sides.

'Can we talk, Ames?'

'I'll never keep you from having a relationship with your daughter, but we have nothing else to say to each other. I think you need to leave,' Amy's eyes flickered to Lamont. 'Both of you.'

———

Shorty didn't speak as they made their way back from Amy's. He had expected resistance from Grace, but he hadn't expected her to run away. Lamont had patted him on the shoulder as they climbed into the car, but that was it. He hadn't tried to counsel Shorty, and he appreciated that.

'L, K-Bar called. He wants a meet.'

Lamont flicked his eyes to him. 'Are you up for it?'

Shorty nodded, hoping his old friend could distract him.

TARGET PART TWO: THE TAKEDOWN

K-Bar waited outside a house on Leopold Street. He climbed into the ride.

'Fucking hell, Shorty. I knew you were getting out, but not so soon! What's going on?'

Shorty grinned at K-Bar's excitement. He had known Lamont longer, but he and K-Bar had struggled together, pitching weed out of a dirty flat, desperate to make money when no one else would give them a shot. When they'd begun running with Lamont, K-Bar played his position, working under Shorty and keeping the streets in line by any means necessary. He'd put on size since the last time Shorty had seen him, judging by how his biceps bulged against the navy blue hooded top he wore.

'You know what L's like about keeping secrets. I missed you, fam.'

It was K-Bar's turn to smile. 'I missed you too. Where are you staying? We need to go out tonight and show everyone you're back.'

Shorty looked to Lamont, expecting him to veto the idea, but his face was blank.

'Yeah, we can go out. You down, L?'

Lamont shrugged. 'I'll go for a few.'

'Won't Jenny mind?' Shorty asked. K-Bar shot him a confused look. Lamont's face remained the same.

'I doubt it. She wants to do something tomorrow night. I don't think she'll begrudge me having a few drinks. K, what's the situation?'

K-Bar's smile vanished. 'Hughesy came to see me. Doesn't want to buy from us anymore.'

'Did he say why?'

K-Bar shook his head. 'Just said he'd had a better offer. Summat's up, though. He looked nervous.'

'We can't force people to buy from us, K. We're not that kind of operation.'

'He's not the first, L. Three people alone have stopped doing business with us in the past two weeks.'

'We're still the best party in town. If we have to raise the price on the people dealing with us, we'll do that.'

K-Bar ran his hands through his dreadlocked hair.

'Is that the right thing to do?'

'Unless you know who they're all copping from, there isn't much to be done about it. It's not a problem at the moment. We have the best stuff on the market. Don't forget that.'

'Those fucking do-gooders, man. They're not making things any easier with their damn meetings,' K-Bar mumbled.

'What meetings?' Shorty asked, remembering Trinidad's earlier words.

K-Bar scowled. 'There's this new community thing. They call themselves the *OurHood* Initiative. They formed last year and started preaching about making changes on the streets.'

'Those types of dickheads have always been around.'

'Not like this, bro. They're growing all the time, proper well-funded and organised. Some poet prick is at the head of it. Can't remember his name, but people are acting like he's some future world leader.'

Shorty mulled over that. He'd known people over the years who claimed to have the best intentions for Chapeltown. They started collecting money, saying they would keep kids off the street and in youth clubs, but they never seemed to go anywhere.

———

'Do you really think that's a smart idea?'

Lamont watched Akeem as the bodyguard paced the hardwood floor of the safe house. Mindful of conducting business in the home, he had a spot he went to whenever he needed to talk. It was scanned for listening devices daily and monitored to prevent surveillance. After they had left K-Bar, Shorty decided to stay at his own place. Lamont knew he was upset over Grace's reaction, but he needed to wait it out. Once the shock wore off, Lamont believed she would want to spend time with him again.

TARGET PART TWO: THE TAKEDOWN

'It's necessary. We need to root out who is working against us, and playing dumb is the best way.'

'I understand that,' replied Akeem, 'but why not bring K-Bar in on it? He's already operating from a position of weakness. You know the messes he's endured.'

K-Bar had taken charge when Lamont was in hospital, but he was a soldier, and people both in and out of the organisation tried to take advantage of that.

K-Bar was a logical thinker but not a diplomat. An argument with a small-timer who wanted to make a name for themselves led to him shooting him in the leg. The man threatened to press charges, but it had been smoothed over.

'You're right, Akeem. I do, but this is better. The less he knows, the more convincing it looks. How is that other thing going?'

'I've got my best people on it. We'll find something. Are you sure it's smart to go out tonight?'

'A few drinks won't hurt. Make sure one of your people is amongst the crowd. I don't want any surprises. I need you on call.'

Akeem nodded. Lamont drank his gin and tonic in silence. The team was still making money, but it felt less secure than in the past. Every day it seemed new crews were starting up, trying to get their piece of the money pie by any means necessary. He'd aided K-Bar in getting things back in order, but was reluctant to divulge his full attention to regulating the streets. There was so much going on at the moment that he was playing catch-up. Having Shorty back could free him up, but he was fresh out of prison. The authorities would be furious that he had slipped through their fingers. They were likely watching him, and by extension, Lamont too. He finished the drink and wiped his mouth.

'Take me home, please.'

SHORTY QUIETLY SIPPED HIS DRINK, sitting in the VIP section of an exclusive club near Call Lane. Lamont, K-Bar and Maka surrounded him, sipping champagne. Lamont insisted on fitting the bill, and so far, he'd paid for everything, from transport, to the overly expensive bottles in the clubs.

Maka kept his eyes on the crowd, not looking in his direction. The pair greeted one another coolly, but hadn't spoken beyond that. Shorty asked K-Bar where Blakey was, only to be told he'd moved on. When he questioned why, K-Bar admitted they hadn't seen eye to eye, and had left it at that. His dreadlocked friend was grinning, trying to get the attention of several barely dressed females, with little success.

Shorty glanced at Lamont, clutching his champagne with a faraway look on his face. He'd noticed how distracted he had looked the entire time they'd been out, but it was pointless trying to get him to talk. He would need to do some digging around on his own. As Shorty watched, Lamont seemed to come out of some trance. He stood, holding his glass aloft.

'Gents, hold up your glasses, and let's toast to the little thug we all know and love, fresh out of prison, and ready to do his thing.'

They all toasted, their glasses clinking as Shorty grinned, despite himself. All day, he'd been thinking about Grace. Deciding to loosen up, he finished his drink and made his way out to the dance floor. VIP was cool, but he felt like an idiot sitting around as people gawped. K-Bar followed. Maka stayed.

'Maka, you need to talk to him and bury this,' Lamont said. He nodded, but didn't move.

'It's not that easy. I shot his family.'

Lamont understood his position; Timmy had held a gun on him the day he'd been shot, and although he ultimately couldn't shoot, Maka hadn't known this when he arrived at the scene.

'You saw a threat, and you reacted accordingly. Shorty would have done the same thing, and he knows that. Trust me, bury this early and don't let it fester.'

Maka nodded again, but seemed more animated now. Slapping his hand, he left the corded-off VIP section, leaving Lamont alone with his thoughts. He watched K-Bar converse with a few females,

TARGET PART TWO: THE TAKEDOWN

gesticulating wildly as he spoke. He seemed to be keeping his distance, though, as if going through the motions. Tonight was about distracting himself as much as Shorty, yet he felt more distracted than ever.

'Yo, can I approach, *boss*?'

A voice snapped him out of his reverie. A man hovered near the VIP partition as a burly bouncer glared at him. He was light-skinned, with cropped hair and a slit in his left eyebrow. He wore a chain almost bigger than him, leaning slightly forward. A short distance behind him stood two men, watching his back.

'Nikkolo, how have you been?' Lamont nodded to the bouncer, who let him through.

'I'm good, man. Just sampling some of these ladies in here. You need to get out there and make summat happen, bro!'

Lamont smiled tightly. 'My lady wouldn't approve.'

'What she doesn't know won't hurt her. Anyway, how's business on your side?'

'Everything is fine,' Lamont replied, his tone neutral.

'I heard people are leaving your camp.' Nikkolo's eyes danced with glee as he spoke, but he couldn't get a reaction from Lamont.

'I don't get caught up in rumours. Say hi to your boss for me.' Lamont shook his hand, then left the VIP section. He didn't notice him glaring at his back.

Lamont made his way to K-Bar, still surrounded by women. The space was cramped, people moving and dancing all around. One of the women, a slim Asian woman with short black hair, smiled at him. He smiled back, not wanting to be rude.

'L, lemme introduce you to my new frie—'

'I'm leaving, K. Here.' He handed K-Bar a stack of notes. 'Watch out for Shorty.' Before K-Bar could protest, he'd gone.

―――

SHORTY CLOSED HIS EYES, enjoying the feel of the body pressing against his as he swayed to the beat of the music. He was sure his dance moves were out of sync, but it was the last thing on his mind.

The girl he danced with had tried talking to Lamont earlier, but had gotten nowhere. Being spurned had hurt her confidence, and he hadn't worked hard to get a dance out of her. As the DJ switched songs, she ground against him, whispering in his ear.

'Let's go outside.'

Shorty didn't need any persuasion. He followed the girl, unable to keep his hands to himself, kissing the back of her neck as she giggled against the thumping tempo of the music. All those months on remand meant he was backed up and in serious need. He was tempted to get a taxi home with the girl, but didn't think he could wait.

The pair stumbled around the corner, Shorty pressing the girl against the wall and roughly kissing her, letting her feel just how erect he was. The hairs on the back of his neck stood, causing him to jerk away from her just as he heard hurried footsteps.

'Yo, give it up,' a gruff voice sounded. Shorty faced the pair, two men. Furious with himself for getting caught out, he glared, causing one to take a step back.

'S-Shorty?'

Shorty peeked at the trembling man. He held a knife, wearing a black jacket, trousers and trainers. His face was half-covered by a bandanna like some wannabe bandit. He recognised the younger man with a sudden jolt.

'Jerome?'

Jerome was a friend of Timmy's; a delinquent from an early age, constantly getting him caught up in his foolish schemes. When Timmy set Shorty up, he went after his cousin through Jerome and another friend. He'd mercilessly beaten the pair with a gun, demanding to know Timmy's whereabouts. After beating them into unconsciousness, he'd fled. When he was arrested, he presumed the pair had snitched, but they never said a word to anyone.

'You know this guy?' Jerome's accomplice snapped. He was

TARGET PART TWO: THE TAKEDOWN

around Shorty's height, with a slim frame, his entire face covered by a balaclava. He too had a knife, still pointing it in his direction. The girl had disappeared. Shorty knew the scheme. She'd meet them later to collect her share, but she would be disappointed. Shorty had never allowed anyone to rob him, and he wasn't starting now.

'You don't know Shorty from Chapeltown? He's a killer.'

Years ago, he would have smiled at the obvious fear in Jerome's voice.

'I don't care what his name is. He needs to give up the money and jewels before I poke him.' The other would-be thief wasn't backing down an inch. Shorty kept his eyes on Jerome, ready to hit him first. Jerome's eyes widened, and he ran just as K-Bar and Maka rounded the corner.

'What's going on?' K-Bar lunged for the robber, hitting him in the nose and causing the knife to fall from the man's hand. Maka sailed in, smashing his fist against his jaw.

'You think you can rob our boy? Are you crazy?' K-Bar snarled, throwing the kid into the wall next to Shorty. He slid to the floor, bleeding, Shorty looking at him in disgust. He yanked the balaclava from the kid's head, but didn't recognise him. He had curly black hair with blonde tips.

'Let him up. Get him out of here.' He couldn't help thinking about his cousin. These silly robberies were the kind of thing Timmy used to do to get his rep up. As K-Bar slapped the kid and warned him not to show his face again, Shorty sighed, wondering if it was all worth it.

CHAPTER THREE
FRIDAY 16 JANUARY, 2015

'HOW HAS IT ALL BEEN GOING?'

Jenny looked around the office, procrastinating as always. It was how their weekly meetings started, but she was never prepared. The office was compact, Jenny perched on a neutral blue sofa. Amanda's chair was a dark brown colour and seemed less comfortable than hers, but the woman's chocolate brown eyes projected their usual warmth. If there was any discomfort, it didn't show.

She'd been visiting Amanda for over a year, after the nightmares from Lamont's shooting became too frequent. She was referred by her GP, willing to pay the additional fees to speak with the counsellor.

Opening up wasn't easy; the idea of being privy to an attempted murder didn't seem real. Jenny had witnessed someone die, and the fact Lamont nearly died from his injuries was a trauma she hadn't known how to navigate. They filled a lot of the early sessions with gaps of silence that took time to overcome. There was a familiarity now, and she respected the older woman, but they weren't friends. She was paying for her time, and that loomed over each session.

Jenny took a deep breath. 'It's old ground we've repeatedly trod. It always comes back to being there in that moment. Me and my partner had everything to look forward to; he was getting away from negative influences, and then it happened.'

'How much influence did you have over your partner's decision; did you pressure him?'

'I don't think I did. I just wanted to be with him, and he wanted to be with me. He said I saved him. And then suddenly, there were men with guns. He was terrified, yet still told me to get away.'

'Why didn't you listen?' If Amanda was aware she'd asked the same question a dozen times, it didn't show.

'I froze. I've never been in that position. I never want to be again. I guess I hoped it was all a bad dream.'

'It wasn't, though.'

She ignored Amanda's remark, rubbing her eyes.

'Nothing is improving, that's the problem. He was shot, and I saw it, and I was covered in his blood, and I thought he was dead. After all this time, after all the effort he put into getting stronger, it remains as distorted as ever.'

'Do you think you may be stuck in the past because you don't want to embrace the change?'

'Of course I don't want to embrace it. We went from real happiness, to this tentative awkwardness.'

'Do you love your partner?'

'I do. The problem is that we no longer know how to act around one another. We're walking on eggshells and won't admit it.'

Amanda paused. 'You said that you spoke to Lamont about seeing someone?'

'He shot the idea down,' Jenny scoffed.

'Why do you think that is?'

'Because he thinks it's a weakness to let people in. He didn't even want to let me in.'

'Why?'

Jenny shrugged. 'Childhood, I guess. I don't know. All I know is that we're stuck.'

'Other than your relationship, how are things going?'

'Work is still a massive slog. I lost a lot of clients, and I'm struggling to get myself out of the hole.'

'Why do you feel you have to do this alone? Your partner is a man of means, is he not?'

'That's irrelevant. It's my business, not his. I don't want his help.'

They sat in silence, Amanda watching her every move. She stared back at the picture of competence sitting in front of her; from the steel grey hair to the cream sweater and demeanour, it all spoke of tranquillity. Jenny recalled wearing a cream sweater the day of Lamont's shooting, choking back a sob at the memory, tears streaming down her face. Amanda handed her a tissue.

'It will get better, Jenny. That I promise you. You need to embrace the possibility that things will not return to how they were, and work with the changes.'

AKEEM AND LAMONT reclined in his office at the barbers. Akeem had swept the room for bugs and locked the door. He sipped a water bottle as Lamont ate some cornmeal porridge they'd picked up on the way, waiting for him to speak.

'I've done some analysis,' the man began. 'I assessed the strength of the crew, and we're weak in certain areas. We're still recovering from 2013, and we lost a lot of key personnel. We ramped up with younger, less skilled soldiers and runners. Police activity has increased, and more of our people are being arrested. They don't know enough to implicate anyone, but it's inconvenient.'

'What are you suggesting?' Lamont valued Akeem's opinion. He had known the man for five years, meeting him when he visited London to see an associate, Vincent. Akeem worked for Vincent and specialised in problem-solving. When Vincent mentioned Akeem wanted a move, he'd taken the fixer into his team.

TARGET PART TWO: THE TAKEDOWN

'We, and by that I mean *you*, need to decide what's going on. You've been out of sorts, and it's causing confusion. K-Bar isn't pleased with the running of things, and he has sway over the younger guys. They don't know you. They saw you very little before; they see you even less now. You need to placate K-Bar if you want to survive.'

'And the people wanting to do other business? You had thoughts on that the other day.'

Akeem shrugged. 'Replace them with new customers. We have the best product. The game is changing and making it harder, though, so we need to change with it.'

Lamont thought of the man he'd seen in the club. He knew who Nikkolo worked for, but he wasn't aware it was public knowledge that he'd lost customers. He hadn't mentioned it to Akeem, but he wondered if Nikkolo was sending a message. Akeem was right, though. The money was lower than it had been in years, the morale terrible. He was in the game, whether or not he wanted to be; he needed to find his form.

———

JENNY SAT in her work office, staring into space. Since Lamont had left the hospital, and they moved in together, it felt like they'd lived under a protective bubble. Everything had been idyllic. Lamont hadn't directly spoken of his plan, but she knew he was leaving the life, and she welcomed it.

Lamont had more than enough money. Marcus had been murdered. Xiyu — *Chink, as Lamont and the others called him* — had been murdered in what police called a botched home invasion. Shorty had been arrested and accused of murder. She didn't know much about Lamont's business, but knew they were the cornerstone of the illegal empire he had built. Now, Shorty was out, and Jenny had no idea what that would lead to.

The conversation with Shorty flitted to her mind. He seemed so different from the vicious, fiery man she'd glimpsed in 2013. There was an air of unpredictability around him then, but now he seemed haunted. Life appeared to have caught up with him and quenched the flames of rage. She didn't know how to feel about that, or about his presence in Lamont's life.

After a while, she heard the ding of the door announcing a customer had walked in. Giving herself a moment, she headed out to the front, smiling widely at the man standing there.

'Good morning,' she said. 'Are you looking for a particular arrangement?'

The man returned her smile. 'I am. Maybe you could give me a few pointers?'

'What's the occasion?' Jenny slipped into worker mode. The man studied her for a moment. It was a speculative gaze, and though not a leer, she felt the look.

'I wanted a nice arrangement for my mum. Maybe with a nice card. Do you do cards?'

'We do . . . Is it your mother's birthday?'

The man shook his head. 'Just thought it might be nice. She likes roses, so the arrangement could include those.'

Jenny ran a hand through her hair. The man looked to be around her age. His face was clean-shaven, aside from a moustache and some stubble around his chin. His eyes were dark. He smiled widely, wearing a lightweight black jacket over jeans and a grey t-shirt. The outfit was casual, but she had a trained eye. She could tell it was expensive, yet he wore it with a disdain that intrigued her.

The man slightly adjusted his shoulders. He was broad, towered over her, and looked like he worked out. Jenny discreetly coughed, focusing on the task at hand.

'We have roses in different colours. Red is the most popular. Does your mother have a favourite colour?'

'We both like purple.' His words were as smooth as his skin, clipped with a slight hint of authority.

'What about purple, some base red, and maybe some raspberry-shaded pink?' Jenny led the man over to the roses section. She wondered if he was checking her out, feeling an immediate stab of

TARGET PART TWO: THE TAKEDOWN

guilt. There was no reason to feel guilty, though. She wasn't doing anything wrong. She was serving a man buying flowers for his mother. And a card.

But was he really? And why did it matter if he was?

Jenny dealt with different customers, and she imagined some bought gifts for significant others. Or mistresses. It wasn't her problem. Her only concern was growing her business.

Something about the man; the cocky smile, the arrogance that seemed to surround him, reminded her of a time that seemed an age ago. She'd been in the shop by herself that day too. Lamont entered, pretending to be someone else. They had a mock interview. She tried putting him on the spot with her questions, but he smoothly answered them, wearing the same arrogance this man had now.

Lamont's had been an act, though. He intrigued her enough that she agreed to go out with him, but it was only when he revealed the inner pain he hid from the world that Jenny truly fell for him. He had trusted her enough to let her in, but wouldn't now.

Jenny blinked, focusing on the customer, watching as he studied the flowers. More customers came into the shop. Most were on-the-spot orders; customers who knew exactly what they wanted and were picking up flowers and gifts before work. One customer wanted a custom order delivered, which she arranged, taking some details and an upfront payment. When she finished, the man seemed to materialise in front of her.

'I'll take the roses we discussed, but I would also like a dozen lilies.'

Jenny nodded. 'Do you have a vase for them, or would you like to purchase one? We have a wide range of custom-made vases, candleholders, candles . . .' her voice trailed off again when she noticed the man smiling at her.

'I like your spirit. You're a right little hustler, aren't you?'

'I'm a businesswoman,' said Jenny with more ice than she intended. The man was equal to it. His maddening smile didn't dissipate.

'That's good. But, don't take me calling you a hustler as a bad thing. I like the spirit. It must be why your shop does so well.'

'It doesn't,' Jenny admitted, before she could stop herself.

'It should. I've seen the way you deal with people. You're efficient, smooth, articulate.' He paused, meeting her eyes. 'And beautiful. Don't forget beautiful.'

'I'm not sure what my looks have to do with anything.' Jenny frowned. The man shook his head.

'Looks are important.'

'Maybe I'm just not as shallow as you.'

'It's not about shallowness. If you were sixty-eight years old, smelling like cough sweets and old mothballs, I'm sure it would influence your business. I think you see that.'

She rubbed her forehead, wanting to rid herself of this arrogant man. He was a customer, though, so she tempered her annoyance.

'You said you wanted a card as well, right?'

He watched her again, slowly nodding.

'I didn't mean to offend you.'

'You didn't,' she lied.

'Good. I've learnt it's always best to be upfront.'

'Is that so?' She decided to test the smooth-talking man in front of her.

'It's most definitely so.'

'Who are the flowers really for?'

The man frowned, scratching his temple. 'I told you. They're for my mother.'

'Why would you randomly buy bouquets for your mum? Are you sure they aren't for a girlfriend, or maybe a side chick?'

'Positive.' He again met Jenny's eyes. 'Mum's been lonely since dad died. I think some flowers, a nice card, the loving attention of her son, should all help.'

Immediately Jenny felt her face heat. 'Oh, I'm so—'

'You didn't know.'

'How did he die?'

'Heart attack.'

'I'm sorry,' she said. The man smiled.

'Don't be sorry, Jenny. Really.'

'How do you know my name?'

'It's on your name tag,' the man said. 'My name is Malcolm, by the way.'

'It's nice to meet you, Malcolm,' said Jenny, her voice warmer now.

'Likewise. So, I'll take a lavender candle, candle holder, two bouquets, and one of these nice custom-vases.' Malcolm helped her carry everything to the counter.

'Regarding the card, would you like me to compose a message?'

'I think I can do that. I'd like you to write it, though. I imagine you have beautiful handwriting.'

'I'll try not to disappoint.' Jenny picked up a fountain pen and a fresh custom card. It was brown, with a heart on the front so dark it was almost scarlet. She held it up to Malcolm to make sure he was satisfied.

'What would you like it to say?'

Malcolm scratched his chin.

'I would like it to say . . . *Mum, thank you for being you. I will protect you. You are the source of my strength, and I hope I can remain as influential to you as dad was. Love your son and Knight.*'

Jenny was speechless. It wasn't just the words that resonated. It was the sincerity. She had seen the cocksure act come down for a moment and witnessed Malcolm's pain. She found herself wondering things; *how he'd coped after his father's death? Had he handled the arrangements? Did he speak at the funeral?*

Jenny thought again about Lamont. When he had told her about his difficult upbringing, his eyes held the same pain. She remembered Marcus's funeral. He'd been gunned down in the middle of the Carnival event last August. Lamont had held him in his arms, just as she held Lamont after his own shooting.

At the funeral, he'd given a moving eulogy, speaking of how Marcus was the best, most unconventional friend he'd had. He nearly broke down giving the speech, and people cried, Jenny included. Malcolm's words about his mother had moved her in the same way.

'Jenny?'

She blinked, focusing on Malcolm again. His eyebrows were raised.

'Sorry about that.' Jenny neatly wrote the card, then passed the pen to him so he could sign it. She noticed he put seven kisses.

'It's her lucky number,' he told Jenny. She nodded. Her thoughts were all over the place, and she was aware of her heart hammering against her ribs. She didn't know why. Or maybe she did.

When she'd bagged everything, Malcolm took the packages, declined her offer to help, and moved fluidly towards the door. He faced her at the last second.

'Would you like to go for a drink?'

'I have a boyfriend.'

He shrugged. 'Beautiful women always do. Still, a drink doesn't mean we will end up naked and sweaty.'

'Do you have to be so descriptive?' Jenny reddened, feeling the hairs on her arms rising. Malcolm smirked.

'I'm a Poet. Being descriptive helps. One drink won't kill you. Bring your boyfriend.'

She shook her head. 'I don't think that's a good idea.'

'You're probably right. I don't know what it is, but I seem to threaten boyfriends.' Malcolm's wide smile showed off sparkling white teeth. 'You take care of yourself, Jenny. I'm sure I'll see you again soon.'

Malcolm left. She went to the window, watching him climb into a grey Range Rover. She waited to see if he would look in her direction as he pulled away, but he didn't. His face focused straight ahead on the road as he zoomed out of sight.

Jenny sighed, closing her eyes for a moment, wondering why she felt such tremendous guilt. She had served a customer. That was all. He had flirted and called her beautiful, but she hadn't reciprocated. She had been nothing but professional. *So, what was it?*

TARGET PART TWO: THE TAKEDOWN

Going back to the office, she called Lamont, wanting to hear his voice, but it went straight to voicemail.

'Jen?'

Jenny gave a small gasp as a woman appeared in the doorway.

'Are you okay? You look flushed.' It was Nadia.

'I'm fine . . . Are you okay? Did you get Toby off to school okay?'

'Yeah, I had a quick word with his teacher and came straight here. I'll just wash my hands, then I'll check everything's okay out there. Do you want a drink?'

Jenny shook her head, watching Nadia leave. She slumped down, picking up the pen and continuing with her paperwork.

SHORTY PULLED up on Leopold Street. He was travelling without music playing more these days. The ride he drove was one that Lamont procured for him. It was a blue Toyota Corolla that ran well. Lamont offered him a range of cars, but Shorty picked a low-key ride. The last thing he needed was to have the police on his back.

Popping a polo into his mouth, he slid from the ride. The terraced house in front of him had peeling paint on the fence, and the brown gate was worn and shabby. The garden, normally well-tended, was overrun with weeds. Making his way towards the front door, he firmly knocked. A woman he hadn't seen in over a year peeked out at him.

'Hello, Auntie,' said Shorty.

'Franklin.' Shorty couldn't read his Aunt's expression. She was open-mouthed, with protruding bags under her eyes. He remembered her as a vibrant woman, and it hurt to see her so defeated. He was sure she would reject him as Grace had, but she sighed and let him in.

Ten minutes later, he clutched a cup of tea. His Aunt sat on her sofa, looking anywhere but at him. The tension was stifling. He wished he had some weed to smoke. His nerves were always shot lately. He detested the feeling.

'How's it been going then?' Shorty felt foolish for asking. She looked at the ground.

'Some days are good, some bad.'

'I'm . . .'

'I know you're sorry. That doesn't help me, though. My son is still dead.'

Shorty didn't speak at first. He couldn't heal his Aunt's pain. At eighteen, Timmy had his whole life ahead of him, but he was determined to walk a mile in Shorty's shoes. He wanted to be known. He wanted a reputation like Shorty. He'd died failing to achieve it.

'I know, Auntie. I wish he wasn't.'

She stirred her drink. He drank his own, glad for the distraction.

'All he wanted was to be like you.'

Shorty let her talk.

'He wanted to do everything you did. He wanted to have the same trainers, same tracksuits. You were his idol.'

Shorty's mouth was dry, and the lump in his throat felt like a golf ball.

'I'm not trying to hurt you,' Auntie's voice quivered. 'I know you loved him. Lord knows the both of you needed your daddies.'

Shorty's body was racked with a feeling he'd rarely felt before; guilt. His Aunt had no idea of the situation, and precisely who'd murdered Timmy. Even he struggled with it. To learn that Maka had ended Timmy's life was harrowing. Shorty understood the circumstances, but Timmy was his blood. He'd played the game and lost.

'I've got a bit of change to help you out, Auntie,' he said. He'd never heard his voice sound so flat.

'You don't have to.' She shook her head.

'I want to. I don't need it, trust me. Let me help you.'

She sighed. Shorty put the cup and saucer on the coffee table, reaching into his pocket. He handed her the stack of money he'd brought. She looked at the amount and then at him; her eyes a question. Neither spoke as she placed the money onto the chair next to her.

'Your friend, the one who was shot a few years ago . . .'

'L?'

His Aunt nodded. 'He sends me money every month.'

That was news to Shorty. Even when they discussed Timmy, Lamont hadn't mentioned giving his mother any money. He knew Lamont took care of the people around him, but Timmy had betrayed them. He'd colluded with Marrion and Chink and helped to set up both Shorty and Lamont.

'L's good like that.' Shorty wondered if Lamont felt guilty over Timmy's death. He stayed a few hours. He let his Aunt make him some food, then hugged her for a long time before leaving. Sitting in his car, he tried making sense of the situation. The money he'd given to his Aunt would hopefully help, but wouldn't appease his feelings. All his life, Shorty had lived and breathed the call of the streets. It had brought him money, respect, fear, and now grief. After another moment, Shorty drove away.

AFTER LEAVING his Aunt's place, Shorty headed to see the crew. Maka was posted up with a few younger guys. He glanced up when Shorty entered, nodding and looking back at his phone. One of the youths paused the video game when he saw Shorty.

'Yo, un-pause it.' His comrade reached for the pad. The kid held it out of reach.

'Long time no see, Shorty. You probably don't remember me.'

He shook the kid's hand. 'You're Darren. Used to roll with your brother back in the day. How's Lucas doing?'

Darren grinned, touched that he'd remembered.

'Still locked up. He goes in and out.'

Shorty nodded. Lucas Lyles, was a goon of the highest order. He robbed everything that wasn't nailed down and liked to hurt people when he did it. Lucas could be cool, but most of the time, he was a complete headache to be around.

'Tell him to send me a V.O. when you see him,' Shorty greeted the other kid. 'Shadow, what's happening?'

'Just waiting for this phone to ring. I've been chatting to this girl for a minute, and I'm trying to roll through today.'

Shorty laughed. Shadow reminded him of when he was younger, running around trying to get with any girl he could. It seemed like a lifetime ago. Maka cleared his throat and slid to his feet.

'Shorty, can I have a word?'

He followed Maka out to the garden. The pair stood in silence. Life seemed to have improved for Maka. He wore a black designer tracksuit and grey Timberland boots. It was strange for Shorty; Maka was one of the few originals remaining. He'd been around for years, doing business outside the crew with his crime partner, Manson. The pair clicked like he did with K-Bar, and they always made money. He knew what Maka wanted to talk about, but held his tongue.

'I'm sorry.'

Shorty waited for him to finish.

'I didn't mean to kill Timmy. He was working with Marrion, but I don't think he was gonna shoot L. I just started dumping when I saw L was down. I wasn't even aiming for him, I promise.'

Shorty studied him. His face was hard, his eyes full of something Shorty identified with. The same guilt resonated from his eyes when he looked in the mirror every morning. Maka wasn't apologising out of fear. He was doing it because it was the right thing to do.

'I know how you feel, fam. Tim violated and tried to get me killed. If I'd caught him in the mood I was in, I would have probably killed him too. I know you weren't trying to, but when you're on the scene, and the President is down, you shoot.'

Maka warily nodded, surprised he was taking it so well.

TARGET PART TWO: THE TAKEDOWN

'No hard feelings, Maka. Tim made his choice. I wish things turned out differently, but they didn't. Let's put it behind us. Cool?'

Maka grinned, and the pair shook hands. They spoke for a few minutes about some old acquaintances, then headed back inside. Darren and Shadow were still playing on the PlayStation.

'One of those idiots tried following me when I linked a sale,' Darren was saying.

'Those *OurHood* clowns are everywhere. Everyone and their other is joining,' Shadow replied.

'What do you lot know about this *OurHood* shit?' Shorty interjected, the reference reminding him of Trinidad's words.

Maka snorted.

'It's some bullshit. Just some do-gooders looking for attention.'

'I've seen them advertising everywhere. That kind of promo ain't cheap. Money's gotta come from somewhere.'

Maka shrugged. 'Probably. What's your plan, though? Are you gonna come back and run shit?'

Shorty considered the question. He was tired of mooching around doing nothing, and while he was sure the police would have an eye on him, he was smart enough to avoid getting caught. He'd spoken with Lamont, and so far, he hadn't said a thing about him returning to his role. He received a substantial weekly wage, but it wasn't the same as hustling for his own money.

'I need to talk with the big man and see what he's saying.'

WHEN LAMONT ARRIVED HOME, he was still contemplating Akeem's words. He needed the crew to be strong while he considered the best course of action for Akhan. He didn't appreciate being blackmailed into maintaining his position, but needed everything running before he could proceed. For now, he was content to play along, and if Akhan saw him replenishing his team, the warlord would grow complacent. When he did, he needed to be ready.

Lamont and Jenny picked at their dinner a while later. She had cooked some fish, with rice and salad, yet neither had much of an appetite. She stared at her plate, her knife and fork abandoned. Lamont stirred his own delicious food around his plate, occasionally eating a portion. He watched the woman, as beautiful to him as the day he'd first laid eyes on her, and felt a pang of tremendous guilt. He'd irrevocably ruined this woman's life, and now he was lying to her about his intentions.

He couldn't tell her about Akhan, or that killing Ricky Reagan with his bare hands had blown up in his face. He didn't know how she would take it, so he would keep her from knowing the truth.

'How was work?' He asked, his high-pitched voice making him cringe. Jenny looked up, hastily smiling.

'I caught up on my paperwork, and a few customers wanted custom orders, so hopefully, that'll drum up some interest. I'm struggling with the social media side of things. Networking is harder than I thought it would be.'

He cleared his throat. 'If it's an issue of money—'

'It's not.'

'I'm just saying, I can help. Martin would even back the investment so we could do it properly. I could just give it to you, even. I mean—'

'Lamont, I said no!'

Lamont stared for a moment, then nodded and picked up his fork.

'I'm sorry, L. I didn't mean to shout. It's been a long day. I had a session with Amanda this morning before work.'

He squeezed her hand, his rosewood eyes full of concern.

'How was it?'

'Emotional. She has a knack for getting me to speak about things. She had the idea that maybe you could come for a session with me, and we could—'

'Thank you, but I'll pass.' Lamont cut her off. He wiped his mouth with a napkin and headed to his study. She had tried so many times to get him to go to counselling, but he had no intention of telling a stranger his problems. Pouring a tall glass of brandy, he resolved to grow stronger on his own, determined to be the person he used to be.

Nikkolo was all smiles as he sauntered into the spacious house on Potternewton Lane. Locking the door, he made his way into what was formerly the living room. Other than two leather chairs, it was devoid of furniture. The walls were grey, the flickering lightbulb giving the room a horror vibe. He bounced into the only available chair and cleared his throat.

'Spoke to Ronnie. He wants to borrow twenty bags. He's aware of the rates and said he can pay back within two weeks.' Nikkolo reached into his jacket pocket and handed a watch to the other person in the room. 'Gave me that as collateral.'

Lennox Thompson took the Rolex without a word, examining it for a moment before handing it back.

'What's going on with the other situation?'

Nikkolo scratched the back of his neck. He'd run Lennox's crew for years, yet the man still made him uneasy. Lennox was wiry, with a thin face and fathomless dark eyes that stared holes through whoever was in the vicinity. He had a quiet presence that radiated malevolent force. It was a lot to take in and didn't grow any easier.

'Our people are saying Delroy has lost his heart. Ever since Teflon humbled him, he's lost a lot of respect. You know my view; we should strap up and take him out. We can get someone to run the drug thing for us and make more money.'

'We don't sell drugs, or did you forget that fact? You wanna be a dealer, go work for someone else.'

He hung his head, abashed. Lennox paid him no attention.

'There are easier ways to destroy a person than charging in and trying to kill them. Delroy is soft. The people he keeps around are softer. Their only goal is to keep making money. Teflon and the other gangs are more of a threat.'

Nikkolo clapped his hands together. 'That reminds me. Did you know Shorty is out?'

'So?'

'I'm just saying. They must have been celebrating the other night. I ran into Teflon.'

Lennox looked up now, his hawk-like expression stilling Nikkolo.

'What do you mean you *ran into him?*'

'I just saw him at the club, and I said hello.'

'What else did you say?'

'Nothing. I didn't even mention you or anything.'

'Tell me exactly what was said.'

'We said hello, then I mentioned that he'd lost a few customers. After that, I kept it moving.'

Lennox's expression remained unchanged, but he felt the tension spike in the room. Lennox held his stare for over a minute before he spoke.

'Why did you mention Teflon losing customers? Did you not think that information wouldn't be public?'

'I d-didn't think—'

'You're right. Get out of my sight. I'll deal with you tomorrow.'

He clambered to his feet and hurried from the room, a bead of sweat dripping from his forehead. As he unlocked the door with shaking hands, he noticed his knees were knocking together.

CHAPTER FOUR
SATURDAY 17 JANUARY, 2015

WHEN LAMONT MADE his way to the kitchen the following day, Jenny had already left. He ate the breakfast she'd prepared, thinking about their previous discussion. He couldn't fathom needing a counsellor. Though he appreciated Jenny's situation, he was in a different predicament. It was hard enough even to comprehend Jenny spilling his secrets and telling some stranger about his life, but he held those thoughts at bay. He trusted her, even if he was lying about his intentions.

Making a cup of coffee, he switched his business brain on. He had meetings today, and the aim was simple; he would get the crew back in line and remind people why they respected the name *Teflon*.

K-BAR ROLLED OUT OF BED, away from the warm body lying there. He padded to the shower. After getting ready, he was spraying aftershave when his phone vibrated. He was tempted for a moment to ignore it, but couldn't.

'Yeah?' He put the phone on loudspeaker.

RICKY BLACK

'Take me off speaker. I can tell,' Akeem's voice boomed on the other end. K-Bar laughed and did as ordered.

'What can I help you with?'

'Meeting spot. We're avoiding the usual place. Meet us at *Number Three*.'

'I'll see you there.' He dropped the phone on the bed.

'You're up early.'

K-Bar turned at the sound of the voice. The woman sat up; the sheet slipping and allowing him to stare at her breasts, which he did until she scowled.

'Early bird gets that worm, babe.'

'Was that your baby mother on the phone? That why you didn't want her on speaker?'

K-Bar frowned. 'Are you silly? Couldn't you hear the dude's voice on the phone at the beginning?'

'Whatever. Who was it then?'

'You're damn nosey. It was your bro, okay? We're meeting.'

Marika didn't reply, her brow furrowed. He wondered if the pair would ever make up. As long as he'd known Lamont, he'd always gone all out for his sister. The traitor Marrion from Manchester had ruined that, though, poisoning her mind and turning her against her brother.

He remembered the dark days after Lamont's shooting, surviving on caffeine and adrenaline, tracking down anyone who had anything to do with Marrion. Marika had called in hysterics, screaming about Lamont murdering Marrion outside her house. She said she'd already called the police, but was shocked when she learned of his shooting. She'd visited Lamont in hospital after the shooting, but only when he was unconscious. K-Bar supported her, giving her money and ensuring she and the kids were okay.

The first time they had slept together came a month later. They'd both been drinking away their anguish and ended up in bed. After avoiding one another out of awkwardness, they began having sex regularly. They couldn't define what it was between them, but it felt right. He'd considered telling Lamont, but he didn't know how his boss would take it.

K-Bar wondered what he wanted. They had spoken the day before, and he knew Lamont had been locked in meetings with Akeem, but he wasn't privy to the inner workings, and he wasn't sure he wanted to be.

K-Bar had been thrust into leadership after Lamont's shooting. The crew had been leaderless, and when Shorty's arrest came to light, people began positioning themselves to make a move against the crew. He'd taken the reins, meeting with Saj to ensure the supply was consistent, then letting people know the crew was still strong. He had tried to deal with all the politics and drama the best way he could, but he wasn't Lamont. His skillset differed; he had street smarts, could hustle, survive, plan and execute murders, but wasn't the analyst Lamont was. This led him to get the short end of a few deals and lose his temper with people. One wannabe gangster ended up in hospital with a bullet in his leg after pissing him off. He'd had to pay and threaten the man into silence, but it was worth it.

Lamont was back now, and as much as K-Bar would miss the money he'd made, walking in his shoes wasn't worth it. It was too difficult.

'NADIA, how are we getting on with completing that order?'

'It's finished, Jen. The husband is picking it up this afternoon. His payment processed.'

Satisfied, she deeply exhaled. Sipping her cold coffee, she brushed her hair from her eyes, trying to focus on the ponderous report in front of her. The shop door opened, but she didn't think much of it until she heard Nadia laughing. Smoothing her hair, she headed to investigate.

Nadia stood by a selection of hand-made vases, shoulders shaking as she giggled. There was a man next to her, but Jenny couldn't tell who it was. Nadia shifted to the right, and then she recognised him.

'Shorty?'

Shorty grinned, but it didn't extend to his eyes.

'Hey, Jen. Your lovely worker here was showing me around.'

'That's fine. Everything okay, though?' She hadn't known he knew where her shop was. Shorty hesitated. Nadia noticed and smiled at Jenny before excusing herself to the back.

'Did L say anything about Grace?'

Jenny had to think for a moment, remembering that Grace was his daughter. She recalled Lamont saying something about him having a son too, but that he didn't see him much.

'No, he didn't. Me and L haven't really spoken, to be honest,' she admitted. She noticed him sizing her up. 'What's up with Grace?'

Shorty shook his head. 'She didn't want to see me when we went over there. She ran out of the room.'

Jenny saw the pain in his eyes, and her heart went out to him. She'd never given children much thought, but it was evident that Shorty's girl had hurt him.

'I'm sorry to hear that.'

'I can't blame her. I was away, and she had to hear all kinds of rubbish about me. She's probably confused. Anyway, I wanted to buy her some flowers to leave with her mum.'

Jenny smiled. 'That's a great idea. Do you have any arrangement in mind?'

'I was hoping you'd handle that for me; I just want summat colourful.'

When Jenny had prepared the flowers and given him his change, the pair awkwardly stood.

'How come you and L haven't been talking?'

Jenny opened her mouth, but he spoke again.

'I'm not trying to intrude. Summat's not right with L, and I can't put my finger on it.'

Jenny took a deep breath.

TARGET PART TWO: THE TAKEDOWN

'Honestly, I don't know.' She glanced at him, then the words tumbled from her mouth. 'He's not all there. Hasn't been in months. First, it was the shooting, and then he nearly killed himself trying to get better because he didn't want to look weak in front of me. He kept straining himself, and his personal trainer tried to speak to him and get him to slow down, but Lamont sacked him. He didn't want to hear what the man was saying.

'I tried getting him to speak to a professional, but he won't. He just broods, drinks, and tries to be strong. I don't need him to be strong, though. I need him to be the man I fell in love with.'

There was a long silence when she finished, her face red with exertion. Shorty wiped his face, placing the bouquet on the counter.

'L's that kinda guy. Even when we were young, he never enjoyed looking weak. None of us did. L took it to another level; didn't want people to see him angry, or sad, or anything. It was mad when you look back at it, but it made him who he is. It's difficult to shake that, even when you love someone.'

Jenny's mouth was agape when he finished. She'd only ever viewed him as a thug and was surprised he could be so eloquent. He'd hit the nail on the head. Lamont considered controlling his emotions the ultimate tool.

She smiled, musing that Shorty, of all people, was helping her with her thoughts.

'What do I do then?'

Shorty shrugged.

'I know fuck all about relationships. Guess you just need to remember how to talk to him. L's not gonna like being given advice. He likes to be the one to tell other people what they should do. You two have summat, though; we all saw it back in the day, and I saw it the other night. Things are just different. It's a different world for everyone, and I think we forget that.'

Jenny wrapped her arms around Shorty. She felt him stiffen, before he returned the hug and quickly let her go.

'Thank you for listening, Shorty, I really appreciate it.'

LAMONT AND AKEEM approached the takeaway restaurant on Roundhay Road, parking on the side of the road and walking straight to the back. On the way, they had seen no less than three police cars — one an undercover vehicle, driving around Chapeltown. Lamont felt their world shrinking. The police had an agenda, and he couldn't predict how it would turn out. As Akeem drove by them, he considered bowing out for good, only to be reminded of Akhan, and his ultimatum.

'I need you to do something for me,' he said as they settled into the office space. The smell of fried food was overpowering, but they wouldn't be long.

'What is it?' Akeem asked.

'Find out everything about Akhan and his team. I don't care what it costs. Just be discreet.'

'Consider it done.'

SHORTY FELT UPLIFTED after speaking with Jenny. She had been right, he realised. He just needed to give things time with Grace, get her used to being around him. It wouldn't be achieved overnight, but it was achievable, and he had a smile on his face at the thought.

Shorty was ready to leave the past behind. Men tried to kill him. He'd put them down and paid a massive price. It could have been worse, but he needed to make the most of the situation.

After leaving Jenny's, he showered, changed his clothes, then drove to Amy's. He clutched the bouquet and a card he'd written, and walked towards the door. After lightly knocking, and not receiving a reply, he left them on the doorstep and headed down the drive.

'Shorty?'

Amy stood in the doorway, eyes widening as she picked up the card and flowers, sniffing them on instinct.

TARGET PART TWO: THE TAKEDOWN

'I didn't think you were in.'

'I was washing up; needed to dry my hands. Why are you here?'

'I just wanted to ask you to give those to Grace,' Shorty's tone was polite, his hands jammed into his pockets as she scrutinised him.

'Grace isn't here. She's staying at a friend's house.'

He nodded. 'It's cool. I shouldn't have just turned up. I just wanted her to get the flowers. I'll talk to you later.' He turned to walk to his car.

'Do you want a drink?'

Shorty sat in the kitchen, holding a steaming mug of tea and watching Amy fuss around, moving plates and cutlery.

'I'm sorry for turning up like I did the other day.'

She didn't speak.

'I wanted to see Grace so bad that I didn't stop to consider it might hurt her. I just thought she'd jump into my arms, and everything would be okay.'

Amy took a moment before she spoke.

'Grace was terrified when it all happened. She asked about you constantly, and I didn't know what to tell her. We tried to keep the police away from her; my mum had her, Diana had her. We didn't want her exposed to any of it.

'And then you handed yourself in, and it was in the paper. We told her you'd gone away, and she cried. We couldn't console her. The last thing we wanted was for her to know you'd been locked up. She's smart, though. Saw the paper, or someone showed it to her. After that, she stopped asking about you.'

Shorty hung his head, his heart aching at the thought he'd caused his daughter so much pain. He didn't regret the killings. They were necessary, and the people he'd put down had come to murder him. They hadn't shown him any mercy, and he'd paid the three of them back.

'Give it time, Shorty. Grace will want to see you again. She's just confused.'

He beamed, recalling Jenny saying something similar.

'I will.'

Amy blew out a breath.

'I still think about that whole situation sometimes.'

'Which?'

'That summer. Everything that happened; Marcus, you, Lamont . . . I still can't believe someone tried to kill him. Even Timmy.' Amy rested her hand on his shoulder for a moment. 'I'm really sorry about your cousin. I can't even imagine what things were like then. I don't know anything about what you were doing, and I don't want to. Timmy was your family, though, and I know you loved him.'

Shorty could have told her why Timmy was shot, but he didn't. It wasn't worth it.

'You're right; that summer was a complete mess, and people are still coming to terms with it. Still glad I clocked your boyfriend with the gun, though. He caused me a lot of shit.'

'He's not my boyfriend.' Amy stared into her mug. 'Chris and I ended things shortly after you were remanded.'

Shorty hid a smile. He'd never liked Chris, even before she began a relationship with him. He'd called the police when Shorty tried saying goodbye to Grace. He didn't know the ins and outs, but knew threats were made to force him to change his story. Chris eventually stated he never saw Shorty with a gun and refused to press charges.

'Are you seeing anyone else?' Shorty heard himself ask. She again paused.

'I'm dating, if that's what you're asking. Nothing serious, nor is it anything I want to expose Grace to.'

He nodded, swallowing down the lump in his throat. They hadn't been a thing for years, but the thought of Amy being with anyone else still jarred him. He understood at the same time. Too much had happened between them for anything to blossom, and where that fact would have made him angry two years ago, now he focused instead on the bigger picture; earning back the love of his baby girl.

TARGET PART TWO: THE TAKEDOWN

―――

When K-Bar arrived at the meeting, he greeted both men and slid into a seat. Akeem remained standing near the door, ensuring he could see anyone approaching.

'What's up then?' K-Bar rubbed the back of his neck. He didn't know what the meeting was about, and hoped Lamont hadn't found out about him and Marika. He eyed Akeem for a second. He knew the man had a reputation down in London and wondered if he could move fast enough to take him if it came to it. Lamont stared at him unflinchingly, as if he knew exactly what was going through his mind. He cleared his throat.

'Things need to change.'

'Which things?'

'The streets. Things have been in limbo for a while, and it's messing everything up.'

K-Bar bit back the words on his tongue. Ever since he'd taken over, everyone had a sad story to sing about him and how he was perceived to be running things. The money wasn't the same as when Lamont was in charge, but the times had changed. The police were everywhere, more people wanted to do their own thing, and he couldn't take things in any direction because he didn't know what the intentions were. He was a soldier who watched over drugs and people, then dealt with anyone who stepped out of line. Admittedly, he wasn't ready for the big seat, and when it was thrust at him, he had to deal with things the best he could.

'I don't blame you, K. You were dealt a shitty hand after I was hurt, and you didn't know if I was even gonna survive. You were still loyal, and dealt with the people involved, and I'll never forget that. We need to establish ourselves all over again now.'

'How?' K-Bar leaned forward in his seat.

'First, I need you to find all the people still owing us money, and get it back. There's too much leeway, and it stops now. People are far too comfortable, and that's affecting our name.'

'I'm down with doing that, L, but I need more people. We're

running low on solid personnel. People moved on, and some got locked up. I'm working with what I've got, but if you're wanting to make moves, it won't be enough.'

'Make a list of capable people, and we'll bring them into the team if they fit. Darren Lyles, he's still down with us, isn't he?'

'Yeah,' replied K-Bar, wondering how Lamont even remembered him. Darren had been a kid when he was last running the crew, and he wouldn't have known him if he'd tripped over him in the street.

'I've heard he's a solid worker; would you agree?'

'He's one of the best we've got, that's for damn sure.'

'Let's do more with him then. Switch things up, get the money in line, and let's show people why we're the best team in town.'

Lamont headed back towards Chapeltown after the meeting with K-Bar. The killer seemed more buoyant upon leaving, which he viewed as a success. He knew how much hassle K-Bar had put up with, simply because he wasn't meant to be in charge. They would get the ball rolling, replenish their funds and armies, and spread themselves out as they always did. With a stronger, more focused team, Akhan would grow complacent, and he would be ready and waiting.

As Akeem approached the barbers, Lamont noted a large crowd of people, some looking angry, others upset. The flashing lights of several police vehicles dominated the road, and there were scores of brightly-clad officers trying to maintain the peace.

'What's happened here?' Akeem murmured. He didn't answer, his eyes searching the crowd. When they parked, he hurried towards the barbers, searching for Trinidad. He let out a huge breath when he saw him standing in the middle of the barbers, consoling a woman he didn't recognise. She was sobbing loudly, her head buried into Trinidad's bony chest.

TARGET PART TWO: THE TAKEDOWN

'Trinidad, are you okay?' He asked, Akeem at his back. Trinidad looked at him, every bit his advanced years at that moment.

'I'm fine, L.'

'What's happened then?'

'Marilyn's son.' He motioned to the sobbing woman, who didn't appear to have noticed them standing there. 'The police badly attacked him, and now he's in hospital.'

CHAPTER FIVE
THURSDAY 12 FEBRUARY, 2015

THE STREETS WERE tense after more details of the violent incident came to light.

The situation transpired when the police stopped a fourteen-year-old boy named Diego. He was allegedly known to them. When they stopped him, they tried to pat him down for drugs or money. He resisted, claiming he knew his rights. They overpowered him, found nothing incriminating, and began hitting him, claiming he was struggling.

Locals hurried from their houses, some recording the incident, others shouting at the police to stop. More people arrived, and the police quickly called for backup, several younger officers losing their heads and attempting to fight with the crowds. It was many hours later before they diffused the situation.

Even now, the tension lingered.

Lamont sat at the kitchen table, reading about the incident in the Evening Post. He'd heard most of the story from Trinidad, but didn't know Diego or which crew he was affiliated with. Even after several weeks, there had been organised protests and demands for the police officers involved to be sacked. The videos of the police violence had gone viral on

TARGET PART TWO: THE TAKEDOWN

social media, and the *OurHood* Initiative had been the most outspoken, spending money on advertising and highlighting the issue.

In particular, a man named Malcolm Powell had been vehement in his demands for action. Lamont had read an article the man had penned on the *OurHood* website:

We had an incident recently, with police storming into our streets once again with impunity, doing what they wanted and attacking our people without the threat of punishment. It's not the first time, and unless steps are taken, it won't be the last.

Whatever Diego Northwood may or may not have done, at this time, he was innocent. He knew his rights, and that police had no right to profile him while he was walking through his own streets and doing nothing wrong. Even after the police found no evidence of wrongdoing, they still assaulted him.

I'd like to ask those officers involved if they feared for their safety to the point it took multiple officers to overpower a skinny teenager? Does it seem acceptable, because, to me, it is galling. When did the lines become so blurred that police brutality was viewed as acceptable? When did we begin to question why wrongdoing was done, rather than condemn it happening in the first place?

Let's go back to Diego, because I refuse to let this incident rest. There has been much talk about him being a local drug dealer. Whether or not he was selling drugs, he likely wasn't working for himself.

Chapeltown has been synonymous with drugs for years, and the increased presence stems from tit-for-tat violence. This is not a rare issue, people! Over the past three years alone, there have been scores of murders, robberies, and even public violent attacks, all stemming from drugs and illegal activity.

I'm not saying anything most of us are unaware of. The money these criminals make is astounding, and with that amount of money on the line, guns and knives are used to increase the market share. So many good people in Chapeltown and other areas are suffering, scared to speak up for fear of being targeted.

We've allowed it to happen for too long, and to all the above, I say no more.

LAMONT READ the article several times. It was well written, and the community had absorbed the message. He'd even heard from Akeem that their workers were openly discussing the article. Closing the paper with a sigh, he went to make himself another drink.

JENNY WAS HANDING a customer their change when the door opened, and Malcolm Powell stepped in. His eyes twinkled as he surveyed her, but he waited for her to finish serving the customer before he spoke.

'Nice to see you again.'

'You too, Malcolm. Did your mum like the flowers?'

Malcolm grinned. He had a presence, she realised. He appeared well-built beneath the expensive clothing, and his eyes resonated with a power she had only seen in a few people.

'Loved them. Asked me to pass along her compliments. I'm actually here to discuss a larger audience. I'm hosting an event in two weeks, and I'd like you to help set it up.'

Jenny hid her surprise. 'There are people who can do a better job helping with that than me.'

'We'll have to agree to disagree. I think you'll be perfect for the role, and the money is good.'

'What's the event?'

'It's a community meeting to discuss the violent attacks in Chapeltown, and what we can do to prevent them in the future.'

'I heard about that. The young kid that was beaten by the police?' Jenny recalled Lamont reading an article on the internet that called out the police for the attack. She read a few lines, and they gripped her, but hadn't read the rest.

'Diego spent time in hospital, and as of yet, nothing has been done. My organisation will keep up the pressure and ensure that he's not forgotten, like so many other victims.'

'How?' Jenny found herself intrigued. Malcolm spoke passionately, and the situation clearly meant a lot to him. She wondered if he had a personal relationship with the boy involved.

'We organise protests against the police, but we also look into the root of the cause, which is the stigma of drugs and crime that has plagued Chapeltown and other surrounding areas for decades. It's an infection passed on from generation to generation.

'I grew up in Chapeltown, and when I was in school, I was ostracised because other parents didn't want their kids playing with me, because of where I came from.'

'That's disgusting,' said Jenny, openmouthed. She wondered if Lamont had experienced this. She recalled their conversation when he spoke of his upbringing, and why he started selling drugs. Malcolm's passion reminded her of him.

'How did you avoid the streets?'

'I wanted more. There's no magical tale. Growing up, the local kids beat me up a few times because they thought I was a victim. I learned to fight back with my mind and skills, and I applied those to education and furthering myself.'

'That's amazing.' Jenny had grown up with the best of everything, and the financial support to do whatever she wanted. She'd rarely considered the opposite end of the spectrum; the need to fight and survive every day. Lamont even called her out on it when she'd tried to lecture him, reminding her that she grew up in comfort.

'Look, whether or not you want to be involved, come along to the meeting. It's in two days' time, and you can get a feel for how people are reacting to the situation. Check out the *OurHood* Initiative. The website is on here.' He handed a gold and black business card to her. 'Hopefully, I'll see you there. Take care, Ms Campbell.'

Malcolm swept from the shop, leaving a thoughtful Jenny in his wake.

———

Lamont drove to the barbershop after leaving his house. He parked around the corner from the barbers, nodding at a few local people. To his surprise, an older woman pulled her jacket tighter, giving him a foul look as she stalked past. He frowned. Normally, she was full of smiles and always asked about his family. Shrugging it off, he approached the barbers. The shutter was up, but the *closed* sign was still on the door. Curious, he tried the handle, finding the door locked. Worried now, he quickly unlocked it and hurried inside. Trinidad sat in his chair, smoking a cigarette, staring at the walls. He didn't even look up.

'Trinidad? Everything okay?'

'Haven't seen you around lately.' Trinidad ignored his question.

'I didn't want the publicity. People see me close to the scene of an incident, they start thinking I'm involved,' he said darkly, thinking about the woman outside.

'You're part of Chapeltown, aren't you?' Trinidad asked. His blunt tone surprised Lamont.

'I grew up around here. You know that.'

'Then that means taking the good with the bad. You should have been here, giving people hope, showing that you care.'

'I care, Trinidad. Never assume otherwise. Chapeltown will always be in my heart, but for me, caring doesn't extend to protesting, or sitting around talking.'

'Take action then!' Trinidad roared, startling him. 'Tell people what they should do, listen to their problems and their issues. Help them. Don't just sit around while your workers take their money. That's foul, Lamont, and I expect better from you.'

'I don't know why you're coming at me like this. I didn't hurt that boy. He doesn't work for me, and I didn't tell the police to target him. You're mad at me for keeping my head down? Do I have to remind you what happened to me?'

Trinidad's face softened. 'I remember; it broke my heart. I care about you. I believe you're a force for good. Always have. You have a lot of power, and if you just used it in the right way, you could help so many people.'

Lamont grew tired of his tone.

'I've helped many people. I've given people money, funded ventures. Most of the time, there was nothing to show for it. I never made a big deal about it, so don't you dare talk about me not helping people.'

'Help now then. Chapeltown made you rich, so stand with us. There's a community meeting, and if you're there; if you speak and show people you care about what happened to Diego, about what is happening to so many of our kids, it will go a long way.'

'That's not how I do things, and I need you to respect that.' He had no intention of going to the meeting. It was being held by the *OurHood* Initiative, and he would not sit silently while they made him a scapegoat. There was too much going on at the moment to be distracted, and he needed to be *Teflon* now more than ever.

Trinidad shook his head, extinguishing his attempts to stand up for himself.

'I know that you're dealing with your own things. You were shot, but you must realise that the community needs you! This community made you a millionaire, and don't give me that shit about *not being that rich*, because I know differently. I may not know everything, but I know that about you. Help them, the way we helped you sling that poison.'

Lamont tightly clutched his water bottle, his jaw clenched.

'Don't try to give me some speech about morality, Trinidad, because it won't fly. I've made money in Chapeltown, but I wasn't the first, and I won't be the last.

'You wanna talk about what I've gained from these streets? Well, let's talk about what I lost too. I lost my parents, and I was sent to live with a monster. I lost friends to pointless squabbles right here in these streets.

'You think the money makes all that welcome? You think it excuses the pain I feel when I cry at my parents' graves, wishing I could give up this money just to see them again? I came from nothing. You know that. I told myself that I wouldn't bend and scrape. I was going to do whatever I could to get what I wanted. I love this community, but before I started doing what I did, who even gave a fuck?'

'And that gives you the right to be selfish?'

'Not at all! I have things going on at the moment that you couldn't even fathom. I'm trying my hardest to navigate through, for me, for everyone else. Do I want what's best for Chapeltown? Course I do. But, I need to fix me too.'

There was silence. The old friends glared. Trinidad again shook his head, his eyes flat.

'I never thought I would see you as a sellout, L. A man that cannot get behind his people, is no real man.'

Before Lamont could reply, there was a sharp tap on the front door. Both men looked, seeing a young woman and her son. She pointed at her son's nappy head with a shy smile. Trinidad shuffled over and let them in. Lamont hurried to his office, shutting the door behind him. He took several breaths, trying to calm down. He knew why Trinidad was angry, but to blame him was out of line. Lamont wondered if there was more he could be doing. Downing the drink, he dropped the empty bottle, staring at his desk. Maybe he needed to be more involved. It was just another thing on his list, he supposed.

Taking another deep breath, he reached for some papers, switched on some *Charles Mingus*, and tried to lose himself in the soothing music.

TARGET PART TWO: THE TAKEDOWN

THERE WAS something about a white Mercedes that made K-Bar envision success. Whenever he saw one, he stared, reminded of his childhood. He saw many a *player* driving them back in the day, rich-for-a-day fools with whatever young girl they could coerce into the passenger seat.

K-Bar had grown up. Life had been good to him to where even now, stuck in traffic, he could still appreciate the beauty as he sat in one himself, *Cadell* pumping from the speaker.

'Do you have to play that so loud?' His passenger complained. She was a slight woman, brown-skinned with poise and tired beauty. He ignored her, still looking at the car, an older version of his. The kid driving was younger, nodding his head to some track he'd never heard of. He had his own girl in the car. Mixed raced with big breasts barely contained in a sleeveless top. She noticed him, glaring at first, then taking in the jewels and the ride. Fiona noticed her looking at K-Bar and shook her head.

'If only she knew.'

'Knew what?' He sped up, driving down Harrogate Road.

'That it's not all it's cracked up to be. Riding with a thug.'

'What are you talking about?'

'Is that how you like them?' Fiona was still looking ahead.

'Are you gonna tell me what you're on about?'

'You don't know?'

'Forget it,' he sighed, turning the music up. Fiona immediately turned it down.

'Don't you know?'

'Why are we doing this shit? Is this why you wanted a lift? So you could talk in riddles?'

Fiona looked at him blankly. He hated when she did that. That was his thing. Giving people the vacuous stare to keep them unbalanced, unsure of his true intentions. He didn't like it being done to him.

'I asked for a lift because I'm going shopping for your child. You think I care if you want to sleep with that slag, or if you want to slip your dick into Marika Jones?'

So that was what this was all about. He resisted the urge to roll his eyes.

'Me and Marika are friends.'

'Me and Dwayne are friends too.'

K-Bar scowled. Fiona and Dwayne were as on and off as she and K-Bar were. Dwayne made a slick comment once when he'd dropped off his child, so he sought him out a few days later and broke his nose. Dwayne had wanted to press charges, but Fiona — with help from Grimer, talked him out of it. Still, it was a low shot, and they both knew it.

'Why isn't he giving you a lift then? No petrol for his shitty little ride?' K-Bar snapped back. Her eyes narrowed.

'Just because he doesn't sell drugs like you—'

'Shut up about what you don't understand.' K-Bar snapped. He drove past the Arena, approaching the Merrion Centre. He pulled to a stop outside the Yorkshire Bank, keeping his eyes out for overzealous traffic wardens.

'How don't I understand? Just remember, I was there in the beginning. I remember when you were a little tramp eating crisp sandwiches for dinner. I still loved you.'

K-Bar couldn't deny that. Fiona had unconditionally loved him. No matter what rumours she heard about he and Shorty, she'd stood by him. Until he got too deep into the game, and cheerful hailings of 'Franklin' and 'Kieron' turned into hushed whisperings of *Shorty* and *K-Bar*.

'Are you gonna pick me up?' Fiona paused with her hand on the door handle. He handed her a twenty-pound note.

'Get a taxi if you can't get hold of me.'

Fiona shot him an evil look, but took the money. She slammed the door and stormed across the road towards the Merrion Centre back entrance. He stared after her, then sped down the road. He was tired of Fiona making slick comments about his relationship with Marika. Turning onto North Street, he headed back to the Hood, passing a blue Vauxhall Corsa near Francis Street.

TARGET PART TWO: THE TAKEDOWN

Lennox noted the silver Mercedes cruising by. He idled at the curb in a blue Corsa, sitting with Nikkolo as they staked out a red-bricked terraced house. It had an attached brown garage, and some sparse plants in the tiny garden. Though similar to the other houses, they knew it to be one of Delroy Williams' spots. He had an office in the area, heavily guarded, where he conducted business. This house was used to house large quantities of drugs, something Nikkolo wouldn't shut up about.

'There's gotta be kilos in there. Delroy only deals in boxes. I bet there's at least fifty. We could have a team in and out of there before anyone realised, Len. Say the word, and I'll—'

'Be quiet.'

He stopped talking. Lennox hadn't raised his voice, nor did he need to. After a beat, Lennox spoke again.

'As I keep stating, we're building, piece by piece. Everything has a purpose, and a silly robbery isn't part of that. This isn't about drugs, and we're not drug dealers. Remember that fact, because I'm tired of reminding you.'

Nikkolo nodded, keeping his head down. The unpredictable energy in the car was unnerving, and he didn't want to say the wrong thing.

'This spot is a weak link. We target weak links. Put a man on Winston Williams. I want to know everywhere he goes, and who he associates with. Don't engage him. Just watch and report. Understand?'

'Yeah, I understand. I'll take care of all of that,' said Nikkolo. He sighed before speaking again. 'Teflon's spending more time in Chapeltown. That was K-Bar, who drove by in the Benz. What do you think they're planning?'

Lennox knew Lamont's intentions. He'd sat idle for too long, and the reputation of his firm was dwindling in certain circles. He was sure Lamont would now rectify that and get things straightened out. Nikkolo waited for an answer, so he gave him one.

'I don't know.'

'What about Shorty? He bust case on that murder charge, and he's out too. Is him being out gonna affect anything for us?' Nikkolo froze at the ugly expression on Lennox's face. The dark eyes held an icy glint that worried him, and he wondered if he had gone too far.

'I'm not worried about Shorty, and you shouldn't be either. If he involves himself, I'll break him.'

CHAPTER SIX
MONDAY 16 FEBRUARY, 2015

LAMONT SULKED for a while after his argument with Trinidad. He saw where he was coming from, but Chapeltown's problems had been there long before Lamont was around, and would be there long after he went. The most irritating thing was the guilt he felt. People looked at him differently now, and he didn't like it. The old woman avoiding his path was only the start. When he went to local takeaways, or to buy things from local shops, he felt the angry glares. He needed to shrug it off and focus.

Driving into the city centre, he parked, took his ticket, and headed towards a little restaurant near Albion Street.

'CAN I get you anything else, sir?'

Lamont shook his head, tucking into the grilled chicken breast. He didn't think much of it, but kept his expression neutral, letting the conversation swirl around him.

'What does Kingsford think then?' His business partner, a doughy, bespectacled man named Martin Fisher, asked whilst shovelling fillet steak into his mouth and washing it down with wine.

The third, a diminutive hook-nosed man with balding hair and a five-thousand-pound suit, picked at his salad, arranging it on the plate. He sipped a glass of sparkling water.

'He's out.'

'How can he be out, Levine? I'm not sure if you remember the talks from last year, but he was our best bloody friend then! What's changed?'

'The climate, Marty. I'm just your solicitor, but I've plenty of contacts in the Kingsford camp. People have been whispering in his ear for months about Lamont's background, and with his unfortunate incident, and all the publicity, he got cold feet.'

Lamont didn't even raise his head. Martin still believed they could salvage a deal, but he saw the writing on the wall. From a business standpoint, he was damaged goods. After his recovery, he'd reviewed news coverage from the shooting. He'd received near national exposure, with talk relating to the fact the shooting was tied to drugs. With Timmy dead at the scene, and eye-witness reports of multiple shots being fired, the press were desperate to unlock the secret of who exactly Lamont Jones was, and why people wanted to kill him.

Thanks partly to the machinations of Levine, the story died down, but the men Lamont was in business with had long memories.

'Commitments were made, and I — rather, we, want to see something for it, Levine. I don't think that's too much to ask.'

'I'm only here to counsel and dispense advice. Reach out if you feel it's necessary; just don't be shocked if you receive a cold reception. That local initiative is making many developers wary about treading into Chapeltown.'

Martin, now red-faced, stabbed his fork into the remains of his steak. The loud clinking sound had heads turning in their direction.

'L, I know you're not enjoying the chicken that much. How about a little input here?'

He glanced at Martin. 'No one is forcing the Kingsfords. If they want out, I say we leave them to it.'

'I agree,' said Levine.

'That means leaving the potential to make a lot of money on the table,' argued Martin.

'If we can finance the housing initiative, we'll have an excellent foundation. The Kingsford's are formidable, but they're not the only game in town.'

Martin shook his head, but didn't reply. He could be short-sighted, but Lamont knew he would have to accept that the Kingsfords had been spooked. He checked the time on his watch.

'I'm going to have to leave you two. I have another meeting.'

'With whom?' Martin demanded. Lamont stared him down, silently imploring him to relax.

'It's personal, not business. Levine, I'll call your office in a few days, and we can iron out the details.' Shaking hands with both men, he left two fifty-pound notes on the table, ignoring the protests he didn't need to. He always paid his own way.

JENNY AND KATE met for drinks after work, heading to a bar they remembered from years back. The music was low, and the bar still relatively empty, meaning they didn't struggle to hear one another.

'So, what's new?' Kate sipped her drink, looking around the room before bringing her dark eyes back to Jenny.

'One day at a time. Martha's helping a lot. She wants me to face the fact things won't be the same, and roll with the changes.'

'So, basically, the same thing I was saying all along?'

Jenny rolled her eyes. 'Yes, Kate, you're great and always right. Can we move on now?'

She grinned. Jenny stirred her drink with her finger, listening to the music for a few minutes.

'Do you know much about Chapeltown right now?'

'Are you going to be more specific?'

'That *OurHood* Initiative. Do you know much about it?'

Kate shook her head. 'I've heard of it, but not in much detail. Why?'

'I was speaking to the guy that runs it. He's come to the shop a few times, and he was telling me about the work they do. He's really involved in fundraising and organising events to raise awareness. He does a lot of writing and blogging about social issues. I was checking out his website, and some of the articles are insightful. You should read them . . .' She trailed off when she saw the speculative look on Kate's face. She'd seen the look too many times before, and it never turned out well. 'What?'

'You said he's come into the shop a few times?'

'Customers do that sometimes, Kate. So what?'

'And you spoke with the guy enough that he told you all this information about an organisation, and interested you enough to the point you checked out the website yourself?'

'Yes, Kate. Are you going to get to a point soon?'

'I'm just asking questions, Jen. Don't be so defensive. What does he look like?'

'Why? I don't know. Tall, really tall. Looks like he trains, and he's black with these really dark eyes . . .' She again trailed off as Kate giggled.

'Sounds like you've got a bit of a crush there, Jen. You went from *don't know* to describing his build pretty quickly.'

'You asked, and I answered. Malcolm's an attractive guy, but it's not like that. He's just interesting. I enjoy interesting people. Must be why I'm friends with your crazy self.'

'You're friends with me because I liven you up and give your life meaning,' Kate stuck out her tongue. 'How's L?'

Jenny sighed. Lamont was a tricky subject. They were happy around one another, but there was an undercurrent of forced interaction they were both aware of. Sometimes, the most difficult thing was to sit at the table, or at a restaurant, and make conversation. It used to come so naturally, yet now they seemed to have to try much harder. Even before they became a couple, they could always talk and bounce off each other. She hoped the disconnect didn't continue, because she loved Lamont, and wanted nothing more than to be happy with him.

'He's not one hundred percent. Hasn't been since it happened. I don't know how to help him, I mean, I've suggested he visit my counsellor, but he won't even consider it.'

'You know what L's like. He wants to deal with it all and get better by himself.' Kate's voice was full of warmth. She'd always had a soft spot for him, and had helped to get them together. 'He nearly died, though, and that's gonna change anyone, especially an alpha male like Lamont. When you think about it, you two haven't been together long, and you've dealt with so much. I guess you just need to wait it out, even if that's not what you want to hear.'

They sat in silence. Jenny contemplated Kate's words, grudgingly admitting that her friend was probably right. They had been together for under two years, and they spent a year of that time dealing with his recovery. It wasn't enough time to get a full understanding of each other. She'd sensed when she began seeing Lamont that he was guarded, but of his own accord, he eventually let her in on his pain and inner demons. Maybe he would do the same now if she remained supportive.

Feeling a sudden warmth in her stomach, she smiled and finished her drink.

'Hey, smiley girl. Have you seen who's just come in?'

Jenny followed Kate's eye, surprised to see Marika Jones and a few of her friends. She hadn't seen Lamont's younger sister since they'd spent tear-filled nights sitting by his bedside in the hospital. He'd still been unconscious, loaded with powerful painkillers and recovering from surgery. By the time he was coherent, Marika had stopped coming.

'Should I speak to her?'

'Yeah, go say hi. I'll get more drinks.'

Jenny slid to her feet and walked over to her. She was in conversation with one of her friends. Jenny didn't recognise the woman, but she was hard-faced and looked ready to break a chair over someone's head. She eyeballed Jenny, and when Marika noticed, she turned, noticing her. They stood awkwardly for a second before she found her words.

'Hey, Marika.'

'It's been a while, Jen. Everything good?'

Remembering the tight, skimpy outfit Marika had worn when she saw her at carnival two years ago, her clothes were almost stuffy in comparison. She wore a blue blouse and grey jeans with heels, her sparse makeup allowing her natural beauty to shine through. It was weird being around a family member of Lamont's that looked so much like him. The eyes were similar, the facial features, the way both could stare through a person. Their personalities differed, though.

'Yeah, just went for a drink after work with my girl. Everything okay with you?'

'I work part-time now, which I'm kinda enjoying. It's good to get out and be around people sometimes. How's L?'

It was a loaded question. Marika hadn't spoken to her brother since before the shooting. Things were said during heated moments. Lamont implied Marika was a leech, relying on him financially because she didn't want to do anything for herself. She'd let herself be manipulated by her ex-partner, Marrion, into thinking Lamont had tried to kill her. Even after all this time, they hadn't found their way back to one another.

Jenny knew that Lamont missed his sister, and especially his niece and nephew, but he didn't say much about it.

'He's good.'

Marika's smile was tight and didn't extend to her eyes. 'I'm glad he's doing well.'

Jenny thought for a second and came to a decision.

'Would you be open to making peace with him?'

Marika hung her head. 'I don't think it'll be that easy. The things we did to each other, you can't really come back from. I don't know if there's any way back.' She smiled now. 'Take my number, though, and we can talk. I should make a better effort to get to know my sister-in-law.'

TARGET PART TWO: THE TAKEDOWN

DARREN YAWNED as he sat in the backroom of a hangout spot, watching his runners playing on the Playstation. The stench of weed hung heavily in the air mingled with the smell of fried chicken and dumplings.

'D?'

He glanced around, startled at hearing his name. One of the youths handed him a phone, his brow furrowed.

'Yeah?' Darren held the phone loosely to his ear.

'Meet me outside in half an hour.'

Recognising K-Bar's voice, he hung up, hoping he hadn't done anything wrong.

'YOU WEREN'T WAITING LONG, were you?' K-Bar asked. He and Darren were in a rented black Alfa Romeo. K-Bar wore a black bomber jacket over some dark jeans and a pair of black boots. His dreads spilled freely down his back, his eyes darting around the streets, always on the lookout.

'Nah,' lied Darren. K-Bar was an hour late, but it would be pointless bringing it up.

'Meeting ran on longer, but I think you'll like what you're hearing.'

'Are we talking here?' He gestured to the car. K-Bar cocked his head and smirked.

'Nah, we're going to a spot.'

He asked no further questions, listening to K-Bar speak about random Hood politics until they pulled up to a spot in Seacroft he'd visited once before. It was a ramshackle red-bricked terraced house with crumbling stone steps leading up to a pale door. They headed inside, slouching into chairs in the makeshift kitchen.

'First up, here you go,' K-Bar reached into his pocket, slapping a wad of notes on the kitchen table, 'enjoy.'

Wordlessly, he scooped up the money, thumbing through the twenty-pound notes with an awestruck look.

'What's this for?'

'People have been noticing the work you're doing on the roads. Keep it up.'

Darren shoved the money into his pocket. 'Thank you.'

'Teflon sees summat in you. We all do. He wants you to be a big part of what happens next.'

'What's gonna happen next?'

K-Bar scratched his head. 'You know shit's been funny since Teflon's shooting, right?'

Darren did. The shooting of their leader, along with the murders of Marcus, Chink and Timmy, had cast a negative spotlight on a crew known for keeping things low-key. Their inner conflicts had been thrust out into the open, leading to a notoriety that made it difficult to do business. They persevered, but there had been little growth, and the crew were surviving rather than thriving.

'Yeah, a few people have noticed.'

'Course they have. People think we're weak, plus the Feds are just waiting for us to mess up. Fact is, though, Teflon is back.'

Darren frowned. 'I thought he was leaving.'

'Who told you that?' K-Bar flinched.

'Heard it in passing.'

K-Bar sized Darren up.

'Anyway, he's recovered, and he wants a push on the streets. We need to re-establish ourselves, and to do that, we need you in another position.'

'Which position?'

'For now, you're only gonna report to me. Your money goes up, obviously. You'll meet a few new people, and you'll keep everything you hear to yourself. Cool?'

'Course it's cool.' He fought to keep the grin from his face. He sensed he wasn't being told the full story, but would not turn down more money or responsibility.

TARGET PART TWO: THE TAKEDOWN

———

Lennox Thompson sat in the kitchen of one of his spots, drinking coffee and writing in a battered notebook. He heard the front door unlock and footsteps heading toward him. Checking his gun was within reach, he resumed writing as Nikkolo bounced into the kitchen.

'What you doing, boss? You writing bars or something?' He chuckled. Lennox laughed.

'Yeah, I'm trying to start a career as a Grime MC. Can you imagine me up on stage with *Kano*?'

The pair laughed. Lennox sipped his drink and motioned for him to sit.

'Is everything in place?'

Nikkolo nodded. Lennox knew he wasn't on board with the plan, but he wouldn't dare speak his mind.

'The police are there now. They got our little tip-off, and they raided the spot.'

'Any word on what they took?' Lennox had ordered Nikkolo to leak the address of Delroy's stash house, wanting to further weaken his fledging power base.

'Only rumours from people hanging around, but there were boxes and boxes in there, and about twenty kilo's of weed. They had some fancy equipment to hide the smell. Couple' guns too. People are still talking about it.'

'Make sure our people are discreetly out there talking it up too. I want everyone to see Delroy Williams for the fat, worthless weakling that he is.'

'I'll take care of everything.'

Satisfied, he returned to writing his notes as Nikkolo poured a shot of brandy.

———

LAMONT LED K-Bar into his study and poured him a drink. They toasted.

'Surprised you didn't want to meet at the barber's,' said K-Bar, noticing his expression darken for a second.

'It's good to switch it up. This room is well-guarded. Akeem made sure of it.'

'You trust him, don't you?' K-Bar remarked.

'I trust both of you. You wouldn't be here otherwise. There aren't many people that know where I live.'

'Mostly women, I'm guessing,' quipped K-Bar. They both laughed, which seemed to take some tension out of the room. K-Bar knew he was right. It had been years since K-Bar had been to any of his houses. The fact he was here was a sign things were changing.

'Did you put that list together?'

K-Bar handed a crumpled piece of paper to him.

'Are these guys available?'

'I've put out feelers. They're all willing to work for the right money. Jamal and Rudy, in particular, will get shit done. They knew Marcus back in the day and had good things to say about him.'

'Bring them all in, piece-by-piece, and put them to work. What about the other thing?'

'We collected most of the money you were owed. A couple people were funny about paying. Akeem went to speak to them, and the money popped up like magic. A few others arranged payment plans as they didn't have the money in full, so we'll make interest off that.'

Lamont smirked. Akeem had already informed him about those people.

'Great.'

K-Bar rubbed the bridge of his nose. 'There's one little problem.' Which is?

'Big-Kev is holding out. He's ducking out of paying, trying to avoid meetings, fronting about paying later.'

'What does he owe?' Lamont scratched his chin.

TARGET PART TWO: THE TAKEDOWN

'Fifteen bags,' K-Bar replied, though he was aware Lamont already knew the amount.

'It's not a massive amount, but enough that people may pay attention.'

'Agreed. You wanna meet with him, see if you can convince him to pay?'

Lamont finished his drink, pouring himself another.

'Kev is the one who shot up Rika's house, right?'

K-Bar nodded. Big-Kev had links in Manchester and had loaned Marrion a large amount of money. Marrion then skipped town and avoided paying him back. After a few warnings, he struck, shooting up Marika's house, then murdering Marrion a short while later.

Lamont's expression became cold, taking K-Bar by surprise.

'Meet with Akeem, sort the situation between yourselves. Send a message, let people know that we're back in the game.'

CHAPTER SEVEN
TUESDAY 17 FEBRUARY, 2015

'I DON'T THINK it'll hurt him.'

Darren Lyles sat in the stash spot with Maka, watching the workers bagging drugs. They were deep in conversation about the raid at Delroy's spot.

'Del's been doing this for years, and I heard the police got like twenty boxes at the most. That can't hurt Delroy,' he kept saying. Maka was more reserved. He had been in the game far longer than Darren and read between the lines with certain situations.

'You think so?'

'Yeah. Twenty's minor when you've got money like he must have.'

Maka shook his head. 'Lesson number one: never assume the other man has money. You don't need to count anyone's pockets but your own. I'm telling you, as a man that's been around, that loss will hurt Delroy a lot. There's gonna be a lot of restructuring behind the scenes. It's the same thing K had to do when Tef was down.'

'What are you lot on about?'

K-Bar entered the spot and greeted the pair, ignoring the workers.

TARGET PART TWO: THE TAKEDOWN

'Just the Delroy thing. Is everything good?'

'I need to talk to you.'

Maka and K-Bar headed to the garden. The cold was biting to the point both men wore large winter coats, hoping that the spate of bad weather subsided soon.

'What's going on then?'

'You hear about Kev?' K-Bar got straight to the point.

'I heard he was ducking L.'

'Well, now he's gotta go. Permanently.'

'For real?' Maka's eyes widened.

'Tef is back, bro. He wants people to know they can't take liberties.'

'That's a big move for him. Shorty used to have to talk him into hitting people. Now he's ordering it himself.'

'Things change.' K-Bar shrugged. 'I'll handle the hit, but I want you to do the driving. Cool?'

'Let me know when. What about the slotting crews in Manny? Didn't Kev use one of those to shoot up Marika's house?'

K-Bar nodded. 'They're not gonna get involved. They're saying it's a personal issue.'

Maka scratched his chin. 'Tef must have given them something to make them step aside.'

'Doubt it was a small amount either. He's gonna have us back on top, though.'

LAMONT SAT IN HIS STUDY, leafing through a file Akeem had given him. Akeem stood in the corner, waiting for him to finish. He took his time, and when he finished, he placed the file in his drawer and locked it.

'Those are the people you could locate?'

Akeem nodded. 'Akhan is a ghost. I couldn't find an address without exposing what I was doing. He stopped using the office on Hares Avenue over a year ago. Another family appears to be staying there now, and I don't know what connection they have to him. It could be family, or random renters. It's hard to get a fix.

'His organisation is all over the place, which makes them harder to track. Saj was easy enough to tail, and through him, my people were able to find some others.'

'Looks like mostly low-level guys in that folder, so we've either grossly exaggerated how powerful Akhan is . . .'

'Or, he keeps his inner circle close to his chest.' Akeem was silent for a moment before speaking again. 'What's the move here? Akhan is blackmailing you, but you decided to keep selling drugs, regardless. What's the endgame?'

Lamont thought for a moment before he replied, appreciating the question Akeem had posed to him. When Vincent suggested he come and work for him, Lamont had quickly taken to his way of viewing things. He kept his own counsel and spoke when necessary. Lamont appreciated those traits. He'd been open with him about Akhan's threats. Akeem listened, then asked what he wanted him to do.

'I can't let Akhan have an edge. If he thinks he has me over a barrel, he'll take more liberties. It's how men in his position work.'

'And are you willing to risk the high-quality drug supply to usurp this man?'

Lamont rubbed his eyes.

'Let's deal with one thing at a time.'

———

JENNY ENTERED a coffee shop in the city centre and waited in the queue. After ordering a drink, she headed upstairs and saw the person she'd come to see. Taking a deep breath, she strolled over and slid into a seat opposite.

'When you asked for my number, I didn't think you'd use it,' she said to the person, who smirked over the rim of their own cup.

'I just thought we should talk. A loud bar in the middle of town wasn't the best place.'

TARGET PART TWO: THE TAKEDOWN

Jenny nodded. 'It always tickles me to enter these coffee shops. My first date with L was in one, believe it or not.'

'I'd have expected him to pull out all the stops.' Marika laughed.

'I did too, but it was nice. Awkward at first. You know how it is when you don't quite have the right back-and-forth. Didn't help that every woman that passed us kept staring like they wanted to steal him.'

Marika laughed again. 'We have good genes in my family.' She ran a hand through her silky hair.

'Things got better from there, though,' Jenny finished. Marika watched her.

'How is he?'

Jenny blew out a breath, rolling her shoulders. 'Like I said, he's getting there. L doesn't like to let people in. He just bottles it up and hopes it will go away.'

'I think he learned that when we were younger. Has he told you about his upbringing?'

'He's mentioned your Aunt, if that's what you mean.'

'I didn't see what it was he saw.' Marika took another sip.

'What do you mean?'

'Ever since we stopped talking, I've spent more time around Auntie, and she'll always find a way to bring up L; how horrible he is. How he doesn't take care of family. It's bullshit, because L always helped me out, and he helped other family members too. L's paid for funerals over the years, family holidays, given people money when they were sick . . .

'I think Auntie's issue is that L doesn't give *her* any money. He doesn't acknowledge her, and the family knows it. I guess we were all avoiding the question staring at all of us.'

'Which is?'

'Why did L hate Auntie so much? L's no angel, but still. He was a top student, never put a step wrong, did all the housework and cooking without complaint. How can you do all that and still have your Guardian hate you?'

'Did you ever see it?'

Marika looked away a moment. 'I saw little things. Beatings here and there. She was always going on about L's appearance, but she bought him rubbish clothing. Mine was a little better, but she used to say that was because I was younger and my clothes were cheaper. I used to try to get him in trouble all the time.' She hung her head.

'Kids do that.'

'It was worse. Auntie didn't need much provocation to punish Lamont, and he just took it. He never stopped loving me, never mistreated me. I was his closest family member, and I revelled in it, even as we got older. I could always count on him for money, and my kids loved him. Still do.

'When we argued after Marcus was killed, though, and he called me a leech and said all those horrible things, it broke me. He was right; I took and took, and I definitely learned it from Auntie.'

'Is that why you stayed with Marrion?'

Marika wiped her eyes, her voice quiet now. 'He wanted to look after me.'

Jenny waited for Marika to continue.

'Marrion came out of nowhere, and he was strong, and he dressed and talked nice. I guess I hoped I'd found someone I could build with; someone who would motivate me to do something with my life. He was a hustler who'd come up from nothing, just like my brother, and I imagined them working closely together and everyone making more money. Marrion had different goals, though, and his agenda was nowhere near mine.'

'In what sense?'

Marika took a deep breath. 'Marrion was behind the shooting.'

Instantly, Jenny's blood ran cold, her hands shaking. She remembered the man who'd screamed for Timmy to pull the trigger, before grabbing the weapon and doing it himself.

'Why?' She whispered after a moment.

'He wanted it all, and L was in the way.'

'L was walking away from the life. Surely he knew that?'

TARGET PART TWO: THE TAKEDOWN

Marika shrugged. 'I honestly don't know. Marrion lied to me and said L was behind the shooting at my house.'

Jenny breathed deeply, trying to rid herself of the memories. Marika clutched her trembling hand. It was just for a moment, but it calmed her.

'What shooting?'

'Turns out Marrion owed some people. They came looking for him and shot up my house with the kids and me in there. Luckily, no one was hurt.'

'How does this coincide with Marrion trying to kill L?'

'Marrion warned me that L would be taken out. I told him that L was my brother. I said that if he loved me, then he would stop it from happening.'

'And then what happened?'

'He stormed out, and he was shot. Right outside the house. I heard about L's shooting afterwards, when the police finished questioning me.'

'That's why you came to the hospital,' Jenny realised. She nodded.

'Look after my brother, Jen. He's not as tough as he wants you to believe, and he needs you. Just help him get where he needs to get.'

The two women from opposite ends of the spectrum surveyed one another for a long moment. Jenny broke the silence.

'I will if he lets me.'

THAT NIGHT, Lamont and Jenny hosted Shorty at home. It surprised him to get the invitation. He'd seen little of Lamont lately, focusing on catching up with old faces and getting the lay of the land. Youngsters dominated the roads, with many of his age group leaving Chapeltown behind, or going legal and working jobs. It was a culture shock.

Shorty vaguely remembered the rise of social media just before he got locked up, but now all he seemed to see were youngsters on their phones. Even Darren and Shadow had posed for a photo the last time he'd seen them, claiming the ladies loved it. They'd tried getting him to take one with them, but he refused.

Shorty hadn't broached the conversation with Lamont about getting started again. He was still collecting money, but, other than giving some to Amy, hadn't done much with it. He'd purchased some new clothing. Having been locked up during the summer, a lot of his clothing was unsuitable.

Back in the day, he would have blown the lot, then hustled up more, but he was wary of the police now, and didn't know how to get in contact with a lot of his independent links. He would need to take things slowly.

Jenny and Shorty spoke as Lamont prepared the food in the kitchen. She offered to help, but Lamont refused.

They kept the conversation light, speaking about her business, his daughter, and the incident in Chapeltown still dominating the local news. Jenny didn't know much about the situation, but was open to the thought of more scrutiny being given to police officers.

They spoke about the *OurHood* Initiative, and Shorty was surprised when she mentioned Malcolm Powell, whom he knew was the driving force behind much of the group's work. When he pressed, she said he was a customer she'd met recently, leaving him to wonder if she was being truthful.

Soon, they sat at the table, consuming Lamont's food. He'd made grilled steak, baby potatoes with asparagus and green beans.

'I gotta say, fam, I forgot you could cook like this,' Shorty admitted, a massive grin on his face as he tore into the food.

'I like to cook at least once or twice a week, maybe more if Jen's tired. It's therapeutic.'

Jenny sent him a wide smile which he returned, squeezing her hand. Shorty watched the pair, happy that they seemed to be getting along. It was the most time he'd seen them spend together since his release, and he recalled how high-strung Jenny was when he'd gone to buy the flowers. Lamont seemed more relaxed now, more like the old *L*.

'Have you two ever told me how you met?' Jenny asked. By now, they had finished eating and were in the living room sipping drinks. Lamont disappeared to complete the washing up, then sat next to her afterwards. Shorty and Lamont laughed.

'How many years ago was that?' Shorty asked.

'Thirty, thirty-one at least. We were in Reception.' Lamont took over the story. 'I was nervous, trying to avoid everyone around me.'

'I was a little shit,' Shorty said. 'I was bigger than everyone else in the class and didn't know how to sit still. I remember seeing L sitting there, trying to read some little kiddie book, and I just started hanging around him. Stayed like that for a few years. People used to trouble him because he was quiet, and I fought them off.' Shorty paused, reminiscing. 'It was just like that, I guess. We lived close to each other, and I guess I liked his quietness. I didn't want anyone else getting more attention than me.'

Jenny smiled. The pair continued to tell stories of things they had done as kids. She noticed the stories were all light-hearted and innocent, for which she was thankful. The last thing she wanted was to hear more stories of Lamont's criminal days. She was tempted to mention the meeting with Marika, but didn't know how. She stayed quiet and sipped her wine.

When Jenny went to bed, Lamont and Shorty retreated to his study, taking their glasses and a bottle of brandy with them. Lamont topped up their glasses, and the old friends toasted in silence.

'It was a good night. We'll have to do this more often,' Lamont started. 'You should bring a girl next time. You got anyone in mind?'

'Amy?' Shorty joked. Lamont grinned.

'They got along when they met. Amy came to visit me, and she and Jenny were talking. I think Jenny met Grace after that, but you know what she's like.'

Shorty grinned. Grace was wary around new people, something he was sure she had picked up from him.

'Amy's dating now, and I don't think we could ever go back to the way things were. I met a girl after I got out of prison, but that was just a one-night thing. I don't even know her name.'

'Typical you then. What about Kimberley?'

Shorty scowled. He and Kimberley had been on and off for years. The last time they had been together was the Bank Holiday weekend when Marcus died. Kimberley got into an altercation with some girls, and he defended her. They slept together the same weekend, but in the aftermath of the shootings, he'd forgotten all about her until he was locked up. He'd tried reaching out and even wrote to her, but she never responded.

'I'd have to try tracking her down, see what's going on. She ducked me when I was in prison, but I could always get her to slip up one-on-one.'

They laughed, remembering some of the altercations Shorty and Kimberley had in the past.

'It really is good to see you out, Shorty. We haven't spoken much, but I never liked the thought of my best friend rotting behind bars. If shit hadn't gone down how it had . . . you wouldn't have stayed in so long.'

Shorty nodded, touched by the emotion in his friend's voice.

'How are you doing, though? I bet it's dodgy trying to get used to everything.'

'Entire world's changed. I remember so many people from before I got locked up, and they're not even around anymore. There's people fighting each other who I'd never have expected. Even this *OurHood* shit, it's mad. Jen was telling me earlier that she knows the man behind it. Some dude called Malcolm. I'm assuming you do too.'

'I've never met him.' Lamont's expression hardened. Shorty blinked, and his face was blank again.

'Think he must have bought some flowers or something. Is that initiative affecting business?'

TARGET PART TWO: THE TAKEDOWN

'Everything is affecting business at the moment. I'm taking steps to get things in order. It won't happen overnight, but it's necessary.'

'About that,' Shorty started. 'We need to talk, L.'

Lamont sipped his drink, topping himself up. He motioned to the bottle, but Shorty shook his head.

'I thought we were talking?'

'I want back in. Put me on so I can start hustling again.'

Lamont didn't reply straight away. The silence stretched, Lamont holding his glass and staring off into space. The longer the silence, the more antsy Shorty grew.

'Did you hear me, L?'

'I think you should stay under the radar for now. The police might still be watching you, and the last thing we need is to give them a reason to look too closely.'

'I know the game. I know how to hustle low-key. The money is running low, and I need to step up so I can fund my kids. You know that.'

Lamont smiled. 'Shorty, you're my brother, and you never have to worry about money. I've more than got you covered with everything you need.'

Shorty's hands twitched as he tightened his grip on the glass

'Listen, I'm not Rika. I don't need a handout. I can earn.'

'It's not a handout. I want to help you, and I don't want you getting yourself in any trouble.'

'Then you need to have some faith in me. It's a handout if you wanna keep giving me money and not have me work for it.'

'Do you not understand where I'm coming from, Shorty? You just got released from a murder charge. You weren't worrying about money when I was paying my solicitor's small fortunes to defend you.'

'What does that have to do with anything?'

Lamont rubbed his face, his jaw tight.

'It means that if you hadn't been so foolish to get yourself arrested, I wouldn't have needed to protect you. You should have left the Manchester situation alone. I told you to be careful, but you didn't listen. You never do, and that's why I have to be careful before I put you back in.'

Shorty let out a harsh laugh. 'Protect me? What can you protect me from? You couldn't even protect yourself when you got dropped in the street like a coward!'

The tense silence that followed his words was palpable, both men scowling. After a while, the ringing of Lamont's phone punctuated the silence. He answered curtly, his expression changing as the person on the other end spoke.

'I'm on my way.' He hung up and leapt to his feet.

'What's happened?' Shorty asked. Lamont rubbed his eyes as he drained his drink.

'It's K-Bar. We need to call Akeem and go. Now.'

CHAPTER EIGHT
WEDNESDAY 25 FEBRUARY, 2015

K-BAR WINCED, gritting his teeth, his hand wrapped around a bottle of the worst-tasting whiskey he'd ever tried. He wasn't in a situation to be picky, resisting the urge to touch the bandages that swathed his upper body. He closed his eyes as footsteps bounded up the stairs of the safe house, resisting the urge to go for the gun under his pillow as Lamont burst in, followed by Shorty. Both froze.

'What the hell happened?' Lamont found his voice first. K-Bar sighed.

'Things were dicey.'

'Dicey, how?'

He swigged the whiskey, making another face.

———

K-BAR WATCHED the surroundings from the passenger seat of the Ford Focus, wearing his all-black killing gear. In the driver's seat, Maka slouched, devouring a packet of crisps as he stared at his phone. The loud chewing was irritating K-Bar, but he shut it out. He needed to be in the zone.

They had been tracking Kev for days, eventually tailing him to a spot near Armley. They were parked nearby, monitoring the house. K-Bar hadn't fired his gun in a while and was trying to slip into his mode of focus. He took a deep breath.

'Oi, put the phone away and make sure you're ready, okay?'

Maka nodded, wiping his mouth and slipping the phone into the pocket of his combat trousers.

'Make sure you're on point. If anything goes wrong, finish the job and get clear.'

'Got it, K. I know the drill.'

It was after ten when Big-Kev lumbered from the house. He was a mountain of a man, standing well over six-feet-tall with the weight to match. Even from his vantage point, K-Bar noticed his chins wobbling as he struggled to move forward. He had to be at least twenty stone.

'Right then, show time.'

K-Bar slid from the car. Kev was paying little attention as his accomplice rambled on about something, waving the keys in his hand excitedly as the Range Rover clicked. K-Bar's black boots clumped over the frosted ground, making little noise. He raised the gun when he was close by, satisfied neither man had even noticed him. His finger caressed the trigger as Kev stopped short.

'Shit, forgot my—'

K-Bar's gun whistled, silencing the rest of Kev's words. His hesitation saved his life, K-Bar aiming for where he expected the man to be. The bullet whizzed past them as his accomplice yelled. Kev trudged back towards the house as his accomplice reached for something, but K-Bar was far quicker, a bullet lodging into the man's chest as he flew backwards. He hurried after Kev, the large man already out of breath after a few yards. Three shots slumped into his back, and Kev fell face-first to the ground with a grunt. K-Bar put his gun to Kev's head and pulled the trigger, finishing the job.

As he turned to find Maka, he was stunned to see a flash of metal, then felt the searing pain of the knife slashing against his chest. The accomplice he'd shot bore down on him, holding the blooded knife, his face contorted with pain. K-Bar saw the red patch on his sweater, but it didn't seem to hold him back. He tumbled over Kev's dead body and fell to the floor, the gun slipping from his hand. The accomplice raised the knife to finish the job, and he cursed himself for not making sure the man was dead. Three shots rang out, and now the man lurched towards him, the knife tumbling from his hand. K-Bar leapt to his feet, fumbling for the gun as Maka dropped his own smoking weapon.

'Come, man; we need to go!'

Maka helped him, and they stumbled towards the car.

'WHY DIDN'T you finish him in the house?' Lamont's eyes seared with fury.

'We didn't know how many people were in there. Figured we'd get him when he came out. It would have worked if he hadn't hesitated.'

'You should have made sure his guy was dead the first time, K,' said Shorty. 'Always clean your plate. You nearly got finished because you were sloppy.'

'I know, Shorty. I don't need to hear this shit right now. My fucking chest is killing, and I just wanna drink until the pain goes away.'

'Did anyone see you?' Lamont asked.

'I don't know. I was too busy trying not to die,' snapped K-Bar. Lamont's expression softened.

'Fair enough. At least he's dead. I'll send word to the Manchester links that he's gone. Did you leave any blood at the scene?'

'I honestly don't know. There was no time to call anyone to clean up, but the Fed's won't be able to prove it's me, anyway. It was dark, and we burnt out the car we used. It's cool.'

Lamont nodded, sharing a look with Shorty.

'I'll send Akeem to see if there's any possibility of a cleanup, but

I doubt it at this stage. For now, lie low and speak to no one. I'll send word when it's cool to resurface.' He swept from the room, with Shorty following.

'I expected better from K,' Lamont admitted, as they climbed into the ride. Akeem motored away.

'These things happen, L. He did the job regardless. If anything pops off, K-Bar will ride it. He's not gonna roll on us.'

Lamont shrugged, thankful that K-Bar's mission had distracted Shorty from their argument. He wasn't ready to let his friend back into the fold yet, but it was growing harder to keep him at bay. He needed to sit down, think, and reinforce his next move.

―――

Detective Inspector Rigby slumped, wiping tired eyes as he pored over several papers on his cramped desk. It was late in the office, and very few were still working, other than the night shift. Sipping his stone-cold coffee, he ran a hand through his greying hair as someone approached.

'Figured I'd find you here.' Murphy took a seat next to him and glanced at the paperwork. 'This couldn't wait until tomorrow?'

'There was nothing to go home to.' Rigby shrugged. Murphy grinned, showing yellow teeth.

'Guess I'm staying here with you then. What do you have?'

'This Kev thing.'

'What about it?' Murphy had been placed on the case of the dead criminal, with Rigby and a few others. The name was one they knew. Big-Kev was a nasty man known for throwing his weight around and taking liberties with people. Murphy wasn't enthused about catching his killer, but it was better than the cases they'd had recently.

'It stinks, to be honest.'

'He was a scumbag everyone hated. Course it stinks,' Murphy pointed out.

TARGET PART TWO: THE TAKEDOWN

'That's my point; everyone hated him, but no one ever made a move. He was a big deal, and he had a lot of connections, so no one could touch him. What changed?'

'I dunno, Rig. I don't see why you think it's so important.'

Rigby shook his head. Murphy didn't get it. He'd lost that desire for police work two marriages ago. Rigby still believed in their work, even in a sparse department, almost threadbare from the redundancies and recent cutbacks.

'Because it's an important part in everything that's happened recently. We've seen more murders in the past four years than the last ten years before that. Doesn't that shock you? Even when we had all the mess between the Yardies and the local kids, it was never this bad. We need to pull the threads and follow them while we still have a city left to protect.'

Murphy wanted to argue, but held his tongue. It was hard to stop Rigby when he was off on a tangent. He was the sharpest detective on the unit, though, and as annoying and convoluted as his thinking could be, it bore results more often than not.

'Do you have a plan?'

Lamont washed and dressed the next day, ate a quick breakfast with Jenny and then left with Akeem, quickly mired in traffic.

'I'm assuming we couldn't get people up to Armley in time?'

'The police had the area cordoned off. Someone got close enough to see that there were two bodies. We should be okay. Doesn't look like K-Bar left much mess behind, and it was late, so it's less likely someone saw anything.'

Lamont was satisfied, for now. K-Bar was in hiding and would remain there until things calmed down. He'd used the situation to get Shorty to agree to back off. He wouldn't be able to keep him at bay forever, and wondered to himself why he didn't want him involved. It wasn't a question of greed; he paid his people well, and

Shorty received a larger share than anyone other than himself. Skill-wise, Shorty was in a different league. He could shoot and maim enemies, but had the charisma to make people want to be around him; an essential trait for the role he'd held.

Lamont wanted him to be safe, though. The police loathed people getting away with murder, and he didn't want them trying to put Shorty down for good. It wasn't the time to think about it, though. He had work to do.

They reached their destination. Akeem led the way, Lamont following. The garden was unkempt. Weeds lived where flowers once rested, and the gate wailed as they pushed it, its rusty shell creaking. They knocked at the door, waiting.

'L?'

A powerfully built, dark-skinned man loomed over them. He wore a rumpled white t-shirt, grey jogging bottoms, and was barefooted. His sleepy eyes brimmed with obvious confusion.

'Hello, Sharma.'

Lamont didn't have many memories of Sharma. He, along with another soldier named Victor, did the running around of Marcus Daniels. Victor had lost his freedom trying to protect Marcus when he was shot. He was serving time. Lamont ensured he was looked after, but money was nothing compared to freedom.

He realised this now more than ever.

'Come in, fam.' Sharma shuffled to the side to let them enter. He'd never made big money rolling with Marcus, and it was clear he was making even less with his death. There was a sofa in the middle of the room that looked like it had been left outside someone's house, some splinter-ridden wooden chairs, and a TV. The floorboards creaked under the weight of the men.

Sharma hung near the door, rubbing the back of his neck.

'Sorry about the mess. Wasn't expecting company.'

'How are you doing?'

'I'm getting by. Juggling here and there. You know how it is.'

'Definitely,' agreed Lamont. It had been years since he'd needed

TARGET PART TWO: THE TAKEDOWN

to scramble around to make money, as everyone present knew. He still went along with it.

'Ring K-Bar. Tell him I said to call. We'll find something for you.'

'You don't have to do that . . .'

'Marcus was closer than family. He trusted you, and I shouldn't have left you out in the cold. Blame the shooting.'

Sharma nodded, humbled.

'I need to ask you something. Need you to be honest.'

'Okay, L. I will. I swear.'

'Reagan. Who got rid?'

Sharma swallowed audibly, his eyes darting between the pair.

'I was there, but Marcus hired cleaners. He needed to leave no trace, probably cos' of where it happened. He knew how much you and the old man loved the spot.'

'Do you know which cleaners?'

Again, Sharma hesitated.

'Some freelancers out of Gipton. They're trustworthy, though.'

'Give me all the info you can on them. You can take down K's number too.'

Sharma rooted around for a pen and some paper. He stopped mid-search, looking at him, the fear and uncertainty dissipating.

'L, I just want you to know, Marcus loved you like a brother.'

'I need the name regardless, Sharma, but thanks,' replied Lamont, noting how empty the words made him feel.

———

'Are you really going to give him a job?' Akeem asked when they left Sharma's. He intended to learn how Akhan had found out about Reagan's murder. There was a camera fitted above the barbers, but they had checked the footage, erasing anything connected to the day Reagan visited.

Lamont thought back, recalling how nauseous he had felt after killing Reagan. He'd expected a massive outcry, but the work he and Chink had undertaken in smearing Reagan's reputation paid dividends. Most people assumed Delroy had him bumped off. The police asked a few generic questions, and then they'd buried the case.

That was why Akhan was able to blindside him, he realised; complacency. He'd forgotten about Reagan until Akhan brought him up again.

'Sharma is a good soldier, and he's loyal. If he cleans himself up, we can put him to work.'

Akeem nodded, focusing on the road. They had called around, pinpointing the exact location. The cleaners were three men in their late fifties. They had experience in the army and had been cleaning up messes resulting from disputes for years. A friend of a friend had given Lamont the address of the ringleader. He lived in a nondescript semi-detached house. As they pulled up across the road, Lamont could see a new model Vauxhall people carrier in the driveway.

'I guess he's in,' said Akeem.

'We don't want him to feel threatened. Say nothing.'

They made their way up the drive. Lamont knocked. A few moments later, a man with balding, silvery-grey hair and a ruddy face looked out at them with hawk-like green eyes.

'Travers?' Lamont spoke directly to the man who had answered the door.

'Yeah. Don't think we've met, though, Teflon.'

'How do you—'

'I've been around enough people to know that you're a force. Do you need something doing?'

'I need information. Can we come in?'

Travers gave Akeem a long look, sizing him up. Akeem met the stare. After a second, Travers stepped aside.

'What do you need information on?' He picked up a can of beer, but made no move to drink from it.

'You knew a friend of mine. *Tall-Man.*'

Travers gave no indication that he recognised the nickname.

'He came to you for some work last summer, didn't he?'

'What if he did?'

That threw a loop into his questioning. *Sharma had already confirmed that these were the cleaners Marcus had used. What could he really learn from this conversation?*

'Tall-Man paid for a job. Wasn't the first time. We don't ask more questions than necessary,' continued Travers.

'How secure is it?'

'Excuse me?' Travers glared.

'Someone knows about the job. Is there anything to find?'

'No one could put that back together. Someone else must have given them the information. Otherwise, the person is lying.'

Lamont wanted to be relieved. If the cleaner was being honest, there was no tangible evidence of his misdeeds. It didn't explain why Marcus would speak to Akhan, though.

'Has anyone else come to speak to you about this?'

Travers nodded now. 'This young Asian lad was here months ago.'

Lamont straightened in his seat. 'What did he look like?'

'Young, like I said. Lots of jewellery. Had a white Mercedes convertible. Tidy Asian bird in the front with him. She was stunning.'

'Did he give you a name?'

'Can't remember it. Summat with an *R*. Gave me five grand too. For my time.'

Lamont stood, his head spinning with all the implications. The young man had to work for Akhan. He was sure of it.

'Thank you. Someone will drop something on you later. For your co-operation. And your silence. Got it?'

Travers again nodded, and he left.

JENNY MOOCHED AROUND A COFFEE SHOP, sipping a bottle of water and staring into space. She didn't want to go home. She and Lamont had eaten breakfast and sent vague texts about potentially going out for dinner throughout the day. Jenny hadn't heard from him since, and decided she needed some alone time.

She had been to visit Martha several times since asking him to attend a session with her, but the woman was sticking to the same line about her leaving the past behind. Jenny wondered if that was what Lamont was doing. The disconnect between them seemed to grow. Shorty had said that she needed to remember how to talk to him, but it was difficult. He could close himself off in a way she had never experienced before.

Ordering a scone and some jam, Jenny pulled out her phone and went onto the Internet. Remembering the business card Malcolm Powell gave her, she went onto his website, impressed with the black, gold and white layout. It was clear as she navigated that a lot of effort had gone into the design. She was surprised when checking out Malcolm's latest blogs that he had mentioned the name of her business and posted a photo he'd taken of the arrangement she had made for him. She smiled, distracted for a moment. She clicked on the most recent blog piece and settled in to read:

Another day, another home invasion.
Technically, this one occurred outside the home, but that shouldn't discount the message. Two men dead, shot multiple times, and the police have no clue. One of the men, Kevin Roberts, or Big-Kev to his cronies on the street, was an overweight gangster who, like so many others, peddled misery. He was a loan shark who lent money to people and crippled them when they couldn't pay it back. He was immersed in this life, and for a long time, no one touched him.
Now, he's dead, and while my thoughts go out to his family, I can't claim to be sorry for his brutal murder.
It ties back to what I'm saying; the criminals run this city of ours, and it

TARGET PART TWO: THE TAKEDOWN

goes much further than just pushing a few drugs and walking around in a new chain.
What if innocents had been caught up in the crossfire of the shooting? It wouldn't be the first time now, would it? When will someone hold the criminals so many of your children look up to, accountable?
It's not a good life! A life built on inflicting pain on others is never a good life, and should never be a measuring stick, nor should it be something to look up to. Yet, so many do! And they shouldn't. Respect your mums, dads, Aunties and uncles, and other family members that are breaking their backs to provide for you.
I understand, though; it's difficult, clawing from the bottom, with temptation and fast money on every corner. I'm talking from experience because I grew up among it. I wanted more, and I type these words as proof that you can do it the right way.
In other news, Police recently seized a large quantity of drugs in the heart of Chapeltown. These were mostly class-A drugs, and there were multiple kilos, enough to do a lot of damage to the community.
I'm no friend of the police, and many of their actions relating to Chapeltown and other surrounding areas have been vile, but I applaud the seizure, and I hope it's a step in the right direction towards ridding Chapeltown completely of drugs.
I've heard people scoff and say it's impossible, because too many people profit from the drug trade, and to them, I say this; maybe you should stop them.

AFTER READING THE PIECE, Jenny had to blink a few times, having forgotten where she was. She knew Malcolm could write, but this particular piece resonated with her. As she finished her scone in silence and made her way home, she was still thinking about his words, and the evident passion behind them.

Lamont's vehicle was in the driveway when she pulled up. He sat in the living room, staring into space with a glass of brandy in his hand. He looked up when she entered and gave her a wan smile.

'Hey, babe. Everything okay?'

Jenny nodded. 'I just went for a coffee after work. Everything okay with you?'

'Yeah, just chilling.'

'Do you want something to eat?'

'I already cooked. I left you some in case you were hungry.'

Jenny kissed him on the cheek and padded to the kitchen. She found the pasta salad and warmed it up. When she'd finished, he still sat in his chair. She watched him from the doorway, noting how weary he looked. She wished she knew what was going on.

'I read an interesting article about Chapeltown today.'

'Tell me more.' He put his empty glass down.

'Someone named Malcolm Powell wrote it. Apparently, he does a lot of work in the community.'

'*OurHood*, yeah, I've heard of them,' replied Lamont. 'What did the article say?'

'Read it for yourself.' Jenny found the page and gave her phone to him. He read quickly, his face expressionless as he handed the phone back.

'He writes well.'

'Doesn't he? I think growing up locally gives him more insight into what is going on. He's passionate.'

'You've met him?'

'He came into the shop to buy flowers for his mum. Do you know him?'

Lamont shook his head. Jenny watched him carefully, noting the tenseness of his jaw, and iciness of his eyes. She couldn't believe it; he was jealous.

'Are you sure you're okay?'

Lamont stood and hugged her, kissing her on the forehead.

'I'm fine. Just tired. I'm gonna get an early night.'

He trudged upstairs, her eyes on him the entire way. She frowned, thinking about Lamont's reaction to Malcolm, and wondered if there was more to it. He had been in that life for a number of years, and it was possible he'd drawn comparisons between Malcolm and himself.

As she collapsed onto the sofa, she wondered something else; *how could Malcolm write about street politics with impunity?* Everyone else was scared to speak out for fear of reprisal, but Malcolm not only seemed unconcerned, but appeared to go above and beyond to antagonise both criminals and people in authority.

She looked to the door one more time, then picked up her phone to read more of Malcolm's work.

'WHAT TIME DID you ask him to meet us?'

Rigby and Murphy sat in Rigby's grey Skoda. He looked out the window as Murphy checked the time on his watch.

'He'll be here shortly. Relax and stop drawing attention to the vehicle.'

They didn't wait long. A man approached the ride with his head down and climbed in the back, a hood and cap obscuring his face. He pulled the hood down, breathing heavily.

'Fucking hell. Dunno why I had to meet you lot all the way out here.'

'Maybe because you don't want people to know you're working with us, did you think of that?' Murphy spat. Terry Worthy waved him off.

'Whatever. What do you want anyway?'

'Don't whatever me, you little prick,' Murphy raged. 'Don't forget who you work for, and what we've got on you. You're the scumbag who got caught trying to sell ounces to an undercover, so remember that and speak properly when you're dealing with us!'

'This doesn't matter,' Rigby weighed in. Terry's face was red with rage, as was Murphy's. He needed to take over the talking before his partner did something stupid. 'The focus here is putting the right people behind bars. Don't you agree, Terry?'

He nodded, shooting a dirty look at Murphy. Rigby grinned. They had caught him on a distribution charge, and he quickly began working with them to avoid prison time. He was relatively low on the totem pole, but had a relationship with Lamont. More importantly, he knew the organisation's rough shape, which helped them identify some key components.

'What do you know about Kev's murder?'

'I know he was a fat bastard who took liberties with people.'

'Tell us something we don't know,' said Murphy, still eyeing him.

'How am I supposed to know what you know?'

'Fine. Was your boss involved?'

Terry tipped his head to the side, then scratched his patchy beard.

'Kev definitely owed Tef some money. Ten, fifteen, twenty grand maybe, and he wasn't rushing to pay it back. People said Kev was connected to some Manchester guys too, the same ones who shot up Tef's sister's gaff, so there was definitely bad blood.'

Murphy and Rigby shared a look.

So, who would Teflon use if he wanted to take him out?

Terry shrugged. 'Dunno. Serious. L never discussed that side of things with me. I couldn't even get him to tell me his favourite colour, never mind which slotting crew he was gonna use to take out some loser.'

'The last thing you want is us to think you're not being useful, Terry . . .' Rigby let his words hang in the air as he paled.

'What do you want me to tell you?'

'Who do you think L would use?'

'Fine, K-Bar, If I'm guessing. Happy now?'

Murphy and Rigby shared another look.

'We've got work to do.'

TARGET PART TWO: THE TAKEDOWN

THAT AFTERNOON, Lamont was surprised to get a phone call asking for a meeting. He made his way to a barbers near Harehills, Akeem at his back as he was led into a backroom.

'I see you're copying my style,' he said to the man waiting for him.

'Behave. I've owned this barbers for nearly thirty years. You've got a long way to go.'

Lamont chuckled. 'How can I help?'

Delroy struggled to rise to his feet, but Lamont pretended he didn't notice. He hadn't seen the Kingpin in over eighteen months. They always had issues, almost going to war at one point, but there was always an undercurrent of respect. He was shrewd enough to know Delroy could have made a lot of situations more difficult for him, and was grateful to him for showing restraint. It was why he was here.

Delroy shook hands with Lamont and Akeem, offering them drinks, which they declined. Delroy was by himself, which was a surprising sign, and Lamont wondered if he should take it in the spirit it was intended; Delroy trusting him.

'I have a proposition for you.'

'I'm listening.'

'I want you to run my team.'

'Haven't we had this conversation before?' He didn't react. Delroy had tried many times to get Lamont to work for him, and even when he was buying his drug supply directly from Delroy, he would still attempt to talk him into it. Lamont enjoyed his position, though, and even when the offers increased to ridiculous monetary levels, he still refused.

'I'll pay you an up-front fee. You'll answer to no one, and I'll only be included when necessary.'

'Up-front fee?'

Delroy nodded. 'I'll pay you one million pounds.'

The offer was astounding, and far more than he would ever expect Delroy to come up with.

'What's this really about, Del?'

Delroy frowned. 'Don't you think I'm good for the money?'

'I don't doubt you have the money, I just think it's a massive step. You must know about what happened to me.'

'You got shot. So what? You're still here, and I know you, L. Shit like this makes you better.'

'Still doesn't explain why you'd want me to work for you. The last conversation we had was basically us threatening one another.'

Delroy sighed, his face lined and older than ever.

'I don't know how much longer I can go on. I need someone to teach Winston the game.'

'You taught Winston, though. He learned from you,' said Lamont, his brow furrowed. He'd grown up with Winston, and thought he was an effective manager, but soft, allowing people, him included, to take advantage.

'The drug seizure was his fault.'

'He set it up?'

Delroy shook his head. 'He should have been paying attention. I left the day-to-day to him. He knows that the main spots either get switched up, or you plant them somewhere to allow you to see everything coming, and protect the fuck out of them. He didn't do that. He left them the same, and people learned the pattern.'

'You think someone tipped off the police?' Lamont had spoken with K-Bar and Akeem regarding the situation, and both believed that Delroy had people in his camp working against him.

'I had three people in mind who I thought might be responsible. Mitch and Lennox Thompson . . .'

'That's two,' Lamont pointed out, as Delroy straightened in his seat and looked him in the eye.

'The third one was you.'

'Fair enough.' He didn't even flinch. 'Lennox doesn't sell drugs, though. In fact, he's always been against them.' He'd known Lennox Thompson through Marcus. He refused to sell drugs, but moved guns and loaned money, amongst other things. Lamont recalled him committing robberies all over the country, including targeting drug dealers. He'd done some time in prison, but had kept a tight grip on his crew.

Mitch was a low-key kingpin, who had been in power almost as long as Delroy.

Delroy scratched his chin, mulling over Lamont's words.

'Lennox is the one I believe is responsible. He's crafty enough not to come out and say he did it.'

'The police aren't stupid, so there's always the chance they just ran surveillance and got lucky.'

'Raids are nothing new, L. We both know that. I've never lost that amount in one sitting, though. It wasn't about taking the drugs, otherwise he could have robbed me. I think he was sending a message, and if it pops off, Winston won't be able to deal with him. You can.'

Lamont sighed. 'I'm not heavy like that anymore.'

'I know about Kev, and I know people have been scrambling around trying to get money because *Teflon* came out of hiding and demanded repayments. You're ramping up for something. We can help each other.'

'I want to ask you something else,' said Lamont, disregarding his statement.

'Go ahead.'

'What is the deal with Akhan?'

Delroy didn't speak for a long time, tapping his fingers on the desk before smirking.

'Why?'

'I'm curious.'

'He turned up the heat on you, didn't he? That's why you're stepping up. You're moving against him.'

He didn't reply, waiting for Delroy to continue.

'L, you're talking about an entirely different sort of power here. Those Asians are embedded, with shooting crews and men all over the place. He's a warlord, and he's got direct links to people abroad that will murder you and your entire crew in your sleep. How can you go up against that?'

'I never said I was.'

Delroy rubbed his eyes. 'You know he was the reason I backed off, don't you?'

'I worked that one out.'

'So, what does that tell you?'

'It tells me you take him seriously, but you haven't told me anything I don't already know.'

'Then let me tell you this; don't engage Akhan. Just keep working, making money, and let me know about my proposition. Stay in touch.'

———

'WHAT DO YOU THINK THEN?'

Rigby took a long swig of coffee. It was again late in the office, and he and Murphy were hunched over his desk, looking over files and making notes. Terry's information had been sparse, but it was enough for them to pay more attention.

'Teflon was definitely behind it. We know that Kev owed him money, and there aren't many people who could take him out without a backlash on the streets. Kev was definitely behind the shooting of Marika Jones's house back in 2013. That's been corroborated by several other informants. Kev was even a suspect in the murder of Marrion Bernette, who was also originally from Manchester. There's a definite connection here. Plus, there are those rumours from back then. You know which ones I mean.'

Murphy did. The time after Lamont Jones was shot was tumultuous. The police were terrified that there would be retaliatory shootings every day, understanding his power and the control he had over his crew. They had tried to penetrate the crew multiple times over the years, but they were smart and difficult to pin down. The rumours were that shooters from Manchester had attempted his life, and that there was beef between the two cities.

'Exactly. There is a definite Manchester connection. Add in the fact that Shorty avoided a life sentence for murdering three other shooters from Manchester, we're definitely looking in the right direction.'

Murphy grinned. He'd wanted to lock up Lamont Jones for years, and potentially recapturing Shorty was also appealing.

'Do we think Shorty was the triggerman?'

'Reports suggest that he's been lying low since his release. There's enough for us to approach the higher ups though. We need to get an investigation into Teflon going, and then we need to take him down for good.'

CHAPTER NINE
MONDAY 2 MARCH, 2015

'WHY ARE WE DOING THIS?'

Darren Lyles paced around his living room, his phone pressed to his ear as he spoke with his girlfriend. The argument was a familiar one that he had never learned how to navigate in the two years he'd been on and off with Clarissa.

'Because, it's not enough. I thought you'd be done with what you're doing by now, and I'm sick of waiting around for you to give me more.'

He resisted the urge to swear. It was the second argument of this magnitude he'd had with Clarissa in the past week alone. He'd missed a dinner she'd set up because he was working with Maka, and she had thrown a fit. He couldn't help it. Like others in the crew, he'd come from nothing, and he had the opportunity to live a certain life if he focused. That would mean he missed a few dinners now and then.

'Babe, I can't make you wait around, but you need to understand I'm doing this for us.'

'You're doing it for you. I see you posing for photos in town and popping bottles. You like the lifestyle, not me.'

TARGET PART TWO: THE TAKEDOWN

'It's not about that. I make appearances with my people, but that's it. You're my girl, and you're the only one I care about.'

They went back and forth for another thirty minutes before Darren told her he had to go. He wiped his face, annoyed with her antics. Times like this, he wondered why he even bothered. She'd stuck by him, though, he swiftly reasoned. She only acted as she did out of concern for him. The streets were deep, and the more entwined he became in the game, the more dangerous it became.

A firm knock at the door jolted Darren out of his thoughts. He jerked to his feet and stomped to the door, flinging it open. The words on his tongue died as he looked at Akeem's inscrutable expression.

'We need to talk.'

JENNY WAS SIPPING coffee in her office when there was a knock on the door.

'Hey, Nadia,' she smiled warmly at her employee who stood in the doorway. 'Is everything okay?'

Nadia nodded. 'That man is here to see you again. Malcolm.'

Malcolm was browsing the flowers when she went out. Smoothing her hair, she headed towards him and shook his hand.

'Thank you for the mention on your site,' she said.

'Thank you for the email response. I'm glad you saw it.' Malcolm wore a navy blue sweatsuit and white trainers. His hair appeared damp, and she presumed he'd gone to the gym before coming to see her.

'It was sweet of you. You didn't have to do it.'

Malcolm shrugged. 'I often do what I'm not meant to. I was wondering if you'd let me take you for a quick coffee?' She opened her mouth to refuse. 'Nothing nefarious, I promise. Just conversation.'

Jenny mulled it over a moment. 'Okay.'

After letting Nadia know, Jenny climbed into the passenger seat of Malcolm's Range Rover. They drove to a coffee shop in silence, the sounds of *Slum Village* providing the melodic soundtrack. She thought about Lamont, wondering if he would mind her being with Malcolm.

When they parked and headed inside, Malcolm ordered two coffees, and they took seats. It was after eleven, and the coffee shop was fairly empty. A couple sat at the far end, and one other person pounded away on a laptop. She noticed Malcolm watching the writer.

'Tell me about your business,' he said as he turned back to her. Jenny smiled.

'I don't know what to say about it, really. I like flowers, and I always wanted a career where I could develop it, and here I am.'

'What's the next step? Expansion?'

She shook her head. 'I need to fix the business first. It's not going so well at the moment, so that means more hours and less profit.'

'What caused the switch? Having seen your demeanour, and having purchased some of your products before, I can speak for the quality. Is it your marketing plan?'

'My partner was involved in an accident. I put everything on hold until he recovered, and the business suffered.' Jenny gauged his reaction to her boyfriend.

'He must feel bad about that.'

'He offered to give me money to re-grow the business. He even offered to invest, but I turned him down.'

'Because you wanted to do it all yourself? I'm sure you know he was likely offering because he wanted to help, not because he assumed you needed it.'

'His heart was in the right place, but what happened couldn't be helped. It wasn't his fault, and the business is mine. He runs his own business, and I stay out of that.'

'What does he do?'

'He's an entrepreneur.'

TARGET PART TWO: THE TAKEDOWN

'Sounds vague,' remarked Malcolm. She flashed another tight smile.

'He wouldn't like me talking about his business. He's very private.'

Malcolm chuckled. 'How long have you been together?'

'Nearly two years.'

'And you live with him?'

Jenny tilted her head to the side. 'This is sounding suspiciously like an interview.'

'I have a curious nature, and I like to ask questions.'

'Understandable, with what you do for a living. There's not much to say. We love each other, but I guess we just struggle to communicate.' Jenny paused, frowning, unsure why she had shared this information with Malcolm. If he noticed her hesitation, he didn't comment.

'I understand. Personally, I struggle in relationships because I can never switch off, and my work keeps me busy. Makes it harder to form connections.'

'How did you get started with that work? I was checking out some work on your website, and the pieces are engaging.'

Malcolm smiled. 'I tried to write fiction novels about people from the streets, but I could never seem to make them work. It depressed me for a while, then I started writing poetry and taking part in readings. I studied to be a copyeditor, got my degree, then ended up working a few free-lance roles. After that, I stumbled into social commentary and blogging, I even co-produced a podcast and internet show for eighteen months.'

'That's impressive,' Jenny admitted. Malcolm chuckled again.

'Sounds over the top, like I'm at an interview, but I enjoy my work and make a good living. I grew up in Chapeltown, and all my life, I saw the good overshadowed by the bad. I decided to bring about change with the tools at my disposal, and here we are.'

It took her a moment to realise Malcolm had stopped talking. She had become so enthralled in his speech and the passion behind it that it was overwhelming. It was a similar feeling to the one she experienced reading his words online. The most jarring thing was that she saw elements in Malcolm that reminded her of Lamont. When Lamont spoke, you paid attention to the words, and they resonated with you. Malcolm was the same. She sipped her coffee, her brain alight with thoughts. They spoke for a short while longer, then she had to leave. Malcolm drove her back to the office, but stopped her before she could climb from the ride.

'I know you weren't interested last time, but there's a community meeting this evening at the church on Chapeltown Road. You don't have to speak, you don't even have to contribute. Just listen, and we can discuss your thoughts another time. Bring your partner.'

Jenny mulled it over. She didn't have any plans, and she was curious about his narrative.

'Will you message me the details? If I can make it, I will.'

Malcolm grinned, exposing dazzling white teeth. 'That's not a problem.'

DARREN SAT in the passenger seat, wondering what had led to this meeting. He'd kept his head down, focusing on business and avoiding the politics. The crew was in a transitional period, and he wanted to be involved in the next steps. Teflon was now back in the driver's seat, and he'd already made moves, collecting unpaid debts and wiping out Big-Kev.

Darren snuck a look at Akeem, who remained as unflappable as ever. He wiped his hands on his trousers, trying to look in control. As they pulled up to a spot, he looked at the house. It was nondescript and white-bricked, a small garden and driveway leading onto a garage. Anyone could have lived here, which he supposed was the intention.

Akeem led the way inside. The living room was far nicer than the outside, the floorboards varnished and immaculate. There was a television that took up most of a wall, a few books, and some magazines. Darren also noticed a chessboard hidden amongst various paperbacks and bits of paperwork. In the room, Teflon assessed him from an armchair. He wore a pair of reading glasses and had a selection of papers resting lazily in his lap. Darren's mouth was dry, hands jammed into his pockets. He hadn't expected to be face-to-face with the boss.

'You know who I am?' Teflon motioned for him to come closer.

'You're Teflon,' replied Darren, his voice hushed. He'd grown up in the same Chapeltown streets Teflon had, living with his mother in a small home with little money. His older brother Lucas was in the life of crime, and as Darren grew older, he wanted to do the same.

School was pointless. No one learned anything there. The streets were where it was at; people could grow rich overnight, turn themselves into legends and drive around in the fanciest cars. He wanted all of that. Lucas had too, but when police caught him with drugs, they had sentenced him to years behind bars. He kept his mouth shut, and he was looked after. Because Darren was his family, he too was brought into the fold, working under the tutelage of Maka, and later K-Bar. He kept quiet, soaking in everything around him, and was eventually promoted to run his own team, receiving a percentage.

Now, he was standing in the same room with the legend who had cheated death.

Everyone knew about Teflon's shooting. He had been shot at close range. The people behind it were all dead. Teflon was still here, probably richer and more powerful. *He looked so normal*, Darren thought. He was dressed similarly to him in a white long-sleeved top, jeans and trainers. His hair was unruly. The eyes and stature were powerful, though. They assessed him with consummate ease, and Darren felt far more self-conscious than before.

'Call me L,' replied Lamont, holding out his hand. Darren shook. 'I've heard good things about you. There are things in the works now, that I want you to be part of. I want to ask you a few questions. Cool?'

Darren nodded, not trusting himself to speak.

'You grew up in the Hood, didn't you?'

'Leopold Street. Lived there pretty much all my life.'

'Do you have a girlfriend?'

'For now.' Darren grimaced.

'What's happened?'

'She's stressing. She knows what I'm doing, and she's worried that something will happen to me.'

Lamont smiled. 'Shows that she cares. I guess you need to look at the positives.'

'You're right, but I'm doing this for me and her; so we can stack money and establish ourselves. This is all I know how to do, and that might seem shit, but it's all I want to do, and I think I'm good at it.'

'I do too. You wouldn't be here otherwise. For you and your girl, I guess you need to spend some time with her and let her know where your heart is. If she's gonna stress, at least let her understand the situation.'

Darren shifted, thinking about his words. He was buoyed at the fact that he'd received positive feedback. Lamont seemed to want to get to know him. He would be patient until he could figure out why.

'Back to you. You wanna stack money, and I can appreciate that. What's the endgame, though? Are you trying to rise?'

'Definitely.' He didn't hesitate. Lamont rose from his seat more fluidly than Darren would have expected. He also noticed for the first time that Akeem had left.

'Do you play chess?'

'I haven't in a while, but I used to when I was little. My uncle taught me.'

Lamont smiled. 'We're going to have a game.' He grabbed the chessboard and spread it out on the table. They positioned themselves on either side, and picked colours, Lamont white and Darren black. They played in relative silence, Darren making his moves quicker than Lamont, wondering why he was being so cautious.

TARGET PART TWO: THE TAKEDOWN

Before long, his pieces were routed, and he was swiftly checkmated. Lamont laughed as he stared at the pieces in disbelief.

'How the—'

'Chess is no different than life, Darren. Stay as many moves ahead as you can, and you'll be fine.'

Darren considered the advice and found he liked it. He didn't like to lose, but at least he'd learned a lesson. Lamont was light years ahead of anyone he'd encountered, and the longer the meeting went on, the more he realised this. It was everything; the effortless panache with which he dressed. His expression. All of it banded together to make him what he was.

'I have a job for you.'

'What is it?'

Lamont paused, assessing him for a long moment.

'I need you to get close to someone. An Asian kid with solid connections. I want you to become his friend.'

'Okay,' Darren replied. If this got him to the next level, he would do it.

'Don't agree without considering the facts. The man in question is connected. I'm talking power on a different level. Do you still agree?'

'Yes. What's the plan?'

'We're gonna test his greed, learn who his boss keeps around him, and see what he says about the people he works for. Akeem will handle it all. He'll give you the information we have, and then it's up to you. He'll also give you some money so you can act the part, and you'll have access to whatever resources you need. Don't take the piss. Eyes will still be on you. Understand?'

Darren fought to hide the grin on his face. This was what he had waited for; the opportunity to prove himself.

'You'll report to Akeem. One more thing; you're going to get a driver. He used to work with Marcus. He's trustworthy, but don't say more around him than necessary.'

'Marcus as in *Tall-Man*?'

Lamont nodded.

'Which guy? Vic's still locked up. Is it Sharma?'

Lamont again nodded. Darren remembered Sharma driving Marcus around the streets. He hadn't seen the man in months, correctly assuming he was keeping a low profile after Marcus's death.

'Any more questions?'

'Nah. Thank you, though. For giving me this chance.'

'I didn't give you it. You earned it. If you pull this off, we will talk about something better for you. Okay?'

It was Darren's turn to nod.

SHORTY ROSE from the barber chair and wiped the excess hair from the back of his neck. He checked out his new trim in the mirror, satisfied with how the barber lined him up. Handing the man a twenty-pound note, he instructed him to keep the change.

'You keep tipping these kids like you are, they're gonna be fighting over who does your hair.' Trinidad patted him on the back. They laughed as he walked with him to the door.

'You spoken to L?' Shorty asked, noting Trinidad's face sag. He sighed.

'Not since we argued. I kinda miss seeing him around here. He kept to himself, but it was still comforting.'

'Me and L argue all the time, Trinidad. I wouldn't even overthink it. L likes people to challenge him, and I think he's just getting used to being in the public eye again.'

Trinidad nodded, his eyes slightly brighter. 'You might be right. Did you hear about the police involved in attacking Diego?'

'I heard they got suspended pending investigation or something. Wasn't one of them in an accident?'

'He's in critical condition. He was in a car crash a few days after his suspension. Wrapped his car around a tree.'

'Good, I hope he dies. I ain't got no sympathy for those devils, especially after what they did to the kid,' said Shorty.

TARGET PART TWO: THE TAKEDOWN

'It's dangerous. You know the police as well as I do; they'll come back stronger and make everyone suffer. There's got to be another way to deal with this mess.'

Shorty shrugged. 'I get where you're coming from, but I'm on that other side, old man. I'm in those streets doing what I need to. It ain't for guys like me to dictate where we go. No one's gonna take me seriously.'

'People know what you've been through, and you're still out here. You speaking up could help change the minds of some of these young kids that wanna be like you.'

Shorty mulled over his words. He'd never seen himself as a role model, but he liked the fact Trinidad believed he could do it. He'd always gotten along with the old man, and while they weren't as close as he and Lamont, there was a mutual respect.

'I'm not trying to force you into anything, but there's a community meeting tonight down at Roscoe Church.'

'Is this to do with that *OurHood* shit?'

'They'll definitely be involved.'

Shorty scratched his jaw, the rubbing alcohol applied after his haircut beginning to itch. Going to the meeting wouldn't hurt, and if he didn't like what he heard, no one could stop him from leaving.

'What time does it start?'

LENNOX THOMPSON's face was unreadable as he strode into a room, several of his people waiting. They surrounded a man who was sprawled on the floor. The room itself was formerly a living room, now bereft of any furniture. The carpet had been torn away, leaving a grey flooring currently covered with plastic.

Nikkolo greeted him with a nod.

'It was easy getting him, Len. He thought he had the drop.'

Lennox allowed a small smile, then approached the man, signalling for him to be turned over. Despite the livid bruising around his left eye and cheek, he was still recognisable.

'Spinks, how have my people been treating you?'

Spinks mumbled an inaudible reply. He had been stripped of his clothing and was trying to protect his modesty.

'You're the one they sent? They thought an idiot like you would catch me slipping? Delroy must be losing his marbles.'

The room filled with laughter and jeers. Spinks tried to get to his feet, but was forced down.

'You haven't been the same since Marcus and Shorty nearly killed you. Your brain doesn't work right anymore. Hold him down,' Lennox ordered, laying into him with deliberate, slow right hands, impacting the face and body of the beaten man. 'Gimme the bat.'

Nikkolo handed him a baseball bat, which he brought down repeatedly on Spinks's ribs, savouring the screams.

'You know how it goes. Slow . . . quick; it's all the same to me. I wanna know all about Winston and Eddie Williams. I want hangout spots, safe houses, where they get their pussy, what brand of baked beans they like. I want all of it.

'You're gonna give it to me, and if you don't, then after I've torn you apart, I'm gonna do the same to your family. Everyone you love. Anyone you've said hello to on the street. I'll destroy them all. Start talking. Now.'

SHORTY SLIPPED into the back of the church just as the meeting was starting. The cramped main room was almost full, with most of the attendees standing. As he pushed his way forward, he was surprised when an arm brushed against his. Jenny smiled at him, but before they could speak, a man at the front cleared his throat. His name was Calvin Newton.

'I'm glad to see so many of us here tonight.' Calvin was a squat man with glasses and a quizzical expression, but he had a presence that reminded Shorty of Lamont. Looking around, he could already see people leaning forward in their seats, not wanting to miss a single word. 'I understand it's hard to get out to these meetings, and your support is invaluable.' Calvin waited for the applause that had started up to disperse before he continued. 'I know that we have several crucial issues to discuss, and I feel that we need to tackle the biggest one of all, which is the police, and their behaviours in our town.'

'They're damn-well out of control!' Ken barked. He was another man Shorty recognised; a regular in Lamont's barber shop who often took on Lamont in games of chess. Shorty had seen him argue over football or one of Lamont's moves, but he'd never heard him speak with so much anger. 'They put Claudette's grandson in hospital, then tried to charge him with assault when the hospital released him.'

Calvin shook his head as the crowd began talking amongst themselves again. He looked pained and gave them their chance to speak before holding up his hands again.

'I believe they are out of control, but the police are nothing but a private army, bought and paid for. They've always come into Chapeltown with impunity, bringing drugs and drama with them, trying to arrest your brothers and sleep with your sisters. I want to understand, why? Why are they suddenly coming in and terrorising people? What is their agenda?'

No one had an answer. Shorty watched Calvin, and he noticed the man stare intently at him for a second.

'We have had some terrible events take place that have rocked our community, and a lot of bad press that has people again vilifying Chapeltown, just as they did in the olden days. I feel that the police and their paymasters are using this situation to their advantage, and I believe it ties into funding. The police force across the country is facing heavy cutbacks. If you can justify certain areas appearing to be dangerous or even on the verge of rioting, you can justify your budget.'

'So, what do we do to stop them?' a man called out. Calvin looked that man in the eye, picking his words carefully.

'We all need to come up with that plan together. In light of that,

I would like to welcome Malcolm Powell, who will share a few words. For those of you that don't know, Malcolm is a key member of the *OurHood* Initiative, and has organised several of the recent demonstrations that have taken place in and around Chapeltown. Malcolm, come on up.'

Shorty watched Malcolm approach the podium, people already clapping and shouting words of encouragement. He looked familiar, and Shorty was sure he'd seen him around back in the day. He had a refined look similar to Lamont, but was broader, his facial features more accentuated.

Malcolm greeted the crowd with a smile as he adjusted the microphone.

'Good evening, and thank you all for coming. Calvin asked me to say a few words, but honestly, he has already touched on most of it. A lot of the recent events have been the catalyst for the agenda of those in authority, which is to subjugate by any means necessary. It goes beyond that, and if you've listened to any of my recent podcasts or read my articles, the fault clearly lies with the criminal element that has dominated Chapeltown for decades.'

A hush fell over the room. Shorty felt several people looking at him, but willed himself to stay calm, keeping his eyes on Malcolm. Malcolm surveyed the room, giving him the briefest look and nod before he continued.

'Many criminals in and around Chapeltown profit from the sale of drugs. People have made excuses for them in the past; anything from a lack of education, to being unable to find work. I can't refute any of that, other than to say that I'm from Chapeltown; I grew up around the corner in a house that didn't have much money. What it had was plenty of love and support, and I used that as fuel to succeed.

'I went to college. I worked, I put myself out there and helped people establish themselves. I wanted it. The fact is, some of these criminals are lazy. It's easy money selling drugs, and they're making a lot, so why not continue? And if someone comes along trying to take your spot, why not murder and maim them? After all, the community will protect you, right?'

'It's not as easy as you're making it sound, brother.' A man stood. He looked to be in his late thirties, stout, dressed in a sweater and faded jeans. 'We have families to consider, and speaking out just puts a target on our backs.'

There were murmurs of agreement. Malcolm nodded along with them.

'Thank you for speaking up, sir. Again, you're not wrong. These people have the means to reach out and silence people. Since I stepped up my work, I've had death threats. People have approached me, warning me to shut all of this down. I'm in the same boat as you guys; I have family and friends at risk too.

'But, you know what keeps me in the game?' Malcolm waited a beat, aware all eyes were on him, waiting anxiously for his next words. 'I'm doing the right thing. It's as simple as that. For as long as we can remember and beyond, there have been people who have been oppressed and ostracised, while trying to make things easier for those around them. Without people stepping up. Without people doing the right thing despite the odds, we'd be nowhere.

'That is why I'll never give up, and you can't either. We succeed as one, or we suffer as one. No matter the consequences, I'm in this until the end. Thank you for listening.'

The applause that followed was deafening, and even Shorty clapped. It continued for minutes, growing louder as the man stood on stage and smiled. Shorty appreciated the guts it took to stand there and say the things Malcolm had. It was puzzling at the same time. Malcolm was walking around without fear, saying what he wanted, and no one was stopping him.

Shorty appreciated his words, but he wasn't as invested as some others. He was a hustler. It was all he knew, and he understood the minds of people like Lamont; champion strategists, used to thinking on their feet and tearing apart plots and ideals that worked against them. If Malcolm thought he would unseat them, he would need to try harder.

Before he could speak to Jenny, Trinidad hailed him, and they spoke for a few moments. Most people had cleared out of the church by then. Shorty saw Jenny approach Malcolm, and they exchanged words before she gave the man a brief hug and walked away. Shorty's jaw tightened, his nostrils flaring. He wanted to attack Malcolm for violating, but the hug had been so brief, he couldn't bring himself to do it. Jenny noticed him and walked over.

'I didn't know you knew Malcolm like that,' he said, hoping his voice didn't sound accusatory. Jenny grinned.

'Looking out for L's interests, are we?'

The comment was perfect for defusing the tension, and he laughed, Jenny giggling at his reaction.

'Summat like that.'

'He bought some flowers from me, and I've been checking out his website. He talks a lot of sense. Are you walking out?'

Shorty followed her out, nodding at a few people he knew. He noted several others were avoiding his eye, and a brazen pair of women glared at him, mumbling under their breaths as he passed. Shorty and Jenny stood near the main road, illuminated by nearby streetlights.

'I haven't seen you around lately.' Jenny stuck her hands in her pockets to stay warm.

Shorty rubbed his forehead. 'Me and L kinda got into it the night of that little dinner we had.'

Jenny studied him for a moment.

'I'm not going to ask what you argued about, but L needs you, so make up.'

He grinned again despite himself.

'Just like that?'

'How long have you two known each other? You're closer than brothers. Like I said, you need each other.'

Shorty shrugged, knowing she was right, but not wanting to admit it.

'How's Grace doing?'

'I've been to see her, but it's early days.'

TARGET PART TWO: THE TAKEDOWN

'And your son?'

Shorty sighed and closed his eyes.

'I acted like a complete prick the last time I saw him.'

'In what way?'

He filled her in on the circumstances of his last trip to Huddersfield. Timmy had been present, and Shorty expected Dionte to be happy to see him. The lack of contact had made Dionte unapproachable, and he nearly attacked him out of anger. Since then, he'd heard nothing from either Dionte or his mother, Stacey.

'You should go and see him.'

'I thought about it, but I assumed he wouldn't wanna see me again. I decided to stay away.'

Jenny impaled him with a sudden glare he was sure Lamont had been on the receiving end of.

'He's a child, Shorty, just like Grace. Personally, you seem a lot more centred than you did two years ago. Don't give up. Deal with your children, and your brother, because they all need you.'

Shorty felt uplifted by Jenny's words. She'd hit the nail on the head, and he was done with moping around and waiting for things to get better.

'Thanks, Jen.'

'Don't mention it. You can walk me to my car now. It's freezing out here.'

CHAPTER TEN

SATURDAY 7 MARCH, 2015

BUOYED by the conversation with Jenny, Shorty hit the motorway early one morning.

After a while, he entered Huddersfield, driving through the Fixby area. It didn't escape his attention that the last time he had driven through, he'd had Timmy with him. After his visit with his son imploded, he'd lost his temper with Timmy shortly after. Shaking away the negative thoughts, Shorty drove up a long driveway, stopping in front of a neat, white-bricked stately home. There was a Mercedes parked up. He parked alongside it.

Stacey waited in the doorway, hawk-like eyes watching his every move. She'd put on weight since they last saw one another, but it was well-distributed. Her skin was a dark brown shade, and she wore her age elegantly the way some women seemed to.

'Hey, Stace.'

Stacey nodded. 'Are you okay, Shorty?'

'Yeah. Thought I'd get here quicker, but the motorway was rammed.'

'I think there was an accident. Traffic probably got diverted.'

That was the extent of their conversation. They awkwardly looked at one another, then away. They were young when they'd gotten together. Shorty was on the streets building a reputation. Stacey was in the clubs taking drugs with her friends, trying to meet a big-timer. She wasn't prepared for him, and their tenure was rocky, filled with accusations of cheating — most of which were true — and violence.

Shorty was more volatile back then and had beaten up at least two men he believed were making eyes at her. Finally, this culminated with him being arrested for assaulting a taxi driver whilst under the influence of drink and drugs. He'd been sentenced, and a pregnant Stacey saw the writing on the wall and moved away.

Shorty reached out to Lamont from behind bars, wanting to ensure his kid was provided for. Despite Lamont's objections, he used most of his stash, getting Stacey the very house they stood in. He'd assumed that after his release, he would move out there with her. This backfired when she made it clear that they didn't have a future and began dating a businessman. Shorty had wanted to blow the house up and kill the man, but Lamont talked him around, and he'd left her alone.

'Is he in?'

Stacey smiled tightly. 'I told you he was. He's watching television in the front room. Can I get you a drink?'

'I'm good.' Shorty started towards the front room. He paused when he realised she wasn't following. 'Aren't you coming?'

'This is about you and your son.'

Shorty nodded, his heart pounding as he walked into the front room. Dionte was playing *Fifa*, the same computer game Darren and the others liked to play. Loud grime music played through a Sony speaker, and he nodded his head in time to the beat as he clicked the buttons with dexterity. He looked up when Shorty entered, and his face changed. His eyes hardened, and he glared up at his father with the same surliness he'd last time.

'How are you doing, D?' Shorty started lamely after a minute, realising that his son would not take the initiative. Dionte stared a minute longer, not bothering to turn off the music. He unpaused his game and carried on playing.

'I'm fine.'

'You look fine. You're growing up to be a strong young man. That's good. Means I did something right.'

'You didn't have a thing to do with it,' Dionte told him. Shorty felt the familiar spark of annoyance, but controlled himself.

'You're right. I could have probably done more, but I guess I thought as long as I was throwing money at your mum, you would be all right. Do you wanna know why I randomly came to see you last year?'

Dionte didn't reply, but Shorty noticed he'd paused his game and turned the music down. He took a seat next to his son.

'My friend died a few weeks before I came to see you. I was outside the wake, drunk, when a man approached me. I didn't recognise him, but he knew me. He knew my mum's name. Even knew I had kids. When I asked who he was, he said he was my dad.'

Dionte still didn't speak, but looked at him, imploring him to continue.

'I hadn't seen my dad since I was about four. He ran out on my mum, and he provided nothing. No money, no visits. He just ditched us. So, when he came out of the blue and started trying to be friendly, I knocked him out.'

Dionte looked like he was trying to hide a smile. His lip quivered, and there was more light in his eyes.

'After I knocked him out, I couldn't stop thinking about you. Not to say I didn't before, because I did. It was just easier to distract myself, and tell myself that you were okay in this big house with your mum and her man, and that I was doing you a favour staying away.

'That was wrong of me. I should have attempted to come and see you and stay a part of your life. There's no excuse I can give for why I didn't. I just want you to know that I'm sorry about that, and that I'm sorry that our relationship is like this.'

More silence. Dionte's body arched towards his now, but he couldn't speak. Shorty patted him on the shoulder.

'You're probably wondering why I'm saying all this crap to you, and the reason is simple; I never want to be that broken old man trying to speak to my son, and I never want to be the reason that you put your hands on me. You ever need anything, tell your mum to tell me, and I'll come to you. You have my word on that.'

Dionte turned back to his game and unpaused it, but his expression was different. He seemed sombre. Shorty stood and walked away, not wanting to push it. He almost bumped into Stacey, who stood in the hallway. She gasped.

'Sorry, I shouldn't have . . . I just wondered what you would say,' she admitted, smoothing her hair.

'It's your house. You don't have to apologise.'

'Come and have a drink. I want to talk to you.'

Shorty followed her to the massive kitchen. The last time he'd been here, he argued with Dionte for not wanting to look at a picture of Grace. The room had the same wide surfaces and light worktops that had been commonplace previously. Stacey poured coffee from a fancy-looking filter. It was very Lamont-esque.

'I thought what you said to Dionte was sweet,' she started. 'I'm not just saying that either. I've never heard you talk like that before.'

'Like what?'

'Honest. You've always been your own man, but I've never heard you speaking from the heart before. Even in the older days.'

'Shit's different for me now, Stace. You know some of the shit I've been through last year since Marcus died. It feels like everything in my world fell apart, and I'm just trying to pick up the pieces.'

'I heard about Timmy. I'm sorry, Shorty. I went to his funeral and spoke to his mum. She was sweet.'

'He should have never been in the life. He always wanted to be like me, and look at the example I set. He should have been out going to college and trying to get laid, not running corners and selling drugs.'

'Shorty, the circumstances weren't the same. Timmy wanted that life. I don't think he would have ever gone to college. Sometimes we have to live our lives the way we want to, regardless of what other people think. Timmy did what he wanted to do.'

'I still could have done more. Do you ever feel like you're realising shit too late in your life to do anything, but you can't help thinking about it, anyway? Like, what might have been?'

'In terms of what?'

'What if I'd been more like L? Setting up businesses, thinking of the future instead of for right now. Things could have been so different. I could have been a proper dad to both of my kids.'

'Focus on the fact you're feeling these things now. That's the important bit. You can still change your life.'

Shorty nodded, recognising the truth in her words. He grinned. 'Thanks.'

'Don't mention it. I've never known this side of you.'

'I don't even know what this side of me is. I just know that I think about Marcus daily, and I think about how abrupt his murder was. The world moved on without me, and it feels like I'm struggling to catch up to everyone.'

'Like Lamont?'

Shorty again nodded. 'L was always ahead of me in terms of thinking. He's been preaching all this shit to me for the longest time, but it's only making sense to me now.'

'How is L doing? I can't believe he got shot.'

'Still the same. He's just still getting used to shit. I guess we all are. How's your man?'

Stacey gave him a hard stare. 'Don't go back to being that guy.'

'What guy?' Shorty frowned.

'The guy that tries to flirt with me in my house.'

'I'm not flirting! I'm just asking you a question.'

Stacey laughed. 'Fine. I'll believe you. We're okay, I guess. Marriage is hard work, and we're both busy, so we sometimes struggle to communicate.' She shook her head. 'I can't believe I'm talking to you about this.'

'I can't believe that I'm listening.'

TARGET PART TWO: THE TAKEDOWN

They both laughed, talking for another twenty minutes. He had another coffee, showing Stacey photos of Grace. After a while, he said his goodbyes, giving Stacey a hug and departing. As he climbed into his car, Shorty looked back. He saw Dionte looking at him from the window. He nodded, inwardly gratified when Dionte nodded back.

JENNY WAS TIDYING the work area when the door clanged, and she was face to face with Lamont. The silence lingered until she broke it.

'What are you doing here?'

'Visiting my girl. I want to take you out tonight.'

Jenny grinned, raising her eyebrow. 'What's the occasion?'

Lamont laughed. 'There's a disconnect with us lately, and that's my fault. Some time to recharge will do us both some good.'

It was surprising to hear him openly taking responsibility for the awkwardness between them, and she cleared the distance, planting a long kiss on Lamont's lips. They held each other for a moment, Jenny enjoying the strength of the man she loved.

'It's a great idea, L. We could go to a hotel, or we could just stay at home?'

'Your choice, so let me know. We can do anything you like.'

SHORTY DROVE BACK to Leeds with a smile on his face. He'd never realised just how tense his situation with his son had made him until now. For years he'd tried to make excuses about his lack of contact, blaming Stacey and her move away from Leeds. He saw now that she had done the right thing, and he was pleased with the life she had made. Dionte had grown up well and while he wouldn't be as close with Shorty as he'd like, being civil was enough.

Driving into the Hood, he parked outside K-Bar's safe house and bounded inside. K-Bar sat on the sofa. He looked better than the last time Shorty had seen him. He nodded at Shorty.

'Where are you coming from?'

'Huddersfield.'

K-Bar's eyebrows rose.

'You went to see Dionte?'

Shorty nodded.

'Stacey flip out again?'

'I called ahead this time and arranged it. We had a long talk, I apologised, and then left.'

'Are you two cool now, then?'

'We're talking, so I guess that's enough. Anyone else stopped by?'

'Darren did, but he's on a mission now.'

'What mission?' Shorty's brow furrowed. Darren had a good reputation, but he couldn't imagine anyone letting him pick his own missions.

'I dunno, fam. Summat for L, but he can't tell me what it is, apparently.'

'You try asking L?'

K-Bar nodded. 'He just said it was personal. You know what L's like. If he doesn't wanna talk about something, he won't. I just fell back.'

Shorty heard the anger in his voice, relating to it. It still annoyed him that Lamont wouldn't put him back on the streets.

'I tried speaking to him about getting back in, but he wants me to keep waiting.'

'I see his point, but still, you're not an amateur. You know what you're doing.'

The friends sat in silence, neither in a hurry to break it. They had been friends for so long that they recognised the other's mood. Shorty thought about Dionte again, wondering if he would try to go professional as a footballer, silently vowing to support him all the way if he did. It brought his attention back to Grace, and he remembered he still had a lot of work to do.

'We ain't chilled together much lately, have we?' He said to K-Bar, who scratched his stubbled chin.

'Different world nowadays, fam. When you were locked down, and L was in recovery, the streets were on a different level. I had to step up in L's place. People turned to me because they were scared, but I didn't know what I was doing, so I had to do what I thought you or L would do. Everyone tried us. We took so many hits in a short space of time that they didn't think we would survive.'

'How did you?'

'L. The guy had all sorts of contingencies in place. After he got shot, and we were running around, I had people getting in touch, leading me to stash houses I didn't even know about. People were in place to do pickups, and everything on the business end was the same.

'The connect sent his people to speak with me, the boxes kept coming, and the money was sent where it was needed. I had to keep shit in line and stop these dickheads on the street from taking liberties. I couldn't just chill and play the background like I used to. People knew me, and they needed me to sort shit out.'

Shorty was silent. He didn't want to praise Lamont, even if he agreed with K-Bar. Lamont had always been forward-thinking, and he was man enough to admit that the money he made with him was more than he would have made hustling for himself. As frustrating as Lamont was, he appreciated his business head.

'What happened to Blakey?' Shorty recalled asking when he first landed, but never getting the full story.

'He quit couple' months after you got remanded, saying he'd had enough of the streets. He works in a bar in town on Greek Street.'

'Which one?'

'I'll remember when I see it. We can go tonight if you like?'

Shorty rubbed his forehead.

'I'll let you know.'

WINSTON WILLIAMS SLUMPED on his sofa, dipping his hand into a packet of Big Eat crisps as he stared at the bland action movie on the screen. He'd lost the plot of it thirty minutes ago, but it allowed him time to centre his thoughts.

There was a war on the streets, and he didn't know how they'd gotten involved in it, nor what the endgame was. Over the past few years, he'd taken control of most of his father's business, with Delroy content to oversee.

Then, Lennox Thompson made waves.

Lennox wasn't a drug dealer, so Winston hadn't understood. He'd tried reaching out anyway, and his offers were rebuffed. Lennox hadn't fired any guns or laid a hand on any of their workers. He was sure he was behind the raid on one of their spots recently, however; a raid his dad chewed him out about. He'd dropped the ball and not rotated the spots frequently enough, allowing the complacency to be taken advantage of.

The streets were looking sideways at the Williams empire, and several amongst their ranks were whispering about how bad things were going. The links were looking elsewhere, and the money was dwindling. Customers were holding back repayments, and he was working overtime trying to get things in line. He'd sent a man to track down Lennox, but no one had heard anything from Spinks. Mack, Spinks' uncle, was in his ear every day asking where he was, and he didn't know what to tell him.

Stuffing more crisps into his mouth, Winston nearly choked when he heard a loud bang from outside, followed by the smash of a car window. Leaping to his feet, he fumbled for his trusty baseball bat and charged outside.

'C'mon, you fucking cowards!' He yelled, tired of the neighbourhood kids and their antics. He saw a bunch of hooded boys running away. Winston jogged toward his Audi, panting. They had smashed the front and side windows, and the jarring alarm pierced

TARGET PART TWO: THE TAKEDOWN

the quiet street. Out of breath, he again looked around the street, then trudged back inside to make some calls.

———

DARREN POURED another glass of champagne, acting like he was having the time of his life, doing his best to hide the nerves threatening to jeopardise his night. Lamont's mission rang loudly in his head, and he was playing up to it. Lamont hadn't given him any sign of how long the task needed to take. Darren was determined to do it properly, playing his position to the max. He'd quickly learnt the movements of Rashad. Akeem had compiled a list of the young goon's likes, dislikes and hangouts, and by checking out Rashad's social media accounts, he quickly built an image of the man. He knew that Rashad had responsibility within Akhan's team, similar to Darren's role in Lamont's. He supervised a crew and did a lot of running around, picking up money and ensuring things were smooth. From what he gathered, Rashad seemed decent enough at it.

At present, Darren was in a club near the train station with some acquaintances who knew Rashad's people. They were serial ravers, so he had been going out with them for the past few weeks, trying to bump into Rashad.

This plan had been a bust so far. Rashad hadn't shown, but Darren had met some other people, including some game women, getting laid twice in two weeks. That wouldn't pacify Lamont, however, and he tried to focus. He hated what he was doing to Clarissa, but when the women were all over him, he couldn't resist.

He was in regular contact with Akeem, giving him progress reports and explaining his plan to the bodyguard, who seemed satisfied. Darren remained worried, which explained his nerves. He needed something to show for his efforts. He had killed himself to get noticed, but now he didn't know what would come next. Darren was no fool. He knew people had been murdered within the organisation.

Despite K-Bar's cleanup of Chink's murder, everyone knew that he'd been killed for betraying Marcus. None of it would deter him, though. The plan would work out, and if it didn't, he would tweak it to ensure it did.

'Next round's on one of you lot,' he said, holding his champagne glass aloft. His beaming, half-drunk acquaintances followed suit.

Behind him, there was a flurry of noise. His friend Nathan was shaking hands with a well-dressed man. Feeling a flutter of relief, he realised it was Rashad. He wore a fitted white designer t-shirt with tight-fitting jeans and white and gold trainers. He was laden with jewellery, wearing two white gold chains and a gaudy-looking Rolex. His arm was around the waist of a slim Asian girl with the most alluringly dark eyes Darren had ever seen.

'Rashad, this is my boy, D. D, this is Rashad.'

Darren shook hands with Rashad. He immediately sensed that he was used to people flocking to him the way Nathan had.

'You good? There's champers if you and your woman want it.'

Rashad helped himself to a glass, leaving his woman to fend for herself. Darren filled her glass, and she softly thanked him. Nathan and Co tried to chat up a group of girls, leaving him free to talk with Rashad.

'It's too packed in here. I remember when only a few people knew about this spot.'

Rashad gave him a measured look.

'How long have you been coming here?'

'Years now. My people are deep in here, so it was a good little moneymaker. Still is sometimes, when people don't mess it up.' He saw the gleam in Rashad's eyes as he moved away from his woman to speak to Darren. He noticed her scowl, filing this information away.

'What kinda business are you talking about?'

Darren looked around, checking they weren't being overheard. This was all for Rashad's benefit, and it seemed to be working.

'Can't really say, bruv. You know what it's like these days.

TARGET PART TWO: THE TAKEDOWN

People talk too much. All I can say is that we were steady stacking. People are making it hot nowadays, though.'

'Listen, I'm not any guy.' Rashad lowered his voice, talking into his ear. 'I've got connections too, and I'm always trying to make money. Maybe we can work together.'

Darren paused, drawing him in. He couldn't react too quickly. To do so would arouse suspicion. He glanced around the club, taking a sip of champagne, watching him grow more restless. His woman was looking at her phone, occasionally throwing dirty looks at her boyfriend.

'Do you want a top-up?' He motioned to the bottle. Before she could speak, Rashad interjected.

'Forget her. She's fine. Tell me about the business. Talk to your guys Nathan and them lot. They'll tell you I'm trusted, G.'

Hiding a smile, Darren spoke.

———

Lennox stared into the bottom of a cup when Nikkolo entered the back room.

'The kids just reported in. It's done. Winnie came out and chased them with a bat. They were gonna stab him, but they remembered their orders.'

'Good. I don't want him touched.'

Nikkolo cleared his throat.

'People are saying Eddie Williams is lying low. Delroy has beefed up his security too. We've got a couple squirrels within their team letting us know their movements.'

'Good. Make sure everyone keeps up the pressure on all fronts.'

Nikkolo hesitated before speaking again.

'Boss, I have to ask; why aren't you just pulling the trigger? We took out Spinks and kept it quiet, and now we're vandalising cars like some amateurs. What's the point behind it?'

Lennox fixed him with a stony glare, freezing the lackey where he stood. He held the look for over a minute. Nikkolo squirmed against Lennox's quiet force. He'd never met a man who put out a vibe like Lennox Thompson. It was malevolent, but twistingly captivating.

'I don't pay you for your advice. Keep doing exactly as you're told.'

Nikkolo left the room without argument.

———

LAMONT AND JENNY were shown to their seats. Both had dressed to impress, Lamont wearing a tailored navy suit with brown brogues and a white shirt. Jenny wore a fitted black Peplum dress, her hair teased and wavy, eyes sparkling. He allowed her to pick the wine, and they stared into one another's eyes whilst waiting for their menus.

'This is a lovely restaurant. Feels like ages since we've been.'

Lamont nodded. 'It has been a while.'

'It feels like a while since we've done a lot of things,' admitted Jenny. Lamont tilted his head.

'Hopefully, we can work towards changing that. So much has changed in our lives, and I'm sorry for how I've acted. I've not been considerate, and I promise you that's not the intention.'

She squeezed his hand.

'I know, L. I've never doubted that you cared. We just seem at opposite ends sometimes.'

They sat in silence. Lamont hummed along with the soft jazz music. The place was packed, everyone in their finery and out to have a good time. After browsing the menus and placing their orders, Jenny spoke again.

'Have you spoken to Shorty lately?'

Lamont's face tensed, but he forced his features into a smile.

'No. We had a little falling out, but we'll be fine.'

'He said the same thing.' She sipped her wine.

'When did you speak to Shorty?' Lamont tucked into his grilled fish with abandon, his brow furrowed.

TARGET PART TWO: THE TAKEDOWN

'I saw him at that community thing I told you about.'

'Shorty was there?' Lamont scratched his chin after placing his fork on the plate.

'He walked me out. He was with the nice man from the barbers, Tommy.'

Lamont mulled it over. It made more sense now.

'How did he seem?'

'Less tense than when he was staying with us. I'm not sure if he agreed with everything Malcolm said, especially the parts relating to the criminal element, which is to be expected, I guess. It was a good meeting, though. Malcolm's words were inspiring. He really cares, you know?'

'That's good to hear.' Lamont hoped his words weren't as stiff as they sounded.

'I went for coffee with him. It's refreshing to hear about—'

'You went for a coffee with him?' Lamont's voice was low.

'Yes. He's an interesting man. Is that a problem?' Jenny's eyes rested on him. He sighed, messing with the remaining food on his plate, feeling less hungry.

'No, course it isn't. Just be careful.'

'Don't you trust me?' Jenny glared. It was his turn to squeeze her hand.

'Jen, if there's one person I'll always trust, it's you. Malcolm is a target, though; you said it yourself. He's playing with fire talking about reforms. I don't disagree with his methods, but even you can't deny that it's a worry.'

Jenny smiled, draining her wine.

'If you're finished, let's get out of here and head to the hotel.'

Lamont gave her such a look that she shifted in her seat. Her face flamed, stomach tingling.

'Yes. Let's.'

Lamont paid the bill, leaving an exuberant tip. They took a black cab to the hotel, at the bottom of the city centre, and checked into their room. The door closed, and Lamont forced Jenny against the wall, cupping her face and capturing her lips.

135

The kiss was slow and tender, and she melted on the spot as he applied more pressure. His hands skimmed her body, everywhere he touched seeming to flame. She gasped and pressed her body against his. They spilled to the bed, Lamont rearing up and kissing her exposed neck, her dress askew and hanging from her shoulders. He pulled back, panting, his eyes still on hers as he undressed, flinging his expensive shirt to the floor and kicking out of his trousers. Jenny mirrored his actions and shimmied out of her dress, removing the black lingerie she had picked.

Lamont surveyed her entire body, his eyes gleaming. She was perfection, and he felt like the luckiest man alive. All the doubts about the future seemed to drift away as he drank in her features. Jenny stared at his ripped frame, the jagged scar from his surgery visible. He looked down at it, then at her. Jenny padded towards him, dropping to her knees and worshipping the mark with her mouth as he hissed and gritted his teeth. When she reached for him, he came to his senses, pushing her back onto the bed and entering her with one fluid motion. They quickly found their rhythm, their mouths and bodies meeting as they pushed the world away for the night.

SHORTY AND K-BAR entered the spot on Greek Street, surrounded by bright lights and loud music. K-Bar quickly commandeered a table and started checking out the talent, Shorty bullying his way to the bar. They had phoned ahead to check Blakey was working. He was handing cocktails to a group of giggling girls who appeared very taken with him. Shorty made his way over.

'Yo, B?'

Blakey turned, recognising his voice over the music. He grinned, coming from behind the bar to greet him.

'Fucking hell, bro. Look at you! You look healthy, man,' He shouted over the music. They moved back towards the bar.

'You too. Heard you were working here, so I thought I'd come check you. How's things?'

Blakey shrugged. 'I enjoy what I'm doing now, y'know? Feels less serious. After you went away, the game wasn't fun anymore. Too much blood, so I ducked out and went legit. K-Bar and everyone else needed to change and adapt to survive. I couldn't do it.'

'You need money or anything?'

Blakey shook his head. 'I had a bit saved. Realised things about myself after I stopped hustling. I was never the same when you weren't around. I thought you were gonna go away for life,' he admitted.

Shorty nodded. 'Me too,' He didn't admit how much that thought terrified him. Freedom was something everyone took for granted, but he'd almost lost his for good. 'I'm glad you're doing well.'

'Me too, bro. You look proper healthy, though. You back working with Tef?'

'Sort of.' He still needed to speak with Lamont and clear the air after their last discussion. Blakey was about to reply when a woman sauntered towards them, placing herself in the middle.

'Blakey, babe, can you get me and my girls more bubbly and bring it to the table, please?' She met Shorty's eyes for a minute, and he didn't back down. She was an inch or so shorter, with milk chocolate skin and curly dark hair. She wore a black blouse and tight trousers, outshining everyone around her with ease.

'Don't worry, Sienna, babe. I'll get someone to bring it over.' Blakey noted that the pair hadn't taken their eyes from one another. 'Shorty, Sienna. Sienna, this is my day-one brother, Shorty.'

They smiled, still taking in the other's appearance. Blakey excused himself to fetch champagne for her table, and Shorty continued speaking with Sienna. He learned that she worked in an office in town and that they'd met years ago at a party. She laughed, saying that Shorty had been drunk and passed out in the corner, which tickled him. They'd just exchanged numbers when K-Bar sauntered over, hugging her.

'Easy, Sienna. Where are your friends?'

'At the table over there. They're all spoken for, so leave them alone.'

K-Bar laughed. 'You're always spoiling my fun. Everything cool?'

'I was re-introducing myself to your boy here. I'll leave you both to it.' Sienna sashayed away, both men watching.

'I'm gonna smash that,' Shorty said, feeling the old hunger returning. He hadn't had sex since leaving prison, not counting the random girl from his second night out. He was attracted to Sienna and looked forward to getting to know her.

'You need to watch out. Her man doesn't play.'

'She didn't mention having a man.'

'They rarely do, bruv. You know that. Did you speak with Blakey?'

'Yeah, he's cool. Enjoying his life.'

'Good. Let's enjoy yours now. You can buy the first round.'

Lamont woke the following day, Jenny's arms tightly pinioned around him. He grinned, remembering the activities the night before. They'd had sex since his recovery, but none he'd enjoyed as much. They'd completely let themselves go in a way they hadn't since they first met, and he liked that.

Reality loomed, though, and he still had a mountain of business he needed to handle. He thought about Jenny meeting with Malcolm, and scowled. He remembered her meeting with him at a coffee shop and finding him interesting. Lamont didn't believe she was cheating, but the fact she wanted to spend time with another man made him jealous, and he hated that. He wondered if she had kept her meeting a secret because she was worried about how he would respond. It was galling. He was supposed to be bigger than that.

Lamont disentangled himself and went to take a shower. When he was finished, she was awake. She smiled, but it seemed strained.

'Do you want to take a shower, or maybe order some breakfast?'

Jenny shook her head. 'I'll get a quick shower, then we can check out.'

The hotel ordered them a taxi, and they sat in silence on the journey home. The energetic driver tried making conversation, but other than a few bland remarks, they stared out of their respective windows.

When they reached home, Jenny headed straight upstairs. Lamont watched, wanting to call after her and say something, but he understood her reaction. A single passionate night wasn't enough to erode their problems, and he wondered if suggesting the night had been a good idea.

Sighing, Lamont trudged to his study, ready to escape his world.

CHAPTER ELEVEN
MONDAY 9 MARCH, 2015

RIGBY AND MURPHY sat in the canteen, food untouched as they devoured the awful work coffee.

'K-Bar then,' Rigby said.

'People are saying he was the Head Chief while Teflon was laid up. He was making all the decisions, and I'm sure he was behind Bernette's murder.'

They had looked into the Manchester murders of 2013. Marrion had been gunned down, then several of his associates were killed in separate incidents months later.

'Just Bernette's? Others were dropped during that period. Daniels, the other Carnival shooter. Schemes. The guys from Manchester that Shorty killed. His little cousin. They were all connected, right?'

Murphy scratched at his stubble, frowning.

'Chink was murdered too. He was Teflon's number two, though, so hard to include him. Looks like we had a war between the two cities. The Manchester lot murdered Chink, that Polo character, Timmy, and the girl we found with Chink. Lots of tit-for-tat murders in retaliation. Teflon and Shorty were the main prizes. Shorty killed his attackers, then Teflon nearly died.'

TARGET PART TWO: THE TAKEDOWN

Rigby considered Murphy's words. It was plausible, but they had no concrete proof.

'We need to talk with people; anyone connected with the murders. We'll shake a few bushes and see what we find. The chief won't like us going off base for long, so we better find something quickly.'

SHORTY LIFTED the barbell in the air, breathing out as he held it up for a few seconds, arms straining under the considerable weight. He lowered it back to his chest and repeated the motion twelve times before stopping. He'd spent more time in the gym lately, working off his frustration. They had cleared the air, but Lamont hadn't changed his mind, only choosing to give him more money. He wasn't doing much with the cash. He purchased some new clothes and gave money to both Amy and Stacey. The urge to splash out like back in the day eluded him.

Shorty had taken Sienna out for dinner and returned to her place, but nothing transpired except some kissing. Shorty didn't mind, which was a change. He enjoyed being around her.

K-Bar was back in business, the heat from Kev's murder subsiding. He and Lamont remained frosty, with more orders being relayed through Akeem. Darren was progressing with his mission, but K-Bar and Shorty remained in the dark. Lamont was stuck on Shorty's arrest, hammering home the point that the police would loathe the fact they hadn't been able to put him away. He understood, but resented the fact Lamont believed him to be sloppy.

When he'd finished at the gym, he went home and ate a quick meal. Slouching in front of the television, his eyes were closing when his phone chirped.

'Who's this?'

'It's B. Listen, have you been spending time with Sienna?'

Shorty sat up.

'Why?'

'Her man has been around the club, asking people about you.'

'So what?' Shorty scoffed. Sienna had mentioned her ex's anger issues. He wasn't phased by Lutel Forde or his so-called crazy reputation.

'He's a rugged guy, Shorty. He's not afraid to make a problem. Even knowing your rep, he's still not backing down.'

'B, I'm an easy guy to find. I'm not studying Lutel.'

'Okay. I just thought you'd wanna know.'

Shorty hung up, sniggering at the thought of someone asking around about him. He assumed people had seen him and Sienna at community meetings. Trinidad was another regular fixture, but he hadn't seen Jenny since the first meeting. Dropping his phone on the nearby table, he quickly fell asleep.

―――

JENNY HURRIED through the doors of the nail salon, rubbing her arms from the outside chill.

'I'm sorry,' she said, spotting the person she was here to meet.

'Don't worry about it,' replied Marika. 'I haven't been here that long myself. Had to beg my boss to give me some holiday.'

Jenny grinned. She'd met with Marika several times, learning a lot about Lamont's younger sister. She worked part-time in a contact centre and had taken an interest in finance, which made sense. She'd relied on Lamont to fund her for years and now saw the importance of managing her own money.

Marika had asked her for financial advice, and she did her best to help, but her situation differed. Struggling business aside, Jenny was born into wealth and, financially, hadn't struggled for anything.

'I'm glad you were able to persuade him. Have you looked into that thing we were talking about?'

Marika nodded, her infectious grin making her features shine. Jenny thought Marika was beautiful, but when she truly smiled, she was in a different league. Jenny noticed other patrons beaming at them. By now, they were being seen to, talking with one another as their nails were taken care of.

'I've seen a few online courses, so I'm debating between those, or going to a physical night school to get qualified. It'll take a few years, but I'll be more established, and I can think more about a career.'

'What about the kids?'

'Keyshawn can look after his sister. He's old enough,' Marika hesitated. 'Auntie is always a last resort, depending how many days a week I'd have to study, but the kids don't like her. The online course might be the best.'

Jenny smiled. 'I'm thrilled you're taking this step, Marika. It's never too late to start a career.'

'Thanks, Jen. I've always messed around, but money is kinda fun when you look beyond how quickly you can spend it. There's something I need to tell you, though. It's kinda personal.'

'What is it?'

'I'm seeing someone.'

'That's great; who is it?'

Marika paused. 'K-Bar.'

'K-Bar as in L and Shorty's *K-Bar*?'

Marika shifted in her seat.

'How long?'

'A year, maybe longer.'

'Seriously?' Jenny's eyes widened.

'I know. At first, he was just comforting me after Marrion, but then we started to like each other.'

'Does your brother know?'

Marika shook her head.

'You're the only person I've told. K can't really tell anyone, not in the position he's in.'

'He needs to talk to L directly about it if he's serious.'

Marika sighed. 'I know, but L's awkward. He hated Marrion because he was involved with me, and he and K-Bar have been close since they were teenagers. K doesn't want to jeopardise that.'

'I understand, but he needs to know, and he should hear directly from K-Bar.'

The pair changed the subject. They were preparing to leave when Jenny blurted something out.

'You should come for dinner.'

'What?' Marika shrugged into her coat and picked up her handbag.

'You and the kids should come for dinner.'

Marika paused. 'What about L?'

'It's my house too, and it's time you started talking again. It's been too long.'

Marika opened her mouth to speak, then nodded. Jenny grinned. Lamont's reaction would be worrying, but she would deal with that when the time came.

―――

Lamont parked around the corner from the barbers and strode toward the building, hands in his pockets. He nodded at a few familiar faces, all of whom gave him blank stares. It was a strange response, but he didn't dwell. The place was in full swing, with all four barber chairs filled, loud music and hearty conversation taking place.

The noise dimmed a little when Lamont entered. He nodded at Trinidad, who nodded back. Pausing his hair cutting, he handed Lamont a stack of letters. Lamont thanked him and headed to his office. He hadn't been since he and Trinidad argued, and there was a fine layer of dust on the desk.

Lamont dropped the letters on the desk, thumbing his old chessboard. The pieces were dusty, but holding them seemed to calm him. He took a deep breath. It had become abundantly clear lately that he had no idea who he was anymore. He'd pushed ahead, struggling to focus on anything around him. He didn't know where to turn, or how he could stop. All he'd wanted was freedom. That dream had changed to include Jenny, but now there was nothing but helplessness. Their relationship was precarious, and he didn't know what to say to fix things.

Everything he had worked toward seemed to have imploded, and he struggled to deal with that fact.

'I've missed seeing you around here.'

He looked up. Trinidad stood in the doorway.

'I'd have thought you'd prefer me not being around.'

Trinidad stepped into the office and closed the door.

'We both said some things. I don't agree with your actions, but I shouldn't have spoken to you the way I did. It's not your fault Chapeltown is the way it is. This is going back before you were born.'

'Even so, I respect your opinion. You're more than welcome to blow off steam now and then.'

Trinidad grinned. 'Glad you feel that way. Is everything good, though? Would you like some food?'

'I'm alright, Trinidad. Just going to catch up on some work. How are you doing, though? Everything good money-wise?'

Trinidad shrugged. 'No complaints. I have money put away for my children, and I send a little something back home. All I can ask for, really.'

'How would you like to buy my share of the business?'

'What?' Trinidad's brow furrowed.

'Seriously, how would you like to buy me out?'

'You can't be broke?'

Lamont wanly smiled. 'I'm far from broke. You should have a business to leave to your children along with the money. I can help with that.'

Trinidad's eyes shone as he surveyed him.

'I've always seen you as one of my children,' he mumbled. Lamont was speechless, touched by the words. They awkwardly looked around each other for a minute, before he spoke again.

'I heard you've been a regular at the community meetings.'

'They're a great place to talk, and there's a lot of positive work

RICKY BLACK

in place because of them. I don't suppose I can get you to attend one?'

Lamont shrugged. 'Never say never. What about this Malcolm dude? Is he as cool as everyone thinks?' He thought of Jenny, who had nothing but positive things to say about the man.

'He's a force,' Trinidad said. 'He lives and breathes what he does. He's always doing something, and he gives people hope when he speaks.'

Lamont nodded, feeling a twinge of what he suspected was jealousy at Trinidad's words. He wondered if it was worth attending a meeting to check Malcolm out. His phone rang, Trinidad leaving the room as he answered.

'Hey, Jen.'

'I'm cooking a special dinner tonight, so make sure you're home for six, if that's okay?'

'I'll be there. Should I ask about the occasion?'

'No, you shouldn't. Bring wine, please. Love you.'

Lamont dropped the phone on the table and closed his eyes. He needed caffeine. Deciding not to move, he allowed his eyes to droop and fell asleep in the chair.

———

SHORTY ROSE from the gambling table with a smirk. He'd been playing cards and dominoes most of the day, making a small profit. The gambling spot was an easy place to hang out. No one asked questions, and he liked the atmosphere. He'd had a few brandies and cokes, and was in the middle of a chat with another old head when he heard a commotion.

'Oi, Shorty; I've been looking for you.'

Shorty turned his head to the speaker, who towered over most in the room, his muscled build evident against the black crew neck and bottoms he wore. He was clean-shaven with closely cropped hair and beady hazel eyes. Shorty didn't recognise him.

'Who the hell are you?'

TARGET PART TWO: THE TAKEDOWN

'I heard you've been sniffing around Sienna, and you need to stop,' Lutel growled. The room was silent, everyone watching the exchange with interest. There was no fear. The older generation frequented the spot, and this kind of standoff was commonplace, especially where women were concerned.

'What's it got to do with you?'

'Sienna's my woman.'

'Forget the talking. You wanna do something, then step.'

Lutel lurched forward just as Shorty sprang from his stool. He swung for Lutel, who avoided the hit and caught Shorty with a looping blow that staggered him. He kept his feet, slipping inside Lutel's guard and smashing his ribs with vicious hits. He clipped his jaw with a nasty punch and flung the bigger man to the floor, kicking him twice in the head. Reaching for a chair, he smashed it against his face and shoulders, feeling the glorious rage. It had been too long since he'd laid into someone, and he repeatedly hit Lutel until Jukie snapped him out of his trance.

'Shorty, get out of here before someone calls the police!'

Shorty glared down at the barely moving Lutel, then left.

———

LAMONT ARRIVED home at a quarter to six, grabbing the bottle of red wine he'd bought on the way. He let himself into the house, surprised to hear voices. He entered the living room after taking his coat off, pausing when he saw Marika and the children sitting with Jenny. When Bianca saw him, she hurtled into his arms.

'Uncle L!' She screamed as he lifted her into the air. He tightly clutched his niece, placing kisses on her face. Jenny and Marika watched, both wiping their eyes, overcome with emotion. It took a while before Lamont released her, his eyes wet. He couldn't believe how big she was. Keyshawn sat close to Marika, regarding Lamont almost warily. He nodded and patted him on the shoulder. He was trying to respect Keyshawn as an adult, and the teenager seemed to appreciate that effort, returning the nod.

'Hey, L.'

'Rika, how are you doing?' Lamont asked, his tone noncommittal.

'Jenny invited us to have dinner,' she said. He flicked his eyes towards Jenny, whose eyebrows rose, daring him to say something.

'I wasn't aware you two were in touch.'

'We're friends,' Jenny spoke up. 'I thought you should talk. It's been far too long.'

Lamont handed her the bottle of wine and faced his sister. Marika's hair was shorter; there were more lines under her eyes, but he begrudgingly admitted she looked well. He slipped onto the sofa, Bianca plopping on his lap and chattering nonstop about all her friends, school, and everything else in her life. Lamont half-listened, keeping his eyes on his sister.

They sat for dinner, Jenny and Bianca keeping up a running commentary of their favourite films, songs, and everything they liked in the world. Keyshawn spoke sporadically, confirming that school was fine.

Lamont was surprised Marika was working, but it made sense. He doubted Marrion had left her any money, and she couldn't claim much from benefits, especially nowadays. When she spoke of studying, he couldn't hide his surprise.

'What's brought this on?'

Marika smiled almost shyly.

'I want to understand money.'

After dinner, Jenny put on some music, and they retreated to the living room. They had some wine, and Lamont showed Keyshawn and Bianca around the house.

'Are we going to see more of you now, Uncle L?' Bianca looked up at him with wide eyes. He felt his heart crack as he stared at his beautiful niece.

'Yes, *Princess Bianca*. I'm not going anywhere.'

Lamont thought he saw a gleam in Keyshawn's eyes, but when he blinked, it was gone. His nephew reminded him of how he'd been in his younger years. Quiet, introverted, and damaged. He cursed himself for not being around; for allowing his temper and circumstances to cost him good years with the few family members he cared about.

It was after nine when Marika and the kids left. Lamont paid for their taxi. When he'd seen them off, he locked the door and headed to the kitchen, rolling up his sleeves to wash up.

'I can do that.'

Lamont didn't even turn.

'I've got it covered.'

Jenny paused before she spoke again, entering the kitchen and standing close to him.

'Don't keep it bottled up. Say what it is you've got to say.'

'You had no right,' he mumbled.

'Pardon?'

'I said, you had no right to interfere in my family business!' Lamont snapped, surprising her with the ferocity. He didn't turn, still washing a plate, but his shoulders shook with barely-suppressed rage.

'Are you serious? I care about you, L. I want you to be happy. I invited Marika because this whole mess has dragged on too long, and you're both too stubborn to make the first move.'

'That's not the point, and you know it. It's my situation to work out. It doesn't need you forcing people together and trying to resolve things.'

'You weren't happy to see your family, is that it, L? Because you seemed really happy to see your niece, I can tell you that much.'

'Stop trying to twist it. My family, my problems. Stay out of it.'

'Don't tell me what to do, L. I'm your partner, I don't work for you, and I expect us to compromise on things.'

'There was no compromise, because you didn't tell me what you were doing. You didn't even mention it. Seems to be a common theme with you nowadays.'

'What do you mean by that?'

'Who else are you going on little coffee dates with? There's Malcolm, Marika, Shorty . . . who's next, *K-Bar*?'

Jenny's eyes narrowed. 'Is that what this is about? You don't like me being around Malcolm?'

'No, the problem, as I clearly said, is you being around my sister and trying to force us together.' He flung the plate to the side and glared at her, soap suds adorning his hands. Jenny was red-faced, chestnut eyes alight with rage.

'I want you to be happy, L. Is that such a bad thing?'

'I'd be happy if I was left alone to deal with my life. Don't speak to my family again without permission.'

'I don't need your permission. I'll do what I think is right. You're not dealing with your emotions properly. Why is that so hard for you to see?'

'Jenny, just shut the fuck up with all that, okay? I don't need help. I don't need you to fix me. I'm not as weak as you, so focus on your own problems with your fucking counsellor, and leave me out of it!'

The palpable silence stretched, Jenny's face whitening as Lamont's vicious words hammered into her. Without a word, she stormed from the room.

Lamont glared at the space where she'd stood, trying to control his trembling hands. He wanted to run after her and apologise, but didn't move. When he heard the front door slam a few minutes later, he grabbed a plate and flung it against the wall. Yelling, he began systematically destroying all the dishes and cutlery he could see until he stood in the kitchen, surrounded by shattered kitchenware.

Lamont stared at his hands, breathing hard, wondering how he would get out of this latest mess.

CHAPTER TWELVE
TUESDAY 10 MARCH, 2015

SHORTY HEADED to the barbers the next day. He'd missed the morning rush, and when he walked in, Trinidad struggled to his feet to greet him.

'Are you okay?' He noticed the stiff movements and pain in the older man's face. Trinidad waved him off.

'People have been talking about you all morning.'

'I bet they have.' Shorty's phone had been ringing all morning. Everyone wanted to talk about his fight with Lutel. Even Sienna called. He'd said little, but he was already tired of talking about it. 'Have you seen L?'

'A few days ago, but not today. Are you sure you're okay?'

'Why wouldn't I be?'

Trinidad squinted, rubbing his ear. 'Lutel is a madman. He's not gonna be happy that you whipped him in a room full of people. His reputation is on the line now, and he's dangerous.'

Shorty shrugged. 'I didn't start this. He did.'

'I understand, but you took it further when you embarrassed him. I just want you to be careful.'

Shorty growled, shaking his head.

'Trinidad, I'm the one people need to worry about. Did you

forget who I am? Did you forget what the hell I'm about? I don't avoid trouble, I end it.' He swept a glare around the room, people cowering from the fire in his eyes. 'Any of you talk to that pussy, tell him I'm easy to find. He needs to worry about me, not the other way around.'

Silence ensued. Trinidad met his eyes, nodding slightly. He seemed almost relieved.

'Do you want a haircut now?'

Shorty nodded. 'Shape me up please, old man.'

LAMONT RAISED the glass of brandy to his lips, looking at his phone as he slumped over the table in his spacious kitchen. He and Jenny's spacious kitchen. She'd packed some things and left the house. He had called Kate numerous times, but couldn't get anything out of her. Lamont wondered for a fleeting moment if she was with Malcolm. He'd received a dossier of information about the man. Malcolm had distinguished himself at college and university level, and his online work was prominent. Lamont had even listened to some podcasts he'd produced without even knowing Malcolm was involved. He was direct and able to control his obvious intelligence without sounding condescending. It was easy to understand why Jenny would enjoy his company.

His annoyance rising, Lamont redialed Kate.

'L, you've got to stop calling,' she answered.

'I just wanna know she's okay.'

'She is.'

'And I want her to know that I'm sorry.'

'She does.'

'And I want her to come home.'

'You need to give it time, then. I know how you're feeling, L, but you can't rush this. Look after yourself, and she'll be in touch, okay?'

'Okay.' Lamont dropped the phone on the table. He hurled the

TARGET PART TWO: THE TAKEDOWN

bottle against the wall with a resounding smash, the pieces of glass joining the destruction from their aborted dinner. He picked up his phone to call her, but it went straight to voicemail. Nostrils flaring, he called Akeem.

'Follow Malcolm; make sure Jenny isn't with him.'

'Okay.'

He lurched to his study, locating a fresh bottle of brandy. Opening it, he dropped the lid on the floor. He was about to drink when there was a knock at the door. Lamont left the bottle and wiped his eyes, smoothing his hair. Opening the door, he sighed when he saw Shorty.

JENNY PUSHED AWAY HER PAPERWORK. There were orders she needed to sign off, but she couldn't focus. She kept replaying the argument in her mind. She didn't believe Lamont had meant the things he'd said, but it didn't make them hurt any less. The argument needed to happen. They had probed one another for months, walking on eggshells, avoiding the major topics until it imploded. The fact he'd referred to her as weak was jarring, and it had her wondering if going to counselling was the right action.

Should she have tried speaking directly to Lamont about her issues?

Maybe he would have confided in return. Now, they were both adrift. Lamont had tried contacting her, but she couldn't face him without knowing what she wanted to do. Jenny slumped on the table, wanting to block out the outside world. She wanted to escape, leave it all behind. It was harder than it should be, and she had no idea where to start.

Dimly, she wondered if that was how Lamont had felt the whole time.

'Are you sleeping?'

'You know I'm not,' Jenny said to Kate, lifting her head and watching her friend hover in the doorway.

'Good. I'm taking you to lunch.'

'It's three in the afternoon.'

'So what? Did you eat at lunchtime?'

Jenny didn't answer.

'Exactly. Get up and put your coat on.'

'I can't go to lunch, Kate. I have work to do.'

'You're not getting any work done, and we need a change of scenery. Let's go.'

They went to a local sandwich shop, Jenny picking at a Chicken Teriyaki wholewheat baguette. She sipped her water and waited for Kate to speak.

'Your man contacted me again today.'

Jenny was silent.

'He didn't sound good. He was slurring, so I'm guessing he's been drinking.'

Her stomach lurched. She forced herself to eat the sandwich as a distraction, hating Lamont being in distress.

'What's your move? Are you breaking up with him?'

'I just need some space right now.'

'How do you think L's gonna take that? Do you think he's gonna stay away forever?'

'I don't know, Kate. I don't know about any of this, but if my staying with you is a problem, I'll check into a hotel or stay with my parents.'

'Go to Hell. I'm not letting you go anywhere. I need to ask these questions, though. You know that.'

'We argued, and I can't help feeling that if we'd talked things out properly before, then it wouldn't have happened. I mean, we had a great night out, and amazing sex. That would have been a great time to get everything out in the open, but we didn't. We went with the facade instead.'

'After the time you've both had, is it so wrong that all you craved was that facade for a while?'

'Look where it's led us,' Jenny replied. 'I'm staying with you, and my partner seems comfortable drinking himself to death and ringing and texting me to the point I have to block him. He's not supposed to act like that, but he's broken, and I'm not sure I know how to fix him.' She paused. 'What should I do?'

'It's your life, and you both love each other. I guess you need to ask yourself if that's enough.'

'It shouldn't be so hard,' Jenny sighed. Kate squeezed her friend's hand.

'When the hell have you ever had it easy where L is concerned?'

'CAN I COME IN?' Shorty wrinkled his nose. Lamont's eyes were bleary, and his hair was more of a rumpled mess than ever. He shakily stepped aside, letting him in. He tottered back toward the study on unsteady legs. Staggering into his office chair, he took a deep swig of brandy as Shorty watched. He offered his friend the bottle, but Shorty shook his head.

'You're a damn mess, L. What the hell happened?'

'You don't know? I thought you and Jen were good friends?'

'What are you talking about?'

'We fought, and she left.'

'What did you fight about?'

'Does it matter?'

'With you smelling like you bathed in brandy, it kinda does,' replied Shorty. Lamont mockingly clapped, the bottle slipping from his grasp, liquor billowing over the expensive carpet. Shorty grabbed the bottle and headed to the kitchen, hesitating when he saw the destruction. Glasses, plates and cutlery were nestled amongst dried liquids and broken glass. He was used to Lamont's space being devoid of any mess or dust, so it was a complete shock to see this state. He headed back to the study. Lamont slumped over the desk.

'Tell me about the fight,' Shorty said, jolting him from his stupor.

'She was seeing Rika behind my back.'

'So?' Shorty knew Lamont and his sister hadn't spoken in nearly two years, but didn't understand why it was such a big deal.

'What do you mean *so*? You remember what Rika was like, right? How she picked that piece of shit Marrion over me? Her family, who supported her and paid for every single fucking thing she needed for years, without ever complaining? You think it's cool for Jenny to go behind my back and then invite her to our house without speaking to me?'

'L, Rika fucked up, but she's your little sis, and you love her. Jenny did what she thought was right.'

'It's not Jen's place to sort things. She's struggling with her business, you know? Ever since she took time off to look after me, her florists has been in the shitter. I offered to help; to give her the money and even treat it as a loan if she wanted, but she refused, so I let it slide. I watch her go into her office every day and come home a little more fucked up. It breaks me that she won't let me help, but I stayed away and let it slide.'

'Women are different, and you know that. They don't look at things like we do. Sometimes that's a bad thing. Sometimes it's good, but it's the way it is, and you can't really control the two.'

'Why are you here?' Lamont didn't want to discuss Jenny anymore. Shorty held his gaze for a moment before answering.

'I've waited long enough. I want back into the game, and I'm not taking no for an answer.'

LENNOX THOMPSON PARKED in Miles Hill and strode towards a door, knocking and entering. The man he'd come to see was in the living room, his face heavily bruised. He glanced up when Lennox walked in, but said nothing. Lennox surveyed the pitiful specimen, struggling to control his annoyance. He was about to speak when a woman sashayed into the room, handing Lutel a drink. Noticing him, she beamed.

'Hey, Len. Is everything good?'

'Everything is fine, Nicole. Do you mind giving us a minute?' It wasn't a request, and everyone in the room knew it. Kissing Lutel on the cheek, she smiled tightly at Lennox and went upstairs. He waited a moment before speaking.

'Are you suffering from some disease?'

Lutel frowned. 'What are you talking about?'

'I'm asking if you're suffering from some illness that stops you from listening. I specifically told you to stay away from Shorty. You can imagine how funny I found it when I heard that not only did you not do as ordered, you were also beaten unconscious in a room full of people.' Lennox clapped his hands. 'Well done.'

'My rep was on the line, Len. I needed to do it.'

'How?'

'Huh?'

'How was your rep on the line? You're not with the silly bitch you were fighting over anymore. You've moved on.'

'Shorty violated. He was warned not to step on toes and did it anyway. Whether I'm with Nicole doesn't mean shit. You've never had two girls at once before?'

Without warning, Lennox sprang forward and slapped him, the sound echoing around the room. Lutel leapt to his feet with a roar, but Lennox didn't move. Coming to his senses, he backed away, wincing.

'You're an emotional idiot. Look at you, jumping to your feet, ready to fight despite getting beaten the last time.' Lennox gripped him by the chin, his nails digging into the injured man's face. 'If your stupidity has messed my up plans, I'll have you pulled apart at the joints while your pretty little girlfriend upstairs watches. Understand?'

Lutel nodded. 'Sorry, Len. I got caught up, but it won't happen again. I promise.'

'Good. It better not.'

Lutel sank back onto the sofa, looking up at his boss.

'What are we gonna do now?'

Lennox turned, looking out the window for so long that Lutel wondered if he had even heard the question.

'You need to clean your plate. Get yourself sorted, then take out Shorty. Don't fuck it up.'

Lamont looked at Shorty, determination etched into his friend's face. He rubbed his temples, trying to blot out the impending headache. His mouth was like sandpaper, and he felt the nausea of too much alcohol swimming around his stomach.

'We've already discussed this—'

'And I listened. I disagreed, but I still followed orders and kept my nose clean. Now, I want back in. I can work with K-Bar.'

'Shorty, there's nothing wrong with being patient.'

'Don't give me that bullshit, L. You're just stringing me along.'

'You're letting emotions get away from you, just like when you beat up Lutel. Yeah, I heard about it directly from Jukie. You're lucky the police didn't come for you.'

'Fuck Lutel. I'm tired of hearing about him.'

'What about Lennox Thompson? Are you tired of hearing about Lutel's boss, because I bet you he knows about the situation.'

'Lutel came for me, or did Jukie not fill you in about that part? He started it, and unlike you, I defend myself when someone attacks me.'

'You're a fucking idiot.' Lamont slammed his hands on the desk. 'Is having multiple people aiming guns at me and being shot something to be ashamed of? What about you, *Big bad Shorty?* You got arrested and carted off to prison like some little runner. What does that make you?'

In the silence that followed, Lamont saw the veins in his thick neck throbbing. Shorty clenched his fists, nostrils flaring.

'You're a drunken mess, losing your shit over your woman like some pussy. You're not in the right frame of mind to lead, so stop preaching, and put me back in.'

TARGET PART TWO: THE TAKEDOWN

Lamont took a deep breath, surpassing the urge to retort. His head was pounding, and he wished Shorty would leave so he could throw up.

'You can't aggravate things with Lennox Thompson. We're not in a position to fight that war. We've hired soldiers, but we're still getting everyone into shape. I need you to keep calm.'

Shorty rubbed his eyes.

'L, I can do it. Please, just put me back in, and I'll stay calm. I'll be distracted. Cool?'

There was another long silence, both men sizing up the other. Lamont broke it this time.

'Fine. You're back in. You and K-Bar can work out what's happening, but make sure I'm kept in the loop.'

Shorty grinned, looking ten years younger in an instant.

'Thank you, L. I mean that. For starters, let's get you some coffee so you can tidy up. You're looking like some drunken loser.'

LENNOX AND NIKKOLO were clad in all black as they entered a restaurant near the Hood. When he saw them, the owner scurried into the back as the pair pulled guns, aiming them at the men in the room. Without warning, they fired, two of the three men falling with cries of pain. Lennox and Nikkolo were unfazed, focusing their guns on the other man, hunched over his plate of food. Lennox assessed him, respecting the fact that he was trying hard to hide his terror.

'You're an unfortunate casualty, Winston. Your daddy is at fault, but that falls on you now.'

Winston itched to reach for his pistol. Both men had him in their sights, though, and the fact they had coldly dispatched of his guards showed they had no qualms about killing. He searched Lennox's bloodshot eyes, noting they looked devoid of emotion. There were tired lines around the man's face, but he seemed composed.

'You don't have to do this. We can still work something out. Kill me, though, all bets are off. You'll be hunted down like a dog. You won't be able to make any money. My pops will see to that.'

Lennox nodded at his words.

'You're not wrong, Winnie. I respect the fact you always try to be practical. You're always looking at the big picture. Your daddy isn't the man he was twenty years ago, though. The fact he thought he could point you at me proves that. He'll learn once everyone dear to him is gone. Please don't take what happens next personally.'

Lennox fired four times, each bullet slamming into Winston, his chair toppling backwards and sending the big man to the floor. Winston spluttered, his tongue lolling as he choked on the torrents of blood billowing from his mouth. Lennox looked at him without pity, then signalled to Nikkolo, who put his gun to his head and fired, finishing the job. Dropping the guns on the restaurant floor, they hurried from the premises.

CHAPTER THIRTEEN
FRIDAY 13 MARCH, 2015

FOR DAYS after Winston's murder, Chapeltown awaited the explosion they were sure would follow. The murder was being investigated, but the police were simply going through the motions, trying to stop a war from escalating.

The owner of the restaurant had been questioned. No one had spoken with or seen Delroy. The streets suspected Lennox Thompson was responsible for the hit, but a small crew from Seacroft were stupidly claiming responsibility.

Malcolm Powell held court outside the health centre on Chapeltown Road, where he spoke at length about the drug war tearing apart the community. Speaking only to a few people at first, others quickly convened to hear what he had to say:

'Thank you all for coming. Another week passes, and there is more strife and bloodshed for us to overcome. What happened to the Williams family was a tragedy, and my condolences go out to them. I don't condone their alleged business, but Winston didn't deserve to die.
'How many more, though? How many more soldiers have to die in this pointless war, caused by greed and the sale of illegal goods? The same

illegal goods that allow police to storm into our ends like overseers and beat us at will.

'This is all linked — a home linked to Delroy Williams was raided recently, the largest drug seizure in years that I can remember. It all needs to stop, and we need to continue working together to allow that to happen. It needs all of us working collectively.

'To Delroy Williams directly, I again apologise for your loss and if you see the light and wish to speak to me in confidence, contact me, and I will do my best to help you, I promise.'

'IT'S ONLY a matter of time until Delroy goes on the attack.'

Rigby and Murphy ate a quick lunch consisting of wraps from a local bakery and containers of coffee. They'd worked through the night leading up to their current meeting. So far, the progress had been pathetic.

'Was it definitely Thompson who took out Winston? Maybe Teflon got his hands dirty?'

'I don't think so. Teflon and Delroy get along, according to intelligence reports. They've definitely done business together; I'd stake my pension on that.'

'We need to speak to Holdsworth again. He's leading that investigation, and it's like he doesn't care.'

'He doesn't, Rig. You know that. We need to make sure it doesn't spill over. If you're finished eating, let's talk to our friend in there.'

The pair left the bakery and headed to an apartment building in the heart of the city centre. After announcing themselves and riding the elevator to the 6th floor, they knocked. The woman warily stared at the pair. Rigby smiled, but this didn't seem to reassure her.

'Can we come in, please? We just have a few questions.'

'About what?'

'About your friend Naomi.'

TARGET PART TWO: THE TAKEDOWN

This startled Adele enough for her to pull away from the door. The flat was one bedroom, but appeared lived-in and comfortable. They sat, pens and notepads out.

'What about her?' She folded her arms, eyes darting around the room.

'We're investigating a spate of incidents around the time of your friend's murder, so we apologise if it seems like we're treading old ground. Did anyone speak with you at the time of the murder?'

Adele shook her head.

'Do you know why it occurred?'

'Why would I?'

'Naomi was murdered with two other people. One of the men, Xiyu Manderson, was in a relationship with your friend, putting her in the middle of it.'

'That fucking cunt. It was his fault Naomi was involved. All of it was his fault.'

Rigby and Murphy shared a look.

'Why?'

'He broke my friend's spirit. Naomi was special; she was beautiful, and she had this quality that made her stand out. Chink . . . *Xiyu* broke that. She wasn't the same when she was with him.'

'How?'

'She was nervous. They argued a lot, and she was feisty and liked to run her mouth. Then she just stopped.'

'You think Xiyu was beating her?'

Adele nodded.

'I saw bruises once. I tried asking her, and she just looked right through me. Even when I suggested getting some help, she just ignored me. She wasn't even mad; it was like she'd shut down.'

'We're trying to understand the crime. Polo, an associate of Xiyu's who we believe was his bodyguard, was shot outside. We believe that it was a planned hit.'

Tears streamed down Adele's cheeks as she choked on her sobs.

'They treated her like trash. She was murdered for the sake of it.'

Rigby nodded. 'I agree. Your friend didn't deserve to be murdered just for being there.'

Murphy hung in the background, making notes and watching Rigby work. This was their thing. Rigby was better at making people feel comfortable. Murphy found it easier to intimidate. Adele slumped onto the chair facing Rigby. He offered her a tissue.

'Why are you really here?' She softly asked.

'We want your help to catch the people responsible. You know about the situation, and I think you know why it happened. We'll find out everything. This lovely flat you've got; is it above board? We'll be thorough in checking everything, including finances. Help us out. Don't let Naomi's killers get away with it.'

Wiping her eyes and blowing her nose, Adele finally nodded.

'If you can guarantee my safety, I'll tell you what I know.'

―――

LAMONT WAITED for the electronic gates to open, allowing him access to a sprawling property on the outskirts of Leeds. Driving up a long, winding path, he parked in front of a multi-room mansion. Even as he climbed from the car, he spotted at least eight armed men patrolling the premises. He was quickly patted down and led into the main room. Delroy and a woman Lamont recognised as his wife sat there. Both were quiet, the grief far more obvious on the face of Delroy's wife. Lamont hugged her and offered his condolences, receiving little reaction. Delroy shook his hand, and they traipsed towards another room to talk. He poured two glasses of whiskey and gave one to Lamont without asking. Silently, they toasted and drank.

'Winston shouldn't have been caught up in it,' Lamont finally said, clearing his throat as the hot liquor attacked his chest.

'I know.' Delroy stared into his glass. 'I wanted you to take over. Winnie didn't have the tools. Not for war, anyway. Spinks went missing, and no one even noticed. Lennox probably forced him to

TARGET PART TWO: THE TAKEDOWN

share Winnie's routine. After Mack's attack, Spinks drove Winnie around. They were close.'

Lamont absorbed the information, going over every little point in his head. He wouldn't say it out loud, but Lennox had played a brilliant move. He had effectively weakened Delroy's position by killing his son, having already arranged for his spot to be raided. The pressure was now on Delroy to strike back, yet looking at him, Lamont couldn't see it happening. Not effectively, at least. Delroy wore every single one of his years on his face. He was finished, even if he hadn't yet realised.

'Where's Eddie?' He asked. Eddie Williams was more in the mould of Shorty; a hothead who needed little provocation to cause destruction. The death of his brother would put him on the warpath. Delroy shrugged, refilling his drink.

'No one's seen him. Either Lennox got him too, or he's gone directly after him. He didn't answer my calls, and he hasn't stopped by. Possible he doesn't know, but I doubt that. Word spread quickly.'

Lamont agreed. He'd had well over a dozen phone calls once the news hit the streets about the murder. A man in Eddie's position definitely had contacts.

'What now?'

'Are you going to take up my offer?' Delroy finally looked at Lamont.

'No.'

Delroy nodded.

'I've got a crew in place. They're gonna wipe out Lennox and the rest of his people,' Delroy held his attention, his lined face hard. 'You might wanna stay out of Chapeltown for a while.'

'It's mad.'

Shorty tucked into some fish soup with K-Bar, Darren and Maka at a safe house. A stream of empty containers and carrier bags surrounded them. He was in his element, happy to be back in the life. He'd spoken with K-Bar and picked up right where he'd left off, but with a newfound calmness. Yesterday, he'd even spent time with Grace, under Amy's careful supervision.

Shorty was re-learning the ranks, but found he spent less time amongst the soldiers, and more time analysing things from a distance. As he'd told Lamont, he understood the risk involved with the police. He had no desire to go back to prison. There was too much to live for.

'What is?' Darren asked K-Bar, wiping his mouth as he finished a dumpling.

'How the hell does someone get the drop on a man like Winnie? He's supposed to have security out of the arse.'

'Winnie never took it seriously. He was probably sitting in the restaurant stuffing his fat face,' said Shorty.

'He had one or two guards with him; they were just a little slow on the draw,' replied K-Bar.

'Lenny was gunning at them. Winnie needed more people, or he needed to avoid being out in public. We've all done dirt before. We know the signs.'

No one argued. Other than K-Bar, Shorty was in a league of his own when it came to warfare. His track record spoke for itself.

'Either way, everyone needs to be careful. Delroy is old, but he won't sit tight on this. He's gonna have his people out there hitting back against Lennox. Lennox's people might not discriminate, so we need to have people out there when necessary.'

'Do you think L's gonna get involved?' Maka asked. No one spoke for a moment. All were aware of the weird relationship between Lamont and Delroy. At times there was a father-and-son vibe. At others, they were at each other's throats. Lamont mentioned an offer Delroy made for him to lead his organisation, but no one expected him to take it. He wouldn't work for another person; it was the one consistent fact about him.

'I don't know, fam,' Shorty finally replied. 'I don't think so,

TARGET PART TWO: THE TAKEDOWN

though. L's playing it different. He's not trying to take on someone else's drama. Not anymore.'

Lamont left Delroy's, his mind full of questions. The situation with Lennox was about to heat up. He hoped Delroy's shooters were good, because he couldn't see them having many chances to take out Lennox Thompson.

Lamont was focused on the future. He'd heard about Malcolm's speech on Chapeltown Road, but didn't know if Jenny had been there. Long-term, he could slide into Delroy's spot if Lennox murdered him. He had the infrastructure in place, which would help placate people if they could earn more money. The positive about the conflict was that it was keeping him from overthinking about his estranged girlfriend. Reaching home, Lamont paused. There was a note pinned to the door. Removing it, he noted it had a number to call. Sighing, he called the number.

'Lamont Jones?'

'Who's asking?'

'A car will pick you up in ten minutes.'

'The person hung up. Lamont called Akeem.

'Someone left a note at the house. A car's coming to pick me up in ten minutes to take me somewhere.'

'I can have someone at your place in five. Go inside and lock up.'

'It's fine. I believe I know who's behind this.'

When the car arrived, he was blindfolded and driven to a location. Despite the circumstances, he felt oddly calm. He was led into a building, and then the blindfold was removed.

'Hello, Mr Jones,' a familiar voice intoned. Lamont nodded, a small smile on his face.

'It's good to see you, Akhan.'

CHAPTER FOURTEEN
FRIDAY 13 MARCH, 2015

LAMONT AND AKHAN STARED, neither man blinking. Lamont recalled their last conversation; when Akhan had calmly blackmailed him under threat of his murder of Ricky Reagan becoming public knowledge.

Akhan looked the same; unflappably calm and fastidiously dressed in a shirt, trousers and dress shoes. Finally, he motioned for Lamont to sit down.

'Would you like a drink?' He asked.

'Some water please,' replied Lamont. Akhan signalled for someone to fetch it.

'How are you?'

'I'm well,' said Lamont, keeping his words succinct. He was aware of the guards posted by the door.

'Our last meeting, things went in a different direction than I'd intended.'

'I doubt that. You wanted to establish control, and you did.'

Akhan shook his head, his expression almost pained.

'I wanted what was best for you. The freedom you desire, it doesn't exist. Chapeltown needs you, especially with the current situation with Delroy and Lennox Thompson.'

'You know about that?'

'Delroy will lose. We both know this. Lennox is more organised, more logical, and he's utterly ruthless. He wants everything, and Delroy is in the way. Even before his son's death, he could not have won.'

Lamont rubbed his forehead, drinking the water, so he had something to do.

'Are you going to explain what this has to do with me?'

Akhan assessed him for a long moment. The guards shifted slightly, but held their positions.

'Lennox is a problem because if he wins, he won't leave you unchecked. You're a threat, maybe the only one he has in Leeds. He doesn't think the same way as Delroy, and he will not co-exist. You'll be taken out.'

'Why do you care?' Lamont understood his concerns, but the fact remained Akhan had blackmailed him, and that loomed over everything else the warlord said. 'You could do a deal with Lennox. He'd be forced to take you seriously. You don't need me for this.'

Akhan grinned. 'I meant everything I said, Lamont. It's only your unwillingness to really get involved that holds you back. If you looked at your whole city the way you do your crew, things would work better, and everyone would profit handsomely. Lennox is concerned only with himself.'

Lamont closed his eyes.

'If I take out Lennox, will you allow me to walk away?'

Akhan again gave him a long look.

'Stay for dinner, and let us talk of other matters. One more thing,' Akhan began as he led them from the study, 'Darren is to stay away from Rashad and any other member of my organisation. If he doesn't, he dies.'

JENNY PLAYED with the food on her plate, her appetite awol. She was in a trendy restaurant near Park Row, but her thoughts were scattered. She looked at the mobile phone resting on the table, thinking of Lamont and what he might be doing. She'd had a lot of time to think about their argument and hated that things had grown so out of control. Several times, she'd considered contacting him and trying to work past things, but she couldn't predict where it would end. The future seemed murky, and she had no idea how to navigate that.

'Aren't you eating?'

Jenny glanced at Malcolm and shook her head. He'd called earlier, inviting her to get some food. She appreciated the distraction and agreed. Malcolm met her eyes, a strong, confident presence in the full venue. Women snuck appreciative looks at him as he ate his food, but he paid them no attention, entirely focused on her.

'Starving yourself won't make things any better. You need to eat something.'

'I'll eat later.'

Malcolm looked for a moment as if he would argue, but shrugged and kept eating. After a while, he wiped his mouth.

'What do you know about the war in Chapeltown?' He asked.

'I try not to think about it. I still have nightmares from what happened to my partner a few years ago.'

Malcolm's face was unreadable as he surveyed Jenny.

'You don't talk about him much.'

Jenny sighed. 'There isn't much to say. Sometimes, relationships are a struggle. I'm sure you've heard all the cliches before.'

'What does your boyfriend think of you spending time around me?'

She frowned. 'Why would you ask that?'

Malcolm grinned. 'I'm a curious fellow. You won't eat, so I'm going to talk at you for a while and see how that works out. So, stop avoiding the question.'

'I'm not avoiding the question. Look, he's a private guy, and he's fantastic at hiding his emotions. If you're trying to ask if he knows about you, the answer is yes.'

TARGET PART TWO: THE TAKEDOWN

'And, he said nothing at all about spending any time with me?'

Jenny thought back to the conversations they'd shared about Malcolm. Lamont had mentioned his name the day they'd argued. Malcolm was a good-looking guy; he was articulate and quirky, and she enjoyed spending time with him. The fact he was a superb writer was an additional bonus. Jenny saw him as someone she could confide in, and wondered if that would upset Lamont. She tried putting herself in his shoes. *If Lamont was speaking with another woman the way she spoke with and spent time with Malcolm, how would she feel?*

Her eyes narrowed, and she shook her head to clear the thoughts from her mind.

'Where the hell were you just then?' Malcolm's eyebrow rose.

'Somewhere I'm not sure how to navigate,' she admitted. 'To answer your question, no, he didn't. He's a closed book.'

Malcolm rubbed his eyebrow. 'Let's talk about something else. What do you want to do with the rest of your life?'

Jenny's face crinkled in surprise. It was such a simple question, but it startled her.

'I want to grow my business. I can make it better than it was before, it's just going to take time. I often have to remember that and stop beating myself up.'

Malcolm nodded. 'I told you before that your passion was one of the things I liked the most about you. I know you're in a relationship, and you're giving that your attention, but you should always put yourself first because, quite simply, you deserve the best, Jenny. Whatever or whoever that may be.'

She couldn't speak at first, moved by his words. They were empowering and touching and warmed her in a way that they shouldn't. They stared at one another for a long moment. Her hands trembled, her stomach churning in a way that had nothing to do with nausea and everything to do with nerves.

'Have dinner with me. Tonight. I'll cook.'

Jenny's heart seemed to stop for a second. She thought again of Lamont, but Malcolm was right. He was invested in her and wanted to spend time with her. With that in mind, there was only one answer to give.

'Okay.'

Lamont met with Akeem. They sat in the study, Lamont pouring drinks as he shared Akhan's words.

'We need a strategy for getting rid of Lennox. Delroy will struggle. He's got shooting crews in place, but Lennox will see them coming. Lennox's team is solid, but he's the key.'

'He's powerful. He has people ready to die for him,' Akeem agreed.

'The police exposure at the moment won't make it easy either.'

'Shorty could kill Lennox?' Akeem suggested. 'K-Bar is still benched. The only other person I'd suggest is myself.'

'I don't want to use you for that. I've no doubt in your ability, but it's a risk, and I need you for too many other things.'

Akeem nodded. 'What's Akhan's game? He could go after Lennox himself if he thought he was a threat.'

Lamont didn't reply. He agreed that Akhan definitely had an agenda he hadn't shared. He was playing a role, and Lamont couldn't predict what Akhan would do if he killed Lennox.

'He seems determined to have me in place. Maybe he wants to keep me distracted? He knows about Darren getting close to Rashad, meaning Darren was sloppy, or Rashad told Akhan what he knew . . .'

'Or, Akhan knew all along and let it happen.'

Lamont flinched. He'd given thought to Akeem's theory, but didn't want to believe he could be outplayed in such a manner. He wasn't on top form. Jenny occupied a permanent place in his mind; he was trying to listen to Kate and stay away, yet felt things would only worsen if he did.

'For now, let's focus on Lennox. Akhan is the long-term plan.

TARGET PART TWO: THE TAKEDOWN

We have a few goons in place now. Let's at least get an idea of Lennox's team, and any potential weak links.'

'I'm on it, boss.' Akeem downed his drink and reached for his phone.

———

'I'M glad you've made up your mind.'

In the middle of doing her hair, Jenny turned to look at Kate, ignoring the wide grin on her friend's face.

'I don't know what you mean.'

'Sure you don't. You and Malcolm going on a date and you going over for dinner is a sign you and L are done, girl.'

'I'm in love with L, Kate. Malcolm is a friend; a good one who has stepped up when I needed someone. We're friends, that's it.'

'Whatever you say. You're wearing that sexy-ass black dress and those *fuck-me* heels. I haven't seen you like this in years, so you can save the *friends* shit for someone who doesn't know you.'

'L knows about Malcolm. He doesn't mind me having friends.'

'Course, and if the position was reversed, you wouldn't mind L going to dinner with a beautiful woman who wrote really well, would you?'

Jenny didn't reply. She didn't know where they were at, but her feelings were unchanged. She loved Lamont, but the confusion and his refusal to let her in were jarring. Deciding to put it out of her mind, she focused on finishing her hair, ignoring Kate's triumphant cackling.

———

JENNY'S HEART HAMMERED. She knew why. She knew how she could stop it. *It's just dinner*, she kept telling herself. She took her car. A powerful red Mercedes. While Lamont was recovering, and she was driving him around, he'd insisted on buying it:

'I don't need a car, L.'

'I know you don't. You're happy with this one, and that's fine, but I want to buy you one.'

'And I don't want you to. Like I said. I have my own money.'

'I know you do,' Lamont smiled. 'We both have money. So, if you're not going to let me buy you one, then I'll treat myself. A nice cherry red Mercedes.' He gently rubbed his stomach. 'But, with my condition and all, I'm going to need you to drive me around.'

So, they both got what they wanted. Jenny got a car and kept her independence, and he got to buy it for her. She quickly found a buyer for her old car, and it was never spoken of again. Jenny wondered what he was doing, but shook the thoughts. She pulled into Malcolm's drive, parking behind his Range Rover. The house was detached and pale-bricked, with a sturdy-looking brown door. Chest fluttering, she knocked.

'You're right on time,' said Malcolm, beaming when he saw her. He wore a green polo shirt, tight around the biceps, khaki trousers and deck shoes. He showed her into the living room. The lights were dimmed low, the TV on, but muted, silently playing what looked like the Evening News. Jenny was surprised at the organised clutter. Books, newspapers, notepads, pens and paper were all over, but haphazardly placed into piles.

'Can I get you a drink?'

'I'm driving, so just a glass of water will be fine,' said Jenny. Malcolm snorted.

'Glass of wine coming up. Take a seat.'

Jenny did as she was told. The comfortable sofa was a dark, murky brown. She watched the news, hearing the music playing in the background. *Al Green.* She had owned several of his CDs when she was younger.

'Here you go,' Malcolm handed her a glass of red wine, 'try this.'

Jenny sipped it. It was strong, but did a lot to ease her nervousness.

'So, how was work after our lunch?' asked Malcolm. She glanced at him.

TARGET PART TWO: THE TAKEDOWN

'Are we doing small talk?'

'If you want to go straight to bed, then that's fine with me,' replied Malcolm. She laughed.

'I guess I asked for that.'

'Ask, and you shall receive.'

'Is that why you've got *Al Green* playing?'

Malcolm shook his head, grin still etched on his face.

'I'm just a big Al fan. If you'd rather have something else on, I can play a bit of *Spice Girls*? Maybe some *Cher*?'

Jenny giggled. 'Al will do just fine.'

They spoke easily. Malcolm told her a little about his latest projects. They ate dinner, a delicious chicken salad.

'I wrote something based on you,' said Malcolm much later. He was pouring them more wine. It was her fourth glass, and she was feeling light-headed.

'Did you now?'

'I did,' said Malcolm, all lightheartedness gone.

'Well, are you going to share it with me?' teased Jenny. Malcolm didn't smile. His eyes locked on hers, and she faltered. As she wondered what was happening, he cleared his throat and began to speak:

The most beautiful thing about her isn't her beauty.
It's not her lips; lips that make you want to hold her, gently nibble, and seduce her.
It's not the body, highly sexual, molten fire from a volcano, though she does not flaunt it.
It's not the hauntingly intelligent eyes.
It's all the above, and the personality on top.
That of a humble woman who knows, understands, appreciates the world around her.
Yet still goes out and grinds for what she wants.

When Malcolm stopped, it took a few moments for Jenny to catch up. The wine glass was frozen in her hand. With a start, she sat back. Malcolm remained unsmiling.

'Wow . . .' She said.

'You like?'

Jenny nodded. 'It's amazing. I don't think I'm worthy of the words, though. You exaggerated. A lot.'

'You would say that, and that's what makes you so extraordinary.'

'You probably say that to all the girls.'

Malcolm drained his wine. His eyes were slightly red, but it didn't seem to affect him as much as Jenny.

'I'm no virgin, but I don't make it a habit of writing personal poetry for women I'm trying to get with. Usually, I just use what I have on hand, and it does the trick.'

'Malcolm, I have a boyfriend,' said Jenny. His reaction was the same as always. He gave a snort and shrugged.

'So what?'

'So, I can't do anything.'

'Can't, or won't?'

'Both,' Jenny put her wineglass on the table. 'I love him, and I don't cheat. I've had it done to me before.'

'It's not supposed to be nice. Cheating is a way of life. I think you're wonderful. For all the words I said above, and for many more. You know why I invited you here. I know you know, because you're smart, yet you came anyway. Why?'

'I—' she couldn't speak. Malcolm was in her space now, his eyes dark, serious, predatory with their intent. She felt trapped, fighting against her desires, trying to remain true to Lamont. Malcolm's lips were on hers now, though, and it felt right. She went with it, forcing her mouth further against his as he stimulated her lips, determined to control what was undoubtedly a good kiss. She summoned her strength and pulled away just as he snaked her waist.

'No!'

'No?' Malcolm breathed heavily, his face incredulous. Jenny's lips still tingled, a growing part of her wanting to continue what they'd started. It had gone far further than it should have, however. She would not do that to Lamont.

'We can't do this. I love my partner, and I can't go any further with you. I'm sorry if I gave you any impression that I would.'

'Are you serious?' Malcolm's voice rose. Jenny glanced at the exit, ready to flee if he grew hostile.

'I am.'

'You love your damn drug-dealing kingpin of a boyfriend, right? Yes, I know,' Malcolm added when he spotted Jenny's stunned expression 'I know all about *Teflon*, and the misery he brings to the community that I love. He's tactless, more concerned with streets and waging war, than seeing the beautiful, driven, perfect woman in front of him! Is that really what you want?'

Her mouth was dry. She couldn't believe Malcolm knew of Lamont, and not just Lamont, but *Teflon*. He'd known the whole time.

'You don't even know him.'

'I know more about Teflon than you could ever imagine. What did he spin you? That he was going legit? Did he blame his childhood? We all have our demons, but we don't all sling poison to the same people we're smiling at, day in, day out. He'll never stop doing what he does. He's too damn good at it, and while he keeps doing it, people will die. You need to get away, and I can help you. I want you by my side.'

She felt sick, part of her hoping that the words Malcolm spat couldn't be true. The air between the pair was devoid of emotion now, the tension palpable. Shaking her head, Jenny hurried from the house before Malcolm could kiss her again.

CHAPTER FIFTEEN
SATURDAY 14 MARCH, 2015

SHORTY KNOCKED on Amy's door, glancing around as he did. He loved the area she lived in. Shorty was a child of Chapeltown. Even when he started making money, he'd always stayed in the Hood. This area had a peaceful vibe, though. He'd noticed this in the past when he used to pick up Grace.

Before he got locked up. Before everything in his world had changed.

After waiting a few seconds and hearing nothing, he knocked again.

'Why do you always have to knock so loudly?' Amy finally swung the door open, glaring at him. She ran her hands through her hair. Her eyes were narrowed and her face drawn, but her natural beauty shone through. *She was so normal*, he thought to himself. Normal and very attractive. She had that in common with Jenny.

'I thought you might have gone out.'

Amy shook her head. 'I'm not feeling all that great, so I'm resting. What are you doing with Grace?'

Shorty had no idea. It had taken multiple phone calls and apologies to get her to spend more time with him, and that tore him apart. Before everything went wrong, Grace had adored him, and then he'd gone.

'I'm not sure,' he finally said.

'Don't get her all hopped on sugar wherever it is, please. She'll be down in a minute. She's just brushing her teeth.'

Shorty nodded, thinking about Dionte. They had spoken a few times since his trip to Huddersfield. Dionte still had his guard up, but it was a start. He didn't deserve a second chance from either of his children, but he would make the most of it. He wouldn't fail them like he had Timmy.

Shorty closed his eyes. He'd brought Timmy into the game, taught him the basics, then expected him to sit around and wait patiently, because that was the way it was. It hadn't been that way for him, though. He'd gone from moving weed with K-Bar and Lamont, to selling Class-A drugs and making real money. Aside from Lamont, he had never worked for anyone. He'd worked with people like Marcus, and a few elders had schooled him, but he hadn't waited around. He wouldn't wait around. *Why would Timmy?*

'Are you okay, Shorty?' Amy's eyebrows drew together. Shorty nodded. There were more footsteps, and Grace Turner stood next to Amy. She glanced at him, and his heart felt ready to burst. She looked so much like Amy, but he saw his sullenness in there.

'Hey Gracey, are you ready to go?'

Grace nodded. Amy hugged her, kissing her on both cheeks.

'I love you, Grace. Be good for your daddy, okay?'

'Yes, mummy.'

Shorty held Grace's hand, settling her into the back of the ride, a Land-Cruiser he'd rented. He started the engine, cringing when the loud hip-hop music blared. She jumped. He chuckled.

'Sorry, baby. I'll turn this off. We can put the radio on.'

Jenny slumped on Kate's sofa, a blanket pulled around her as she stared at the television like a zombie. The kiss with Malcolm plagued her mind. She'd enjoyed it far more than intended. It would have been easy to succumb further and sleep with Malcolm. At first, she'd dismissed his parting words as a petty attempt to break up her and Lamont, but they'd stuck with her.

Lamont's attitude had changed, and she had put it down to the aftermath of the shooting. He'd told her he would leave the street life behind, and she had taken him at his word. When she thought about it, there was no proof that he'd done so.

'Have you been sat here all day?' Kate called out as she came through the front door. She kissed her on the cheek and took off her coat.

'I want to give you some money,' said Jenny.

'For what?' Kate's lip curled.

'For letting me stay here.'

'You're my best friend, and I'm not taking your money. That's the last I want to hear about it,' said Kate. 'I was going to ring you earlier.'

'Why?'

'Why do you think? I want to hear all about your date.'

Jenny shook her head. 'It wasn't a date.'

'Sure it wasn't. Anyway, tell me all about it.'

'Fine. He made me dinner, we talked, and he recited a poem he wrote.'

'A poem about what?'

She paused. 'About me.'

Kate giggled.

'Wasn't a date, right? But the man crooned poetry to you? What happened after that?'

'He kissed me.'

'And you pulled away?'

'After a minute, I did.'

Kate's eyes widened.

'Wow. I teased you, but I didn't actually think you had it in you. Was he a good kisser?'

'Yes.' She still recalled how Malcolm made her lips tingle, and how badly she'd wanted to go further. She felt another crippling wave of guilt.

'What happened after you pulled away?'

'He started talking about L. He was saying all this stuff about him murdering people, and how he was still a presence in the streets.'

'He convinced you, didn't he?' Kate watched her now.

'I don't know. Do you think L is still selling drugs?'

When Kate hesitated, she felt a lurch in her chest that had little to do with guilt.

'Fuck,' she whispered. Kate grabbed her hand.

'Look, I don't think L wants to, but I also don't think he can leave that life so easily. Not at the level he's at.'

Jenny didn't reply, staring at her hands, her eyes watering.

———

'THANKS FOR COMING,' Lamont said to Darren when he entered the office at the barbers.

'No drama. K said it was important. What's the drill?'

'You need to cease contact with Rashad. Immediately.'

Darren's face fell.

'Did I mess up?'

'You played the role brilliantly. Rashad wasn't as careful as you were, and the wrong people found out.'

'Well, thanks for giving me the opportunity, anyway.' Darren turned to leave.

'Would you like a promotion?'

Those words stilled him. He whirled around, staring at Lamont with abject disbelief.

'What?'

'I want you working with K-Bar. You'll have people reporting into you. Can you handle that?'

'Course I can handle it,' exclaimed Darren, forgetting himself in his excitement. 'Are you sure?'

'I've been hearing good things about you for a while, and this just solidifies that. If you're interested, I'm happy to make the transition, and I know K-Bar and Maka will be too. Do you want it?'

'Yes, thank you, L. I mean that.'

'Take the day off. Someone will contact you with more instructions.'

After Darren left, Lamont ate lunch and headed from the barbers with a quick nod to Trinidad. People were still distant with him, likely the result of Malcolm's speeches. The streets were quiet. He was waiting for things to escalate after Winston's death. Climbing into his car, he drove up to Chapel Allerton, stopping in front of a semi-detached, cream-coloured house. He headed through the well-tended garden, enamoured with the different coloured flowers. It was the type of garden Jenny would like. He knocked, smiling at the bespectacled brunette who answered. She returned the smile and invited him in after a small hug.

'Can I get you a drink?'

'Some tea, please. No sugar or milk.'

Soon, he perched on the sofa sipping his tea. The woman sat beside him.

'I'm sorry for not stopping by sooner. Life has grown extra complicated.'

'You don't have to apologise for living, Lamont. Do you want to talk about what has become complicated?'

'Not really,' Lamont admitted, 'but I will. After everything with the shooting, I've tried to do more on my own. Jen's been after me to speak to someone impartial about my issues. I didn't feel comfortable doing that. Things are happening in Chapeltown. They're making people look at me differently, and I don't like it.'

'Are you referring to the thing with the police? Malcolm's been on a right tear with his writing.'

This surprised Lamont. 'You know Malcolm?'

'I've met him a few times at different writing events. He's definitely a character, but he has star power, if that makes any sense. He reminds me a lot of you, actually.'

'Great,' mumbled Lamont.

'Why is that an issue?'

'He's been spending time with Jen.'

'As in, your girlfriend?'

'The same one.'

The woman assessed Lamont. 'What aren't you telling me?'

'Jenny and I had a massive fallout. She's been staying with a friend.'

'Why did you fall out?'

'Life. My refusal to get help. I called her weak for speaking to a counsellor. She went behind my back and spoke to a family member I'd fallen out with, trying to force a reconciliation.'

'So, her intentions were pure, at least.'

'Yes, but I flipped my lid, and now we're on the outs. I have no idea how to even begin fixing it.'

'Start by talking to her.'

'I've tried.'

'Have you? Or have you tried telling her she should come home? You both need to sit down and talk about what the future is for you both, and if you will stay together. If you stay like this, it'll just fester.'

Lamont shrugged. 'No harm in trying, I guess. How's the book coming along?'

The woman rubbed her eyes. 'It's such a struggle. When I agreed to take this on, I had no idea what I was getting into. Justin's first book sold really well within the community and did okay within other cities. Trying to write more books from scratch is fun, but time-consuming. I've had to reduce my hours at work so I can keep up with it, which everyone tells me is stupid, but I have to do this, you know?'

'Justin left money, didn't he?' Lamont asked. Justin Holmes had been a drug dealer on the rise years ago. After getting locked up, he was released, re-entering the street life. He'd had a desire to write, but he'd been gunned down two years ago. His ex-girlfriend, Charlotte, took up his mantle and began writing, setting up a publishing press in his name. She tidied his novel with the help of some professional editors, then released it. The book had been well-received, and she'd continued writing. She and Lamont first spoke after Justin's death. After his own shooting, he had been less available.

'You're still running the business then?'

'I took on a business partner. They do most of the day-to-day stuff, but I manage the books.'

Lamont nodded, scratching the underside of his chin. Charlotte had given him a lot to think about. The pair chatted a while longer, and he knew he was delaying the inevitable. Charlotte was right about one thing; the longer he and Jenny waited, the harder it would be to come back.

'Don't be a stranger, L,' said Charlotte as she led Lamont to the door. They shared a longer hug, and he kissed her on the cheek, happy he'd stopped by.

'Gracey!' Shorty's mum exclaimed as Shorty walked into the living room holding Grace's hand. Serena Turner was a short, fleshy woman with beautiful cocoa features and a big smile. She immediately smothered Grace with hugs and kisses, paying Shorty no attention. He left the pair to it, making a drink and checking his phone. He headed back into the living room. Grace sat comfortably on Shorty's mum's knee, giggling at whatever story her Nana was telling her.

'How could you take so long bringing this beautiful little thing to come and see me?' She demanded, finally acknowledging her son.

'I've been busy, mum. Sorry,' he replied. He hadn't told his mum about her not wanting to see him. It was too painful.

'Well, she's here now, I suppose. That's better than nothing. C'mon, Grace. Come with me, I've got some things upstairs that I want to show you.'

LAMONT THOUGHT about Charlotte as he drove home. He admired her putting everything on hold for Justin's sake. Justin was full of potential, and he'd wanted to work with him. Justin turned him down and ended up being murdered pursuing a silly street feud.

As Lamont pulled into the drive, he was surprised to see Jenny's Mercedes already parked. He stared at the ride for a moment, trying to evaluate what to do. After a minute, he took a deep breath and headed inside.

Jenny sat on the sofa listening to music when he entered. There was a long moment as they took the other in. She was still the most beautiful woman in the world. He saw the changes, though; the pinched tiredness in her face. He felt a wave of guilt, realising how much he'd impacted her life in a few short years. Everything wrong with her was down to him, and he freely accepted that.

'I've missed you.'

Jenny didn't smile. 'I've missed you too, L.'

'I'm sorry for the things I said. I don't think you're weak. The opposite, in fact. You're one of the strongest people I know, and I know I wouldn't have been able to handle everything you have.'

'I appreciate what you're saying, L. But it's a bigger conversation than that now.'

Lamont wasn't surprised by Jenny's words. The leaden feeling in his stomach expanded, but he steeled himself. Jenny took a deep breath, tears pooling in her eyes.

'For my health and sanity, I need to leave you, L. I love you, but I need to do this for me. You're . . . in too deep. Even after the attempt on your life, you're still doing it. Don't deny it.'

Jenny watched him for any glimmer of a reaction, but his face was like stone.

'Does any of this relate to Malcolm?'

'I find him appealing, and I've spent time with him. It's not about him, though. I love you, but I can't be with you. I can't be with anyone.'

Lamont twitched with anger, furious at the thought of Malcolm spending time with his Jenny. The information Akeem had given him on Malcolm had yielded nothing. Rage meshed with the utter devastation he felt. Opening his mouth to reply, his phone rang.

'This isn't a good time,' Jenny watched as Lamont's eyes widened, his mouth agape. 'Find him. Send people to the hospital. I'm on my way there, and I want it locked down.' He faced Jenny, his jaw tight.

'I need to go, Jen. Something terrible has happened.'

SHORTY AND GRACE RETURNED HOME. Grace held bags full of clothes and toys. After leaving his mum's house, they'd gone shopping. Shorty bought her a happy meal from McDonald's, then they headed back. Since leaving town, she had become distant, content to stare out of the window and communicate with nods.

'Gracey?' Shorty stopped the car. She faced him. To try to make her smile, he'd let her sit in the front seat.

'I'm . . . sorry it came to this. You're the only good thing that daddy ever did in his life. I know I left you alone, and I can never make that up to you, but I'm here now. I'm not going anywhere. Anytime you want daddy, all you need to do is tell your mummy, and I'll be there. Okay?'

Grace stared at Shorty for a long time. The doubt in her big brown eyes made him want to cry. This wasn't supposed to happen. No child should ever be so disappointed by a parent. Shorty blinked back tears, searching for the words to comfort her.

TARGET PART TWO: THE TAKEDOWN

He heard the sharp acceleration of another vehicle. Instantly, he knew.

'No!' He lunged towards a stunned Grace just as brakes squealed, followed by the unmistakable roar of gunfire. Shorty covered her body with his own as bullets bombarded the ride, showering them with glass. Grace was screaming. He had no weapons, but even as that terrifying thought gripped him, the car was gone.

Shorty hurtled out of the Land-Cruiser in time to see a Vauxhall Astra pulling around the corner.

'Shorty?' Amy hurled the door open. Shorty whirled around as her eyes widened.

'GRACE!' she screamed. Dumbfounded, Shorty looked down, his entire world shattering. At first, he thought she was sleeping. Then he saw the blood.

'No,' he gasped, frozen. Amy wrenched open the vehicle door, holding Grace, screaming her name, tears streaming down her face. He still hadn't moved. His own tears harboured his vision. He blinked, his entire body and mind on standby.

This wasn't real. This couldn't be real . . .

'CALL AN AMBULANCE!' Amy shrieked at him. He dumbly reached for his phone, dialling the number, waiting for someone to answer.

'My daughter, she got shot . . . Please, send someone,' he said, his voice shaking when a woman answered.

People gathered on the street, wearing expressions of shock and disbelief. Amy hadn't stopped clutching Grace. Shorty heard sirens wailing, but he didn't dare tear his eyes from his daughter. He didn't know where she'd been hit, but she was deathly still. As the ambulance screeched to a stop, followed shortly after by two police cars, he finally let the tears fall.

CHAPTER SIXTEEN
SATURDAY 14 MARCH, 2015

IT WAS easy to shake away thoughts of Jenny as Lamont strode through the hospital with Akeem at his side. The breakup hurt, but the present situation was far more critical. People would die from the results of what transpired today. Lamont ignored his ringing phone. Akeem barked orders down his, ignoring the onlookers. People were already in place, securing the perimeter in case of attack. Others were combing the streets for immediate answers.

Shorty slumped against a wall, his face tear-streaked, his agony almost palpable. Lamont had never seen him so devastated. Even after Marcus's murder, when they drank and cried together. This was different. The fringes of Shorty's sanity were on the verge of exploding; a pulsating aura of destruction. Lamont sensed it, and a glance at Akeem showed he did too.

Amy tottered towards Lamont, pale and red-eyed, flinging her arms around him. He held her tightly, muttering pointless platitudes, telling her everything would be okay.

'I'm so sorry,' he repeated, over and over. He felt the wetness on his chest from her tears. After a moment, she released him. Lamont approached Shorty, placing his hand on his friend's shoulder.

TARGET PART TWO: THE TAKEDOWN

Shorty didn't look up, but he felt the resonating rage, his muscles almost vibrating.

'I don't even know what to say, Shorty. However you want to do this, I'm with you: the team, money, anything you need. We've got people out there now. They'll find something.'

'It was Lutel,' Shorty croaked. 'He's the only one who fits. The only one dumb enough to try to hit me when I'm with my girl.'

Lamont didn't argue. It made sense.

'Did you tell the police that?'

The vicious look Shorty gave was answer enough.

'I'll target Lennox's people until he comes forward. No one is gonna rest on this shit. I love Grace too. Do you know anything?'

'They've taken her in for surgery. Bullet hit her in the lung, she's barely hanging on. I don't know too much about all that technical shit, but she's fighting.' Shorty's shoulders shook. 'My girl's a fighter.'

'I know she is. Just like her parents. Stay here with Amy, and I'll take care of everything.'

'I'm coming too.'

'Shorty . . .'

'Don't fight me on it, L. You said however I wanted to do it. I'm no good here. I've already nearly scrapped with security and screamed at the nurses. I need to be out there making things happen.'

'I agree.'

Both men gave a start. They hadn't noticed Amy approach. Her face remained pale and drawn, but her blazing eyes kept them tethered to the spot.

'I want you to go, Shorty. I let you back into Grace's life, and now she's fighting for it. Go be you, do what you need to do, kill who you need to kill. You will never see her again.'

It was a testament to how devastated Shorty was that he didn't argue. His shoulders slumped, and he let out a breath before following Lamont and Akeem from the hospital.

GRACE'S SHOOTING sent a ripple through the streets of Leeds that it hadn't felt in a long time. There had been scores of incidents, murders, shootings and beatings, but nothing that matched a young girl being shot on a quiet suburban street. The fact it was Shorty's daughter only added to the tension. Everyone on the streets began mobilising, and people pulled back, content to wholesale their drugs for now. It was only a matter of time until the drama started.

Lennox and Nikkolo strode to Lutel's spot in Ebor Gardens. He was watching a TV show with his feet up when they stormed into the room.

'It's fucked up that I missed, but—'

Lennox hit him in the face, feeling the satisfying crunch of his nose breaking under his fist. Lutel fell to one knee and was kicked in the face, toppling to the ground. Lennox kicked him several times, not uttering a sound. Nikkolo watched in grim silence.

'Why do I bother?' Lennox finally said, over the sounds of Lutel's pathetic whimpering. 'You're an absolute liability. Missing Shorty was the worst thing you could have done, you cretin. I said *clean up*, not make the situation worse. Did you not understand your orders?'

'Listen, I panicked when I saw the little girl. I just let a couple' shots go thinking I'd pop Shorty and be done. I didn't mean to hit her.' Lutel coughed, holding his battered ribs.

'You're weak. Weak, petty and emotional. The girl is nothing to me. I care about one thing; ruling Chapeltown. I don't know if I've ever bothered to tell you why, but now I will; I'm the only one who can give the streets structure. I can stop the tit-for-tat, *my-strap-is-bigger-than-yours* nonsense. More money for everyone. Less police interest. No drugs. It makes sense. It benefits everyone, but now, you have ruined that with your foolishness.'

'If you'd backed me earlier, none of this would have happened!'

TARGET PART TWO: THE TAKEDOWN

Lutel snarled, forgetting himself. 'If you just took Shorty out, there wouldn't have been any problems. But no, you just left him.'

Lennox stared at Lutel for so long that the man started to tremble. Even Nikkolo stepped back, marvelling at the quiet force emanating from him. After a moment, Lennox scratched his cheek.

'Hide out until we can sort the mess. Nikkolo will get a spot for you.'

When they left the house, Lennox didn't speak until the pair were back in Nikkolo's car.

'Lutel is a loose end. Leak the spot to Shorty. He'll take care of it. It might even placate him.'

'Do you really believe that?' Nikkolo couldn't keep the scepticism from his voice. Shorty was a maniac. Lamont had kept him on a leash since he left prison, but that was done. Lennox ignored Nikkolo, already deep in thought.

'Let me know when you hear anything else.'

K-Bar hung up on Darren, putting his hands on his head. The streets were about to be locked down. He knew exactly how it would go. He'd spoken briefly to Akeem about the situation. They had dispatched men to find out the location of Lutel and whoever had driven the car. He'd tried ringing Shorty, but his phone was unavailable, and Lamont was flat-out ignoring K-Bar's calls. Marika wrapped her arms around him, kissing him on the cheek.

'Have you spoken with Shorty or L yet?'

'I can't get hold of either of them. I've got all kinds of people ringing me, trying to find out what's happening, and I can't say shit to them.'

'Good. People are too damn nosy,' said Marika, though she wanted to know what was going on just as much. 'What happens now?'

K-Bar pulled her closer, running his fingers through her hair as she leaned further into him. They stayed this way for a few moments. K-Bar was sure he was falling for Lamont's sister. It was dangerous, and he needed to speak with him before feelings grew any deeper. He had no idea how the conversation would go, but he would step to him like a man. There was no way around it.

'War, babe. That's the only thing that can happen. We all know what Grace is to Shorty. People are gonna die. Simple.'

LAMONT LEFT Shorty planning with Akeem, heading home. Two of Akeem's men followed in a separate vehicle. They were expensive, highly trained bodyguards, but he wasn't thinking about the cost. When the guns started going off, things would grow even more expensive. He had people watching out for Amy, Stacey, Shorty's mother, and his Aunt. He hadn't asked Shorty if he wanted any of this; he'd just done it.

Lamont walked past Jenny's Mercedes, not knowing if she had left since he'd rushed away to the hospital. Hearing noises from the kitchen, he headed in that direction. Jenny and Kate spoke in hushed tones. They stopped when he appeared in the doorway.

'L, are you okay?' Jenny asked. Lamont's eyes brimmed with passion, and for a moment, she was reminded of the dangerous man she had fallen for. He hugged Kate.

'I'm fine, Jen. Nice to see you, Kate. Surprised you're here.'

'I heard about Shorty. Jen rang me after you rushed off, and I came over,' Kate looked from Lamont to Jenny. 'You two are through then?'

Lamont jammed his hands in his pockets, thinking about Shorty's situation to prevent his own from overwhelming him.

'It's for the best. Especially now.'

'Is Shorty okay?' Jenny didn't want to think about the breakup anymore than Lamont did.

'I can't discuss anything that's happening, or is gonna happen, Jen. I don't want you becoming an accessory. In fact, I'd appreciate it if you let me have someone guard you, just in case.'

'That's not going to happen.'

'Jen—'

'No, L. I'm not part of your world, and we're not a couple anymore. I'll be fine.'

'Grace isn't part of that world either, but she was still hit,' he argued. It was futile. Jenny's mouth was drawn, and her eyes were hard. There would be no fighting her on this one.

'Forget it, L. I'm going to the letting agency when it opens in the morning.'

'You don't need to do that. I have plenty of places to stay, and I'd prefer you to keep the house,' said Lamont. She shook her head.

'I want a fresh start. You can understand that, right?'

Lamont could. A lot had transpired, and he couldn't blame her for wanting to be away from it all. The night caught up with him, and he stifled a yawn, his eyes burning. He needed to be fresh in case there were any new developments.

'I'll sleep in the spare room. You have the bed, Jen. I need to get some rest.' He bid Kate good night, surprised she'd stayed so quiet. He was halfway to the door when Jenny spoke again.

'L?'

He spun around just in time to catch her as she hurtled against him, her mouth finding his. For a delicious moment, all was well, her lips causing a whirl of desire to surge through Lamont's body as he gripped her closer. She moaned in his mouth as the kiss deepened, then pulled away, her legs weak with sudden lust and love.

'Be careful, L. I love you, and I'll always care for you.'

'I love you too, Jen, and I'm always careful.'

THE FOLLOWING DAY, a group of men sat in a meeting room in a local police station. Mumbled greetings were exchanged as tired hands stirred sugar in cups of coffee, needing the caffeine to get them through the torrent of mess in Chapeltown.

Rigby and Murphy were at the front, ready to speak. At a signal from their superior, they began.

'Through careful investigation, we've linked Kieron Barrett, AKA K-Bar, to numerous murders from September 2013. He was responsible for the deaths of Paul 'Polo' Dobby, Xiyu 'Chink' Manderson, and Naomi Gateworth.'

'What *careful investigation* are you referring to?' A man asked. 'This all sounds very circumstantial. Does any of what you're saying connect to the mess on the streets, because if the intel is correct, we're going to have another gang war on our hands.'

'There's enough for us to bring in K-Bar and question him. A friend of Naomi's will testify in court. She was present when K-Bar approached Naomi and offered her five thousand pounds to set up Chink. Half the money was paid upfront, the rest to be paid after. Instead, they murdered her too.'

'We found two different gun calibres at the scene if I recall; who else was there other than K-Bar?'

'At this point, we don't know, but K-Bar could prove more forthcoming. There are several within Teflon's organisation with the reputation to pull it off, but we haven't narrowed it down at present.'

'I'm not sure about any of this,' another superior spoke up. 'Again, it all seems rather thin, even with the tie-in. K-Bar works for Teflon, who has money and a lot of political might behind him. We can't afford to fail.'

'Agreed. Adele being willing to testify is huge, though, ma'am, as it offers motive. We believe it's connected to the murder of Marcus Daniels in August 2013, and that everything after was a direct result. Chink was behind the hit on Marcus in the park and was murdered in retaliation.'

'I thought Chink and K-Bar both worked for Jones? That's what the last report I read showed.'

Murphy and Rigby shared a look. They hated the whole show of having to justify every piece of police work they did. They understood the need for clarity, but as veteran officers, they knew the politics, and were always committed to putting together airtight cases. They wanted to catch bad guys and stamp out crime. That was it. Neither was interested in climbing the police ladder, or getting recognition. It was simply the job. They had planned to brief their immediate superior this morning, but they had been blindsided and forced to present the meeting to half a dozen higher-ups.

'There was definitely a fall out. We believe Chink was engaged in a sexual affair with Marcus's girlfriend, Georgia Pearson. We tried to track her down, but she's left Leeds, and no one has heard from her.'

'What about the more recent shootings? That's where we should be focusing. All the protesting and press from Chapeltown by that blasted organisation has caused a lot of issues. We need to be seen to be doing the right thing on this, and I don't know if that involves digging up cases from two years ago.'

Rigby swallowed down his annoyance as he replied.

'I appreciate what you're saying, sir, but K-Bar is a key piece of Teflon's organisation. He's linked to several murders and ran the team while Teflon was recovering from his own shooting. If we can get him, he could be the key to unlocking the story behind numerous murders, past and present. The intel suggests Teflon was behind the recent murder of Big-Kev. K-Bar would have detailed knowledge of that.'

'We need a resolution, Detective Rigby. Simple as that. I want arrests, and I want to show people we're not sitting on our arses doing nothing. I suggest you get back out there and find more information.'

SHORTY SAT IN A SAFE HOUSE, rag in hand, as he cleaned a selection of guns. Every time he thought about Grace's shooting, he grew angrier. She was in critical condition. The surgery was apparently a success, but the doctors remained tight-lipped about her chances of recovery. Lamont had spoken with Amy and passed on the information. A few of Akeem's shooters were nearby, keeping their straps close as they waited. He wasn't sure if they were guarding him or keeping him detained. It didn't matter.

Lennox hadn't been seen, nor had Nikkolo or any of Lennox's higher-ups. Shorty planned to smoke out Lutel. When he poked his head out, he would annihilate him. Shorty's phone rang. He was tempted to ignore the private number, but decided to let out some anger on the caller. He put the gun and rag down, picking up the phone.

'What?' He snapped.

'Is this Shorty?' A muffled voice asked.

'Don't play dumb. You wouldn't have called if you didn't know who it was.'

'The guy you're looking for, he's at a spot on Grange Park Road. It has a blue gate and a white door.'

'Who is this?' He clutched the phone tighter.

'Don't worry about who I am. Check out the spot if you don't believe me.'

The person hung up. He looked down at the phone, his mind alight. It was possible they were lying, or trying to set him up. Shorty weighed up the risks and decided it was worth it. Rising to his feet, he shrugged into a bullet-proof vest and readied his weapons.

———

'THE CALL HAS BEEN MADE. I already had the driver taken care of.'

Lennox nodded, approving of Nikkolo's initiative.

'Any word on Teflon?'

'People are definitely looking for us. They're connected to him, so he's working with Shorty on this. People are reluctant to talk. It's like they think we're already finished.'

Lennox had expected this. As soon as he'd heard about Lutel

shooting Shorty's child, he'd scaled back his war with Delroy Williams, refusing to get caught out on both fronts.

'Contact Teflon directly. Arrange a meeting on neutral ground. Use a go-between if you have to. Someone Teflon will trust.'

'Are you sure about this?' He blurted. Lennox shot him a sharp look. Nikkolo sighed, then pulled out his phone to make another call.

SHORTY STUDIED the address he had been given, unable to see anything out of the ordinary. The gun resting on his lap had a silencer attached. He wanted to take his time with Lutel. He had no idea how many people were inside, but he'd called off Akeem's shooters, wanting to handle this on his own.

Pulling up his hood, he climbed from the stolen car, strap held low. The street was deserted. It was early evening, and the cold cut through his hooded top with ease. He ignored the chill and kept his head down. Spotting the blue gate, he hopped the wall, landing stiffly on the other side, wincing as pain shot up his ankle. He tested his leg a few times, and seemed to be okay. He saw lights on both up and downstairs, and the curtains were closed. Disregarding the front door, Shorty headed to the side door and tried the handle, unsurprised to find it locked. He had no tools to pick the lock. Stepping back, he kicked in the door, which smashed open with a satisfying crunch.

Shorty was inside, following the voices as he charged to the living room, spotting two men. The younger man went for his gun, but a bullet smashed into his throat, knocking him back with an awful choking sound. Lutel was slow to respond, giving him ample time to shoot him in his right knee. He fell with a scream. Shorty bounded over, hitting him three times in the mouth, then kicking him in the stomach.

'Shut the fuck up. I don't wanna hear your damn mouth. Is there anyone else in the house I need to kill?'

He hesitated, causing Shorty to shoot him in the other knee at point-blank range. His gloved hand covered Lutel's blooded mouth, muffling the scream.

'Answer me.'

Lutel jerkily shook his head, twitching in pain. He aimed the gun at his face.

'Where's Lennox?'

Lutel didn't reply, trying to glare whilst grimacing.

'Talk, or I'm gonna make you.'

Still, he said nothing. Kissing his teeth, Shorty dragged him by his leg to the kitchen. Turning on the stove, he reached for a knife, heating it under the flame. Advancing on Lutel, he sliced at the man's skin, relishing the growing screams of pain. He poured table salt on the wounds, a demented smile on his face.

'Tell me, before I slice your nuts off!'

'Alright! Alright! L-Listen, he m-moves around, but he's got a main base near Cottingley. It's g-guarded, but he spends a lot of time there.'

'What's the address?' Shorty took his phone out. When he'd typed the address into a notepad and saved it, he faced the cowering man at his feet.

'You would have died anyway, but when you went for my daughter, you violated.' He placed the gun to Lutel's stomach and fired once, feeling his body jerk. Straightening, Shorty fired the next bullet into his neck, watching Lutel's body twitch one last time. He breathed deeply. There was still a massive debt to be paid, and Lennox Thompson was next on the list.

CHAPTER SEVENTEEN
THURSDAY 19 MARCH, 2015

OVER THE NEXT FEW DAYS, Chapeltown played host to increased street violence. Fights and ambushes broke out all over the Hood, with doors being kicked in, people being interrogated, and several isolated incidents involving drive-by shootings on certain houses. The *OurHood* Initiative held two meetings, but participation and attendance had dramatically dropped. No one wanted any part of the situation.

The body of Lutel Wood had turned up on the streets, his injuries consistent with repeated torture, followed by execution. The police had a host of suspects, including Shorty, but no one had seen him.

Lennox Thompson climbed from a navy Ford Focus, two goons with him, and strode into a house. The man he'd come to see was pacing around the living room, mumbling to himself. When he saw Lennox, he paused, his eyebrows knitted together in a frown.

'What the hell is going on?'

Lennox went to the kitchen and put on the kettle. When it boiled, he added coffee, then hot water to a cup, stirred for a few moments, and took an immediate sip. The man stood in the doorway, bristling with impatience.

'Are you going to answer me?'

Lennox studied the man, resisting the urge to smirk at his less-than-immaculate appearance. There were circles under his eyes, and he needed a haircut.

'Answer you about what, exactly?'

'People are saying you ordered the shooting of Shorty's kid, which led to Lutel's murder. How am I supposed to spin this?'

'You're the wordsmith, you tell me,' replied Lennox, his dry tone showing a lack of interest.

'Len, I run the meetings, and I can steer people towards certain perspectives, but even I don't know what I'm supposed to do with this one. Did you do it?'

'Does it matter? My name isn't even supposed to be in it. Blame it on someone else. Isn't that what I keep you around for?'

'Don't talk to me like that!' Malcolm snapped. 'You need me. Without my work out there, opening eyes and controlling the masses, all eyes are on you. You think you can get your little *Hood Utopia* if you make an enemy out of me?'

Lennox glared at Malcolm until some of the bluster went out of the scholar. He held the stare a moment longer.

'Understand one thing; you're a tool I use. You have no power. You're not a threat. You're only relevant because I gave you purpose and direction. You're a failed writer turned blogger, nothing more.'

'Bullshit! I was successful long before I met you, and the *OurHood* project is mine, not yours.'

Lennox smiled icily. 'You still don't get it. Without me, there *is* no project. Do you really not know what I was doing behind the scenes? People wanted you dead. You ranted with impunity, because of me. I intimidated everyone who wanted to silence you. If I made it known I was withdrawing my support, you wouldn't last twenty-four hours. If you want to look at it objectively, you failed.'

Malcolm had paled throughout his cutting tirade, but now he found his voice. 'How did I fail?'

'You were supposed to seduce Teflon's lady. You didn't do it.'

'I broke them up!'

Lennox's smirked. 'Do you really believe they'll stay broken up?'

Malcolm didn't reply. He continued.

'You got caught up in feelings and fell for a woman you could never have. Now, scurry back to your laptop and get to work. It'll be open season if I pull support. Remember that.'

Malcolm hurried to the door, wrenching it open. Before he left, he glared at Lennox.

'You'll always be nothing, Len, and that galls you.'

———

SHORTY GLARED at the four walls of the living room of his safe house, coiled and ready to act on the information Lutel surrendered to him. He'd surveyed the spot, but hadn't seen Lennox yet. His body ached with tiredness. He hadn't slept, running on adrenaline and rage. He was tempted to ring K-Bar and Maka for backup, but they worked for Lamont. He wasn't sure Lamont would agree with his plan of action.

Trudging to the kitchen, he made another cup of coffee. While the kettle boiled, he cracked open a Red Bull and chugged it, wiping his mouth and leaving the can on the worktop. He grabbed the cup and headed back to the living room, turning on his phone. Checking his messages, he saw one from Jenny, asking him to call. Without even thinking, he dialled her number.

'Shorty?'

'Hey,' he replied after a few moments.

'Where are you? Are you okay?'

'I'm fine. I'm safe.'

Jenny paused before she spoke again. 'Can I see you?'

'Why?' He sharply asked.

'I just want to make sure you're okay. If you want to talk over the phone instead, it's fine. I . . . guess I understand just enough to see why you might be paranoid.' Her voice broke.

'Where are you staying?'

JENNY LEFT the door unlocked for Shorty, and he walked in, nearly tripping over a pile of boxes.

'Sorry about that,' said Jenny. 'I only moved in yesterday. Still getting all my things in order.' She led Shorty to the living room. He looked around. There was a CD player stuffed in the corner, an old coffee table, two sofas and an armchair, all of which looked like they had come with the house. She wore a black hooded top with leggings and thick socks. It tickled him that she was so comfortable being casual around him, and it took away a lot of the tension.

'You look tired. When was the last time you slept?'

Shorty shrugged. 'There are more important things than sleep right now.'

'Like revenge?'

'Exactly.'

'That won't make Grace magically better, you know that, right?'

Shorty wanted to rage at her, but didn't. He couldn't. Something was keeping her out of the range of his wrath, and he didn't quite understand it.

'This is me, Jen. This is what I do. They went at my daughter, so now they go. That's it. It doesn't get less complicated than that.'

Jenny didn't offer a response, and the silence lingered until he spoke again.

'I'm surprised L didn't give you the house.'

She smiled wanly. 'He offered. I said no.'

'Why?'

'I wanted to start again. I loved that house, but it had too many bad memories, mainly revolving around my deteriorating relationship with Lamont.'

'I get that,' said Shorty. 'No chance of y'all getting back together then?'

Jenny sighed. 'I don't see how we can. He's following his path. I'm trying to figure out what mine is. L said that I saved him once. That I made him see a future for us. I bought into that.'

Shorty didn't reply, absorbing the words. He remembered Lamont's change after he met Jenny, but if he was honest, the signs were there before that. He'd dominated the drugs game, but there had always been a reluctance to his actions. He'd carried himself differently, engaged with women differently, and played the game his own way. It had taken a lot out of him, Shorty realised. Jenny had been his salvation, but it hadn't lasted. The revelation reeled him, making him think about his own path.

'What does the future hold for you, Shorty?'

Shorty shrugged again. 'Honestly, I don't care. I'll murder Lennox. Beyond that, nothing else matters. I don't know if you get that, but it's about as real as I can be.'

No more words were said. They sat for a long time, both understanding the other's view. He opened his mouth to speak, but held back. It wouldn't help the situation.

'I'm gonna take off, Jen. There's a lot to do.'

He stepped toward her, and she met him halfway. The embrace lingered, and they clung tightly as if the action was essential. He finally broke the hug, kissing her on the cheek.

'Good luck. I know you'll smash whatever you do.'

'Thank you, Shorty. Please, please be careful.'

Shorty had already closed the door on Jenny's pleas.

———

LAMONT AND AKEEM entered the city centre club on high alert. The club was located on Call Lane, currently closed to the public. A shot-caller who had links with Lamont and was deemed to be neutral territory, owned it. The terms of the meeting had been outlined to both attendees: No weapons, no trouble. He wouldn't break the terms.

The man he'd come to see, sat at a table overlooking the club with another man. He made his way up, and they shook hands.

'It's been a while, L.'

'It has, Len.'

Lennox sent Nikkolo downstairs, and Lamont asked Akeem to go too. For a while, there was silence, the pair content to let it play out.

'I'm trying to remember the last time you and I needed to meet about something,' Lennox finally said.

'Marcus was alive, I know that. Wasn't it that thing with one of your guys trying a robbery, and some of my guys got involved, and we squashed it?'

Lennox shrugged, a half-smile on his lips.

'Might have been. We've both been doing what we do for a while, throughout the difficulties. You've had a couple more ups than me, I think.'

'We're in different businesses; it's expected.'

'Yeah. You sell poison, and I don't.'

'Indeed. You kill and maim people instead,' replied Lamont, matching Lennox's calm tone.

'So did Marcus, and you still cried over his body.'

'He was my brother.'

Lennox turned to Lamont. 'You can appreciate what I'm saying, though, right? Your *brother* did the same dirt I did.'

'I didn't necessarily agree with him doing it either.'

'You allowed it. Turned a blind eye, tolerated it. Any way you want to put it, facts are the facts.'

'Marcus was a grown man. We collaborated when necessary.'

'You have an answer for everything. I like that,' said Lennox, grinning. It held no mirth.

'I guess we're getting down to why we're both here?'

Lennox nodded. 'Do you mind if I start?'

'Not at all.'

TARGET PART TWO: THE TAKEDOWN

'Chapeltown is in a funk; it needs more funding, there's a loss of community spirit and influence. The influence comes from the money, and the money comes from drugs. Drugs are the problem. Drugs bring in the police, other gangsters, and it needs to stop. I'm going to make it stop. That's my mission.

'You wanted to walk off into the sun and leave it behind, so do that. Leave the drug game to its death. Walk away, leave Delroy and Shorty to their fate.'

Lamont respected the strength of Lennox's words. This wasn't a ploy; he sensed Lennox was being honest.

'You shouldn't have shot Shorty's daughter. That goes against everything you just said. There's no structure that involves the shooting of an innocent girl.'

'What about an innocent woman? Is that different? Because there are a few innocent women whose deaths are connected to your people.'

'I've never authorised the murder of anyone who wasn't in the game,' said Lamont. Again, Lennox grinned.

'That's not the point, and you know it. I agree with you about Shorty's little girl. Lutel fucked up and was eliminated because of it. I didn't authorise her shooting, and I didn't tell him to get into a pissing contest with Shorty. As you know, my attention was focused elsewhere.'

'Meaning Delroy.'

Lennox nodded.

'Delroy won't stop, because his son is dead, and he needs to save face. Shorty won't stop, because he could never comprehend backing down. You've done all you can, L. You need to leave them to their fate.'

'Your plan is doomed, Len. There's too much money, and too many people depending on a wage from the drugs game for you to come in and stop things. You don't have that sort of power.'

'You just don't know. That's the problem.' Lennox's hands balled into fists. The eerie grin had vanished, replaced with a malevolent look.

'You *think* you know, Len. There are level's beyond you, and that lack of understanding will ruin you.'

'You know what the problem is, L? It's all about money to you. Money and the opinions of people you don't even like. I understand it. You came up hard, broke and disrespected by people you saw as beneath you. I was there, remember, chilling with Marcus, blasting people when you were in town buying drinks for girls you could never get without your status. It's everything to you, Shorty and all those other dickheads.

'Me, I'm about order. I want power, and I want to be left alone, but you know what? That can't happen while you lot are moving powder and warring over turf. So, I need to take drugs out of the equation. I need to control the street so that the structure is there. One leader. Me. No drugs, no reason for police to patrol our territory. *My* territory.

'You're a threat to that, L. The biggest threat because you actually have a brain in that head of yours. You're flashy. You have expensive tastes, and you're influential enough to cause problems, so you're my enemy. But, it's nothing personal.'

Lamont remained calm through his words, but the atmosphere had changed. He noted Nikkolo and Akeem looking up at the balcony, both tense and alert.

'It feels personal. You won't disrupt the flow, Len. Simple as that.'

Lennox rubbed his hands together, his dark eyes boring into Lamont's.

'It's a game of sheep masquerading as lions. You're the only anomaly, and you don't even want to be in the game,' Lennox slid to his feet, no hint of a smile on his face. 'Leave them to their fate, or go down with them. Last warning.'

'They broke up?'

K-Bar was at Marika's, bored of hiding out. The noise

surrounding Big Kev's murder had dispersed, but Lamont insisted on K-Bar remaining low-key, which irked him. He understood why Shorty had been so tetchy. So much was happening, and few were as qualified when it came to killing and handling drama as him. He was relying on his people keeping him updated, but no one knew much, other than Shorty being on the warpath and dropping bodies to get to Lennox Thompson.

Now, Marika had dropped another bombshell.

'I spoke to Jen today. She's not living at the house anymore. She moved out.'

'Over what?' K-Bar had been around them in the past and believed they were well-suited.

'She didn't say. When I went for dinner that time, there was definitely tension. I think they argued after I went. Maybe L cheated on her? We know how he used to get down.'

'Maybe she cheated on him?' K-Bar felt compelled to defend Lamont. He had indulged in his day, but K-Bar couldn't imagine him cheating.

Marika shrugged. 'Doesn't really matter, anyway. What's Shorty saying?'

'He's doing what he needs to do.'

'And L?'

'I dunno, Rika. Why are you asking me so many damn questions?'

Marika jerked back, her eyes flashing.

'Listen, if you're gonna snap, fuck off to your own house.'

He took a deep breath. Arguing with Marika would fix nothing.

'Sorry. This shit just gets me mad. Lennox is out there doing what he wants, and people aren't moving against him quick enough. Shorty can't be expected to go up against a whole crew by himself. It's mad.'

Marika squeezed his hand and cuddled up against him. He kissed the top of her head, her presence calming him.

'I was running things, doing what I needed to do, then suddenly I'm just out. Everyone is leapfrogging me.'

'Do something about it then. When you think about it, Shorty might have the right idea.'

'What do you mean?' K-Bar shifted so he could see Marika.

'You know Shorty better than anyone. He doesn't really ask permission. He just does shit, and L kinda has to go along with it.'

K-Bar didn't reply. Marika had given him a lot to think about.

THE NEXT DAY, Shorty played *Blade Brown* as he completed sit-ups in his safe house. His arms burned from the press-ups he'd finished a short while ago, but he pushed through, determined to finish his workout. His phone ringing brought him out of the zone, and he snatched it with venom, pausing the music.

'What?' He snapped. The person on the other end spoke for a few moments, then hung up. Shorty tidied and waited for the coded knock on the door. He let in Akeem, who remained standing as Shorty slumped onto the sofa.

'What does L want?'

'He met with Lennox Thompson, but nothing was agreed.'

'What was the point of meeting him? He should have killed him instead.'

Akeem didn't respond. Shorty wanted to punch him in his stupid face. He was as non-committal as Lamont.

'To try resolving the situation with as little bloodshed as possible.'

'It's too late for that. He shot my girl.'

'Lutel shot at your daughter, and you took care of that. Lennox is much harder to get at.'

'I know where he is. I've got a location, and I've got a guy watching. I'm just waiting for the word that Lennox is at the spot.'

'I'm assuming you got the location from Lutel before you finished him,' Akeem started. 'It may have been abandoned, especially if Lennox feels it's compromised.'

'Lutel said he wasn't supposed to know about this spot. No

reason for him to lie when he's about to die. That's the plan, though. Once I get the call, everyone's gone.'

Akeem headed for the door. 'Do what you need to. Grimer, Maka and Rudy are available at your convenience. L said you would know the number.'

'L's authorising this?' He scratched his head, trying to keep the surprise from his face.

'Did you leave him a choice?' Akeem asked as he left the house.

ANOTHER FORTY-EIGHT HOURS passed before Shorty got the word. Lennox had turned up at the spot with Nikkolo. He made the calls, got his people together, and laid out a plan.

Maka and Shorty drove to the spot in one car, Rudy and Grimer in another. They communicated by pay-as-you-go phones as they approached Cottingley. He expected the roads to be busier, but the way the bodies had dropped, the police probably had no idea where to start. The car was silent. Maka drove, but kept looking at him and then looking away. Finally, he cleared his throat.

'How's Gracey doing then?'

Shorty was quiet for so long Maka thought he was ignoring him.

'She's had two operations. The survival rate in children isn't high, and the bullets fucked her up. That's all I know. Her mum doesn't want me anywhere near the situation.'

'I'm sorry, Shorty. She doesn't deserve that shit. We'll take everyone out and try to leave Lennox to the end, so you can take your time. You clipped the shooter, didn't you?'

'Yeah.' Shorty's jaw tensed as he remembered ripping Lutel apart and slicing at his body.

'I'm gonna ring Zero, make sure Lennox hasn't left yet.'

THE GANG PULLED up in their cars around the corner from where Lennox was holed up. The Cottingley area was quiet, which was a surprise. It was normally far more thriving, even in winter. Zero had already left.

'Right, we need to handle this quickly,' said Shorty, when the four of them assembled. 'We're kinda close to that police station, so use silenced weapons. The cocaine and drink is on me when we're done here.'

Everyone grinned and checked their weapons. They all wore bullet-proof vests underneath their jackets. Rudy and Grimer would sneak around the back. Shorty and Maka would approach from the front and take care of any resistance. Shorty had an Uzi. Rudy the same. Maka had a silenced 9mm pistol, and Grimer grimly clutched a shotgun that had belonged to Marcus Daniels.

They split into their teams and moved. Shorty and Maka tread silently down the path, tense, looking for scouts. Timmy flashed into Shorty's head for a moment, but he put the thought aside, signalling for Maka to move forward. They'd approached the garden when all of a sudden, gunfire erupted.

Shorty dived for cover behind a nearby wall, but Maka wasn't quick enough. He took a hit and went down, men emerging from seemingly nowhere, firing shots at Shorty. He popped up, hitting two of them with the same burst of gunfire, causing the others to back off.

'Maka! Get over here,' he screamed, letting off cover fire. Maka stumbled towards him, clutching his chest and wheezing.

'Did it go through?' He yelled, firing at the attackers. 'The bullet! Did it go through?'

'Nah,' gasped Maka.

'Good. Start fucking shooting, then. We need to get back to that car.'

Maka took aim, sending a target spinning backwards with a well-placed chest shot.

'Now!' Shorty yelled, sprinting down the path towards the car. He expected to see more assassins, but the pathway was clear. He reached the car ahead of Maka, climbed into the driver's seat and started the engine.

'Drive!' Maka shouted.

'Not without the others,' Shorty shouted back.

'They're dead, man! You heard them shots.'

Shorty didn't reply, but knew Maka was likely correct. The gunfire had started at the back of the house. They hadn't done a walk-around. He didn't know what kind of cover was in the back garden, but if he hadn't been able to get behind the wall, he would have been a goner. They both would have.

Shorty's hands hovered near the steering wheel as Maka warily aimed his pistol out of the wound-down window. They had killed everyone attacking from the front. Acrid gun smoke was everywhere. His foot teased the gas pedal, and then he heard a shout and saw someone stagger around the corner, holding his stomach, followed by four more assassins. Shorty started spraying, cutting them down when he realised they weren't any of his people. With another lurch, he realised Grimer and Rudy weren't coming out, and sped away.

———

The mood of the safe house was only comparable to the night of Marcus's murder. Shorty swigged brandy from the bottle, perched in the corner. Lamont had summoned a friendly doctor to dispense painkillers and stitch up Maka. Luckily, the bullet that had breached his vest only grazed his stomach. He'd lost some blood, but would be okay. After the doctor had patched him up and collected his payment from Akeem, Lamont steepled his fingers.

'I don't know how Lennox laid a trap so quickly, but it's possible he was never even at the spot, Shorty. Where did the Intel come from?'

'Zero said he was there. He drove away afterwards as arranged.'

'Have you tried ringing him?'

Shorty frowned. 'His phone was switched off.' Zero was an old acquaintance from back in the day.

'He was in on it. He sold you out,' said Lamont.

'You don't know that,' snapped Shorty, noting everyone in the room giving him the same pitying look.

'Lennox wanted us to hit that spot, and he wanted us to hit it hard. He knew you would get to Lutel. He probably leaked that information. He's been a step ahead this whole time.' Lamont was about to add more when his phone rang. The number was blocked, but he knew who it was.

'Put me on speaker,' Lennox ordered. Lamont forced the swear words back and pressed the speaker button without a word.

'I knew you lot would come, so I left some gifts. You're lucky my people only got two of you. You may have protected Shorty's family, but you know what, L? You didn't protect your main prize.'

Lamont's brow furrowed. He and Shorty shared a look, both saying, 'No!' at the same time.

'Lennox, don't do it. I mean it,' Lamont's voice shook.

'All the best, L,' replied Lennox, hanging up. Lamont and Shorty hurtled towards the front door.

'Wait!' Akeem yelled, leaping to his feet as Maka sat there, stunned.

JENNY TURNED up the *Definitely Maybe* album, debating running a bath. Her phone buzzed, but she ignored it. It was probably Kate, but it was all about her tonight, and Kate would understand that. She headed to the kitchen, not noticing the phone stop vibrating, and then start again straight away.

'HAVE you got hold of her yet?' Shorty yelled. They were in Akeem's ride, the bodyguard zooming through traffic like a

TARGET PART TWO: THE TAKEDOWN

madman.

'Does it sound like I have?' Lamont shot back. They glared at each other, then he again dialled Jenny, hoping they were being paranoid. Lennox was a Child of Chapeltown, just like them. He wouldn't involve her in their issues.

'She's probably working late. Tell Maka to send someone to Jen's work.'

Shorty clutched his own phone, glad to have something to do. Akeem warned them to brace themselves as he swerved around a corner. Lamont's breathing intensified, fear threatening to overwhelm him. Lennox wouldn't hurt her. It was probably a ruse.

'Maka's sent two guys to her work. They'll stay with her if she's there.'

Lamont's jaw clenched as he dialled Jenny's mobile a third time. Just as he was giving up hope, he heard a click.

'L?'

'Jen?' he gasped into the receiver. 'Where are you?'

'I'm home. Must have missed your other calls. Is everything okay?'

'Jen, there's no time. Get out. Now.'

'Excuse me? What the hell do you mean?'

'Look, people are coming. You need to leave.'

'L, wh—'

Lamont's stomach lurched as he heard a loud crash, then a blood-curdling scream.

'Jen? Jenny!' he yelled, Shorty watching. 'Jenny, answer me!'

———

JENNY LEAPT BACK as three men burst into the living room. She screamed when one lunged, instinctively smashing the wineglass against his face. He went down with a hiss of pain as the others grabbed for her.

'Jenny, answer me. We're nearly there!'

Jenny heard Lamont's voice, but couldn't reply. One assailant held her wrists, but she was struggling too much. His partner tried to grab her, but she kicked him in the face before flinging her head back. There was a crunching sound followed by a bellow of pain. Jenny didn't hesitate. She sprang for the door, but the man she'd hit with the glass gripped her leg, pulling her to the ground. She struggled, but he was too strong. He held her arms firmly, his full weight pressed against her, hot breath in her face causing her to gag.

'Keep still, and we won't hurt you,' he grunted. She kept kicking her legs until she could break free, hurtling for the kitchen door, which was closer, the man on her tail followed by the others.

There was a knife on the kitchen sink, and she lunged for it as the man's hand clamped down on hers. She slashed at him with the knife, hearing him scream as he hit the floor in a flash of red. The remaining assailants slowly moved into the room.

'Get back,' she hissed, her hair bedraggled as she tightly held the knife. 'Teflon will be here soon. He'll kill you all.' She was shocked at her words.

'Put the knife down, love. Come with us, and nothing else will happen. We swear.'

Jenny didn't believe the man for a second. He wore a balaclava like the rest of them. She advanced toward them, noting with relish that they were backing up, not wanting to be stabbed.

'Get out of the way and—' Jenny's back arched, and she staggered forward. The fist smashing into her kidney made her head spin, a wave of nausea crashing over her. The knife was still in her hand, but her weak thrust was parried. She wrestled with the man she had stabbed. He panted, but she couldn't tell where she'd struck him.

'Stop struggling,' he roared, but she wouldn't listen. Fear and adrenaline had taken over, and she was beyond reason. The hand clamped over hers as she tried to jerk the knife towards him. There was a twitch, another jerk, and then more pain.

TARGET PART TWO: THE TAKEDOWN

'Hurry!'

Lamont recognised the roads. They were nearly there. As they hurtled to a stop outside of Jenny's, he saw the front door wide open, along with the gate. Her car was still in the drive. Neighbours had converged, but had gone no closer. One of them was talking rapidly into his phone. Shorty was right there with Lamont, gun in hand. They charged towards the house.

'Jen! Jenny!' Lamont yelled, bursting into the house, and stopping short in the kitchen.

'NO!'

The heart-wrenching scream was uttered by both men when they saw the slender figure stretched out near the dining table, so still she could have been sleeping. Lamont hurried to Jenny's side, turning her over. Shorty hung back, angrily blinking away tears.

'C'mon, Jenny, get up. C'mon, quick, babe. We need to go. We need to go away and be free,' Lamont babbled, paying no attention to the billowing wound near her heart. Her lifeless eyes were glassy. All around were signs of a struggle. There was blood near the kitchen door, but he couldn't tell if it belonged to Jenny, or someone else.

'L, we need to go,' Akeem urged. 'Quickly before the police come.'

'I'm staying. You two go.'

'L—'

'I said go.' Lamont's tone brokered no argument. Akeem nodded once and left. Shorty stared at Jenny, his eyes red. Shaking his head, he ran after Akeem.

'Just the two of us,' Lamont said shakily, holding her cold hand. 'You want to be free. If you wake up, I swear I'll walk away. I'll tell you everything. I promise. I'll tell you why I had to stay. Just wake up, and I'll tell you. I promise.'

Lamont's body shook as he held her frame to his. Tears splashed against her, and he closed his eyes, wanting only peace from the hell he felt, as he realised that Jenny was truly lost to him.

CHAPTER EIGHTEEN

SUNDAY 22 MARCH, 2015

LAMONT SAT in the police station. He hadn't requested to speak to his solicitor, or even uttered the words *no comment*. He'd clutched Jenny's body in a daze, tears staining his face until the police came. They had taken him to the station and given him a plastic cup of piping hot coffee, now lukewarm. He still clutched it, lost in thought.

All his life, he had tried to remain vigilant, guarding his heart and emotions. Now, Jenny was dead, and Lennox was his ultimate enemy. He would be hunted down and terminated. He and his team would fall. Anyone foolish enough to get in the way would be dropped. It was as simple as that.

'Look at the poor sod.'

From across the room, Detectives Hardy and Murphy watched as one of the top kingpins of Leeds sat on a chair, staring blankly into space. Hardy was a younger detective with good instincts. Rigby and Murphy liked him, and he looked up to the pair.

'From what I gather, their relationship was the real deal.

TARGET PART TWO: THE TAKEDOWN

Nothing concrete, but *Prince Teflon* over there was seriously sweet for her. Head over heels from day one.'

'It will be crazy on the streets. Whether or not Teflon goes psycho, bodies are gonna fall. We need to tell the boss not to let him go.'

'How are we going to do that?' Hardy asked. 'We have nothing to keep him here. It was a hit, but he came afterwards. We've got his people on some traffic cams driving like madmen.'

Murphy scratched his face. 'Don't overthink it. We know that Teflon there is a criminal. When we have a criminal on our turf, we break them. C'mon.'

'We haven't even read him his rights,' said Hardy, aghast.

'So what? He's away with the fairies. Let's have a chat with him.'

THEY LED Lamont into an interrogation room. He faced the officers blankly staring straight ahead. Hardy looked to Murphy, who had his eyes on Lamont.

'What happened then, L? Why did she end up dead?'

Lamont didn't reply. If he'd even heard Murphy, he didn't acknowledge it.

'We know you had a problem with someone. We know that you were in love with Jenny Campbell. Why did they knife her?'

Still no response. Hardy shifted in his seat. He didn't want the wrong people seeing what they were doing. Murphy was already on thin ice within the department, and he didn't want to go down with him. He'd been warned by Rigby about getting caught up, but hadn't listened.

'Tef, we all know that you wanted to walk away. We applaud that decision, but this is serious. An innocent woman is dead. A woman who had ties to you. Don't let her murder be in vain. Help us.'

Lamont didn't move. Murphy's face twisted from fake pity to fury.

'Listen, you little prick. I'm talking to you. Do you understand me? Fucking answer me.'

Lamont's eyes flickered towards his, but before he could speak, a man strode into the room, still wearing an overcoat over his suit. He was red-faced and appeared agitated.

'Please tell me what you're playing at?' he snapped. Murphy glared.

'Who the hell are you?'

'I'm the legal counsel for Mr Jones. Please explain why my client has been arrested?'

'He hasn't. We were just talking about the circumstances of his little girlfriend getting knifed. Just a chat amongst friends.'

'Lamont,' Levine called to him, 'let's go.'

Lamont shuffled to his feet and left the room without a word. Levine glared at the officers one last time, then followed his charge. Hardy sighed.

'Guess that didn't work out how we wanted it to.'

'Worth a try,' replied Murphy, revealing a yellow-toothed smile.

SHORTY SAT IN A SAFE HOUSE, pounding shots of white rum. Jenny was dead. Lamont should have made sure she was safe, and he hadn't. That wasn't Shorty's fault, but the escalating issues with Lennox Thompson were. He hadn't heard from Lamont since leaving him, but he knew that Lamont's solicitor, Levine, had been called. Akeem was in another room, and Maka was upstairs making phone calls. Shorty's phone was blowing up, but he didn't want to talk to anyone.

When Lennox became a problem, he hadn't considered the possibility of losing. He knew the streets; he knew how to hurt people and get information out of them, so to envision loss was inconceivable.

TARGET PART TWO: THE TAKEDOWN

Until now.

Lennox was a terror. Worse, he was a terror who knew their moves, who had come up alongside Marcus and his crew, just like him. No one had ever got one over on him. He'd ripped apart the inner workings of Delroy's organisation with ease, then adopted similar tactics in luring Shorty into a trap.

Everything had been planned; he now saw that. Lennox leaked the location of Lutel's safe house, knowing he would give up the main location, and he waited patiently to spring the trap, causing their team to lose two good men. Taking out Jenny was ruthless, the sort of move Marcus had done in the past. It was clear where Lennox had learned.

Shorty closed his eyes, tears sliding down his face. He angrily wiped them, not wanting anyone to see. He'd downed his fourth shot of liquor when he heard a key jangling in the lock. He reached for his gun as Lamont trudged into the room. He looked a mess, wearing a faded grey sweater and jogging bottoms. His eyes were blank, shoulders slumped.

'Did they take your clothes as evidence?'

Lamont might have nodded, he wasn't sure. He grabbed a second glass and filled it to the brim, handing it to him.

'Here.'

Lamont took the drink and held it like he didn't know what to do. He collapsed into a chair, spilling a bit of the liquid, then downed the rest.

'L, I'm sorry, bro. Jen shouldn't have gone out like that.'

'It's fine.'

That was it. Those were his only words. He reached for the bottle of rum, but Shorty moved it out of his reach.

'Fam, she was your girl. It's not fine. It shouldn't have happened.'

'It did. That's the game. It's the life we live, and I should have known that before I involved her,' replied Lamont. His hands shook as he closed his eyes, feeling them burn with the urge to weep, but he wouldn't do that. Not anymore.

'For fuck's sake, L! She was your woman. This isn't street shit anymore. Man the fuck up and stop trying to fight how you feel.'

Lamont turned cool eyes on Shorty. 'You wanna know how I feel? Really?'

'Yeah, I do.'

'All of this is your fault, Shorty. You let all of this happen.'

'What did you say?' Shorty's eyes widened.

'You wanted me to be honest? You couldn't just leave the situation alone, could you? God forbid Shorty ever back down, right?'

'Are you serious, thinking you can blame me? You've always been soft, hesitating over shit rather than taking action. We lost Marcus because of you. You were right there, and you did nothing. Everyone close to you ends up dead, or wishing they were.'

'Lennox got to Jenny because of you!' Lamont roared, silencing him. 'Killing her was a shot at *both* of us. I had Grimer watching the house, until the point you needed him for your little suicide mission. You visited her, and I guarantee you that led Lennox's men to the house. I may hesitate, but you got Jenny killed. If Grace dies, that too will be your fault.'

Lamont regretted it as soon as he'd said it. Shorty's face was harrowing. He stared at him as if he'd never seen him before. For a moment, there was a lull. Shorty broke it, letting out a strangled yell and diving at Lamont. He expected it, but Shorty's mass still sent them toppling to the floor. Lamont was about to try to reason with him, but he saw the fury in Shorty's eyes. This was a fight.

Shorty struck first, a short jab to the ribs. He tried mounting Lamont, but he kicked him off and sailed in with a knee, catching him in the stomach. Shorty let out a moan of pain, grabbing him around the throat and slamming him into the wall. Lamont struck with his elbow, catching him in the eye. He hit him twice more, sending his friend stumbling. Shorty came back, dodging the next two blows, clipping his jaw with an uppercut, then hitting him twice in the ribs. Lamont sagged to one knee, but only for a second. When Shorty lunged again, he evaded it, shoving Shorty into the wall. There was a noise, then strong arms pulled him back.

TARGET PART TWO: THE TAKEDOWN

'Enough.' Akeem stood between them. Lamont and Shorty breathed heavily, giving each other death stares. Something had shifted between them. They had argued many times before, but they'd never once raised their hands to each other.

'You're a cancer,' spat Lamont. Shorty tried to pass Akeem, but the guard was too strong. He pushed Shorty against the wall, keeping his eyes on Lamont.

'This isn't the way to deal with this.' Akeem's words fell on deaf ears.

'This is on you, Shorty. You're responsible for all of this. All you've ever done is weigh me down with your bullshit. I should have left you in prison.' Lamont used his jumper to stem the blood from his nose.

Shorty's eyes blazed. Lamont braced himself, expecting him to try again. Instead, Shorty spat blood on the floor and stormed from the house, holding his gun.

'BLOOD, what the hell is going on?'

K-Bar didn't know what to say to Darren. His phone was ringing off the hook. There were rumours Shorty and Lamont had been murdered by Lennox, but he'd spoken with Akeem, who had set him right before hanging up.

'I don't even know,' He admitted after a long silence. The pair were holed up, smoking weed and waiting for word.

'How is Lennox still breathing? I mean, he's got half of Leeds after him, so what's the drill?'

'I know they moved on him last night,' said K-Bar, annoyed he'd been left out of the action. 'I dunno what happened, but it doesn't sound like they got him.'

'This is bullshit. I need to get hold of something, because I'm feeling vulnerable when I'm moving around. I can't even go see my girl, because I'm shook that someone's gonna come for me.'

'You definitely need to be strapped,' said K-Bar. 'I'll get you one to hold, and we can practise shooting to make sure you're ready.'

Before Darren could reply, they heard a voice shout POLICE, and then a boom as the door was smashed open. Officers surged into the room, ordering Darren and K-Bar to fall to the floor without giving them time to comply. The officers slammed them to the ground, restraining them and cuffing their hands behind their backs. Neither man struggled. The safe house was clean. Police would find no evidence of illicit activity there.

'What's the charge, pigs?' Darren spat, only to have his face pushed further into the carpet. The leading officer, a greying man with a paunch and tired eyes, began reading them their rights, but K-Bar tuned him out as they dragged him to his feet.

All across Leeds, there was a similar spate of activity, with fifteen people being picked up in coordinated raids. Some were part of Lamont's crew, and the others had similar crew affiliations.

Drinking in his living room at home, Lamont made sure Levine was aware of the situation, in case they tried to take him in. He had Akeem searching for Lennox, whereas Levine's team would represent his men and get to the bottom of the situation.

LENNOX HAD his feet up at an out-of-the-way spot in Adel. He had mixed feelings about the current climate. People had been arrested in connection with various drug cases. The streets were all looking for him, and Lamont seemed to be sparing no expense in having his killers prowl around the streets of Leeds. Lennox moved around when necessary, but refused to have security watching his every move. It slowed him down, and he couldn't afford that.

Deep down, he knew they could have avoided the situation. He'd told his men to kidnap Jenny and bring her to him. The plan was to use her to force Lamont to back down, allowing him to deal with Shorty and Delroy unchecked. Instead, his team had panicked when she fought back, and ended up killing her. Now, he would have to contend with a fully invested Lamont. Emotions aside, he knew that Lamont wouldn't back down. One of them would end up killing the other. His people were organised and knew their roles. It was up to him to engage.

'I can't believe you.'

Lennox looked up, seeing Malcolm framing the doorway. Malcolm's face was haggard, bags under his eyes, his hair unkempt. His hands shook as he stared Lennox down.

'This spot is for emergencies only.'

'How could you do it?' He ignored Lennox's response.

'You'll need to be more specific.'

'How the hell could you murder her?'

Lennox resisted the urge to roll his eyes. He'd never understood how so many men allowed themselves to become enthralled by the women around them. Malcolm was no different.

'These things happen.'

'That's not enough.' Malcolm stepped further into the room. 'She was a good woman. She wasn't mixed up in your shit. You didn't have to kill her.'

'You have no idea what's going on,' said Lennox. 'This situation is so much bigger than you. I don't have the time for sentimentality. I have an actual war to win.'

'A war? Who the hell do you think you are, Lennox? You're not a general. You're not some great revolutionary. You're a basic gangster, and that's it. There's nothing special or noteworthy about you. I'm sad it took me so long to realise it.'

Lennox was about to reply when a noise distracted him. He heard the click, then the pounding gunfire as he was knocked out of his chair. Malcolm was clipped twice in the neck and jaw and crumpled to the ground, unmoving.

Eddie Williams stepped into the room, aiming his gun at Malcolm and shooting him twice more. He approached Lennox, his jaw clenched and his eyes wide with fury.

'You're next, you piece of shit.'

As Eddie aimed the gun at Lennox, he surprised Eddie by

lurching to his feet, gun in hand. He didn't hesitate, popping Eddie in the head, then firing four more shots into the man. Gingerly, he touched the bulletproof vest beneath his hooded top. The bullet had hurt like hell, but at least it hadn't penetrated. Firing one more shot at close range into Eddie, he snatched his phones and hurried from the house.

K-BAR STARED AHEAD, not taking his eyes from the police officers. He was being interviewed and had been advised of the reason for his arrest. He'd thought he was being picked up on drugs charges, which were easy to fight without concrete proof. When the police told him he was being charged with murder, it completely blindsided him.

'Kieron Barrett, for the benefit of the tape, please tell us where you were on the night of Wednesday, 11th September 2013?'

'No comment.'

The questions continued in a similar vein, with the police asking about his connections to Chink, Polo and Naomi. K-Bar *no-commented* everything, inwardly wondering who had given him up. Grimer was his co-conspirator, but he was dead. Unless he'd snitched while alive, K-Bar didn't understand where the police were going.

'Kieron, we know all about you. We know everything that has transpired over the past few years. We even know about the Manchester war, and the job you did on Big Kev. Make it easier on yourself and cooperate.'

K-Bar looked at his solicitor, but the man didn't seem to have a game plan. Lamont had been onto him for years about making sure he had a legal team ready just in case, but he hadn't taken heed. He had no rapport and minimal relationship with the solicitor he'd hired, and it showed. The man was content to let the police control the interview.

'I have no idea what you're talking about.'

TARGET PART TWO: THE TAKEDOWN

'We have a witness who has stated you paid Naomi Gateworth five thousand pounds to set up Xiyu Manderson, better known to you as *Chink*. She was given two and a half thousand pounds up front and agreed because of an abusive relationship she was in with Chink. You killed Chink's bodyguard, then you murdered both Chink and Naomi. Stop me if there's anything that I've gotten wrong.'

K-Bar fought to keep his expression neutral. He didn't know how, but the police were spot on.

'We know the meeting spot. We know what was said between you and Naomi. You'll take the full force of the punishment, unless you start talking about the people you work for. Help us fill in the blanks. Don't go down with the ship when you don't have to. We know Teflon is behind this. You don't need to protect him.'

'Like I said, I have no idea what you lot are talking about, so you may as well just let me go.'

The officers shared a look with one another, then shrugged.

'Have it your way then; Kieron Barrett, we are charging you with the murders of Naomi Gateworth, Paul Dobby, and Xiyu Manderson. You do not have to say anything. But, it may harm your defence if you do not mention when questioned something which you later rely on in court. Anything you do say may be given in evidence.'

CHAPTER NINETEEN
FRIDAY 27 MARCH, 2015

ON THE MORNING of Jenny's funeral, Lamont slumped in his living room, staring at a bottle of Red Label rum, debating whether to get drunk. He was already in his black suit, his tie dangling precariously over the bottle. He'd considered skipping the funeral, not wanting to face a venue full of people who blamed him for Jenny's murder. If they didn't, they should. The police had cleared him, but none of that did anything to blot the stain around his heart. Shorty was right; people around him did end up dead. Street activity was at its lowest for years. No one was making much money, and police were an almost permanent presence in the Hood.

No one had seen Shorty, but Grace Turner was in recovery after several operations. Lamont had spoken with Amy, who had been grimly pleased, stating there was a long way to go before Grace would be better. Amy hadn't asked about Shorty, nor had he volunteered any information.

People had swept all of his known spots, to no avail. Lennox was also on the missing list, but Lamont and Delroy had dedicated teams tracking him down. The murder of Malcolm Powell was another talking point, as was the fact he'd been gunned down alongside Eddie Williams, a known gangster and son of Delroy.

TARGET PART TWO: THE TAKEDOWN

Rumours were flying around about Malcolm's involvement, people believing he'd been associated with gangsters from day one. Lamont believed this. A person saying the things Malcolm had, shouldn't have been able to walk around with impunity. It was just another part of Lennox's diabolical plan he had to admire. The man had covered almost every angle, and he saw now that the plan had been to destabilise him on the streets, and to break up his relationship.

K-Bar remained on remand, charged with three murders. Lamont had been unable to contact him, and had no idea what he might have said. Regardless, Lamont had a go-bag ready, just in case he needed to flee. Proper instructions had been meted out. There would be no messing around this time; everyone would know what to do if things went south.

OurHood was still going, yet had floundered in the death of its leader and public face. Figures such as Calvin were still prevalent, calling for harsh punishment for the drug dealers responsible for the wrongdoing. More civilians were beginning to cooperate with the police, who continued to make scores of small-time arrests. The public and the police were, for a time, united.

Lamont was wholesaling his drugs, letting the younger, crazier outfits take the risk of selling during a police lockdown. He couldn't bring himself to care. He sat, mourning Jenny, waiting for the news that Lennox had been taken care of, but there was nothing so far.

With a start, Lamont clambered to his feet and went to finish freshening up. He had a funeral to attend.

AS FUNERALS WENT, the service was fairly brief. Lamont noted several people he recognised, including Jenny's friends. Kate was there, her face already wet with tears. He didn't approach. Nadia and several others who had worked for Jenny were present.

Even Marika had shown up, dressed in her black clothes and

standing near Jenny's friends. She locked eyes with him, but neither moved to speak. He spotted two people who could only be Jenny's parents. They were greeting several attendees, their faces heavy with their grief. Jenny favoured her mother, who had the same dark hair and cheekbones, but she had her father's eyes. He was a thin man with a lined face, chestnut eyes and a slight Mediterranean tan to his skin tone. Lamont debated whether to introduce himself, but decided against it.

He drove alone to the cemetery after the service, watching in silence as they buried the woman he loved. Lamont didn't move, even as others around him made their way toward a gathering being held at a prestigious hall in Shadwell. When people started to file away, he noted one figure still stood by the graveside. He debated whether to approach.

'Hey,' he said, walking over. Kate glanced at him, then turned back to the graveside.

'If there's one person on this planet who deserves not to be in there, it's her.' Kate's voice was full of the pain he was internalising.

'I know.'

'She loved you, L. Even after the split.'

Lamont didn't speak. Kate looked back at him, her eyes swollen with the tears she'd already shed.

'Was it your fault?'

He didn't hesitate to reply to Kate's loaded question.

'Yes.'

'Why couldn't you just walk away?'

'I wanted to, but I couldn't. Don't ask why.'

'Wasn't she worth it?' Kate's voice rose. A few stragglers looked over, but no one approached.

'Of course, she was worth it! You should know that better than anyone. You were there. At the beginning. You saw how I felt about her. She was the first person in a long time that I thought could help me navigate away from the darkness.'

'So, what happened; the darkness won?'

TARGET PART TWO: THE TAKEDOWN

'Does that answer your question?' Lamont pointed at the graveside.

Kate didn't speak, fresh tears rolling down her face. Lamont resisted the urge to hug her. They had been close, but it directly resulted from Jenny. Their only conversations had been about her, and she defined them. Now, she had been stripped away. She had been in the middle of a war, and they'd all paid the ultimate price. The cool wind whistled through the cemetery.

Lamont jammed his hands into the pockets of his suit jacket, looking around. Akeem was a respectable distance away from them, monitoring the surroundings.

'I'll leave you to it.' He turned to leave. Kate's words stopped him.

'Do you know who did it?'

Lamont met her eyes. She had stopped crying, the recognisable fire back. He debated lying, just to spare her feelings.

'Yes.'

'You're going to kill them, aren't you?'

He stared, gauging whether to reply.

'Yes, Kate. I'm going to eradicate them.'

'Good.' Kate smiled for the first time. 'Make them suffer.'

LAMONT AND KATE drove to the hall in Shadwell in silence. Declarations had been made, and he'd made a vow that he would see to fruition. Lennox would be torn apart. He was putting money on the heads of everyone involved. He was tired of the waiting around.

Lamont led Kate into the hall, full of people milled around, telling stories in large groups. Lamont wanted to drown himself in the liquor but remained composed, instead drinking water, ambling around the fringes of different groups, not getting involved in conversation. He saw Marika watching, and as she made her towards his corner, he didn't move.

'Hey,' Marika said.

'Hey.'

The siblings stood in silence a moment.

'I'm sorry,' she started.

'I know.'

'Jenny was nice. She was good for you.'

'How do you know that?' Lamont stared at her.

'I saw you together. Everyone did. You were at peace when you were with her.'

It hadn't been peaceful when Marcus Daniels had been murdered in front of them, or when he was almost killed, but he appreciated the sentiment.

'I'm not gonna ask about what comes next, because I know you. Just, be careful. Whatever is going on with us, you're still my brother, and I love you.'

Lamont didn't respond. Marika squeezed his hand, and for a moment, he forgot his pain, remembering the bond they shared, and how much he loved her.

'Come by and see the kids sometime. I'll make you some dinner.' She left him to his grieving, and he'd never been more grateful to her.

The event crawled by. He eventually spoke with a few of Jenny's friends, all of whom were nice, but in a guarded manner that told him quite starkly that they blamed him for Jenny's death. He saw Jenny's parents and couldn't avoid them any longer. Swallowing his courage, he forced himself to approach.

'Mrs Campbell, I'm so sorry for your loss. I . . .' Lamont didn't know what to say, and as fresh tears formed in Jenny's mother's eyes, his throat tightened. 'Your daughter shouldn't have died, and I wanted to tell you that. I loved her more than I can put into words, but this isn't about me. It's about you; your loss. I just wanted you to know that.'

Jenny's mother flung her arms around him, tightly hugging him. Lamont held the embrace, pouring all the anguish and emotion he felt into the gesture. When they pulled apart, both their faces were wet. He sniffed, shaking hands with Jenny's father. He was about to leave, when he felt the man grab his shoulder.

'I'd like to talk to you. Come to our home when everyone leaves.'

LAMONT ARRIVED at Jenny's parent's home, not knowing what to expect. He'd never met them before today, but Jenny often said she got along with her mother more than her father. The pain of losing her hadn't diminished, but it fed the volcanic rage simmering within. He needed to absolve himself by murdering Lennox.

Perhaps Jenny's father wanted to shout at him about the murder?
Lamont wouldn't mind.

Shortly after knocking, he was shown into a study. It was at least three times the size of his, filled with books, a fine leather sofa, a roll-top desk in the far corner, and a liquor cabinet. Jenny's father stared out of the window. He turned, motioning to the sofa. He sat in an armchair facing Lamont.

'So, you're the famous *L*?'

Jenny's father seemed dwarfed by the simple brown chair. Watery brown eyes and rumpled hair were the main signs of grief. Lamont had the impression he was a man who knew how to manage his emotions. He could relate.

'*Lamont* is fine.'

'My daughter spoke of you. Mainly to my wife. I was always protective over her. But, I knew of you. She said you were special.'

'I think she was the special one, sir.'

'Call me Stefanos.'

Lamont nodded, but didn't try the name. Stefanos was testing him, trying to gain the measure of him. It was a tactic he had used in the past.

'Do you have a code, Lamont?'

'Pardon?'

Stefanos cleared his throat.

'Do you have a way of life that you adhere to?'

'I try to do what I believe is right in order to survive.'

Stefanos nodded. 'Survive. I like that. My daughter may have been right about you. From what I've gathered, you are a man of means. You dress well, you lived with my daughter in a large house that you paid the rent on. You drive nice cars. I can spot a pretender, but you're the real deal. So, how are you surviving?'

'I live in a world I shouldn't. I wanted to take the steps into another world with your daughter, but I wasn't able to do that.'

'Are you telling me it was your fault she died?' Stefanos's expression and tone were unchanged, which surprised him.

'Yes.'

'How?'

'I brought her into my life, and I shouldn't have. I realised a long time ago that people who grow close to me seem to end up broken. Like I am.'

'You're broken?'

Lamont met Stefanos' eyes. 'More now than ever.'

'Because of my daughter?'

'Yes.'

'So, why go after her? You wanted a pretty girl on your arm, to sit with in the clubs? To take lots of little photos with?'

'Are we speaking freely here, sir?'

'Stefanos, not *sir*.'

'Okay, Stefanos, sir. Are we speaking freely?'

'Yes, we are,' Stefanos replied, his eyes glittering.

'You've had me checked out, which means you know I'm not the sort of person who sits in the clubs posing for photos. I went after Jenny, because she made sense.'

'Explain.' It was a request that came out as a command, and they were both aware of the fact.

'I was searching for the way out. Your daughter was that way out, and when I first spotted her, I knew she was different. She didn't even have to open her mouth. I had to get closer to her. Jen didn't make it easy. She never made anything easy. I jumped through hoop after hoop to grow close, and I don't regret that.

'I don't regret telling her I loved her. I don't regret telling her my deepest secrets. I regret that I was stupid enough to bring her into my life, but not do everything in my power to keep her safe. I was at war. Still am. I know my enemy. I knew them before they became my enemy, but I still thought they would leave her alone. I'm still here. She's dead. I can't let that stand.'

Stefanos cleared his throat, but still said nothing. After a moment, he opened his mouth.

'I don't doubt that you loved her, Lamont. The fault doesn't lie with you. It lies with me.'

Lamont frowned. 'What do you mean?'

'Answer another question; do you know exactly who was responsible for my daughter's death?'

'Yes, I do. I will handle it.'

Stefanos didn't speak for a long time. Lamont strangely enjoyed the silence. It was comfortable, similar to the silences he'd shared with Jenny once upon a time.

'You have . . . ways of handling this situation?'

Lamont slowly nodded.

'I won't pry. Please, make sure you punish them, and leave with my blessing.'

Lamont's brow furrowed, but he rose to his feet, shaking hands with Stefanos. His grip was like iron.

'Hopefully, we will speak again soon, Lamont. Stay safe and watch the surrounding angles.'

'What's the update then?'

Rigby and Murphy were in the office of their superior. They had been up most of the night, and it showed in their rumpled clothing and haggard expressions. Their cases seemed to grow harder every day, with little breakthrough, and it was causing the pair a lot of stress.

'K-Bar still isn't talking. We've remanded him, and he hasn't tried to get in touch with anyone. He didn't even react when we read the charges.'

'Do you think he might be innocent?' Superintendent O'Hara asked. Rigby shook his head.

'He's definitely guilty. He's also loyal, and either doesn't think we've got a case, or he's more scared of the people he's working for than us.'

O'Hara rubbed his eyes, looking just as bedraggled as the men who worked for him. His job wasn't any easier than theirs at the moment. There was such a spotlight on Leeds and Chapeltown that the past year alone was a blight on their administration. Multiple assaults, riots, demonstrations and murders had made his role more tenuous than ever.

'No word on Jones?'

Rigby again shook his head.

'There hasn't been any retaliation for the death of Jenny Campbell, but it's coming. Unfortunately, our informant is low in the pecking order. He overheard just enough to get us to K-Bar, but Teflon is different. He's far more organised and hands-off. Word is, he's depressed over her murder.'

'Wouldn't surprise me,' Murphy mumbled. 'Did you see his face when we had him in here? I've never seen a more broken man.'

O'Hara clutched his mug of cold coffee, staring at the liquid.

'Broken or not, he's one of the most dangerous men in our city, and must be taken down. Lamont Jones, *Teflon*, or whatever his name is, is key to this situation. He has the power, the clout, and a tremendous amount of resource. If we can smash his organisation, we can save our city, gentlemen.

'Get me something, anything that we can use to go on. Put more pressure on K-Bar, squeeze his people. He has a wife, a girlfriend, a brother, anything. Use it. All eyes are on us, and we need to make something happen, and quickly.'

CHAPTER TWENTY
SATURDAY 28 MARCH, 2015

LAMONT TRUNDLED OUT OF BED. Strangely, speaking with Jenny's father had helped. He still felt the same level of guilt, but the fact Jenny's parents didn't outright blame him had boosted his mindset. After a quick shower and two cups of coffee, he left his house flanked by Akeem. They drove toward Chapeltown.

'Anything?'

Akeem shook his head. 'We're slapping his runners and middlemen around. This is Lennox we're talking about. He wouldn't tell them anything, and even if he had, I'd think twice before acting on the information.'

Lamont mulled this over, knowing Akeem was right. Lennox had been one step ahead of him so far. He'd been trained by Marcus, but had none of Marcus's apparent weaknesses. As far as Lamont knew, he didn't take any drugs, and if he drank, it wasn't to excess. He couldn't think of any women Lennox had been linked to. That was a problem.

'Could you reach out to Vincent? Let's cast the net further if needed. There's no guarantee that Lennox is still in Leeds.'

'I'll make some calls down south and around, but Lennox won't leave Leeds. He's not hiding. He's waiting for something.'

'Is this how it's gonna be?'

Darren continued ironing his hooded top. Realising she wasn't keeping his attention, Clarissa stood and turned him toward her.

'Watch I don't burn you,' he warned, placing the iron on the ironing board.

'Daz, please don't avoid the question.'

Darren sighed. He knew she cared, but he still had a job to do. With everything transpiring, she worried every time he left the house. For the first time, he had real responsibility. He had been picked up by the police along with K-Bar. The police interrogated him for hours, even getting a warrant to search his place. They found nothing, but the events scarred Clarissa.

The game was wide open. Money was low, but it was just a period he was determined to ride out. Lamont had given some of K-Bar's responsibilities to him, and he was doing his best to act on them.

'Babe, I know you're worried, but you don't need to be. I'm fine, and I'm not moving sloppy out there. I promise.'

'People are dying though, Daz. You can't blame me for being scared that the same thing might happen to you.'

Darren finished ironing, then pulled on the hooded top. He held Clarissa, stroking her hair.

'All I can tell you is that I'm watching my back, babe. Why don't we go away somewhere when it blows over?'

'Really?' Clarissa's face brightened, and he felt a warmth in his heart as he realised how much he loved her.

'Start looking for places, and we can go in May or June. Anywhere you like.' He kissed Clarissa's cheek, then gave her a lingering kiss on the lips. 'I've got to jet for now, but I'll see you later on.'

Darren left the house, a car already waiting. He scanned the street before he climbed in. Sharma pulled off.

'Don't you ever listen to the radio or anything?' He'd asked

TARGET PART TWO: THE TAKEDOWN

Sharma the same thing previously, but he never said much. Sharma shrugged as they turned onto the main road.

'Marcus used to flip out about it, saying we needed to be on point.'

Darren nodded. He'd never worked alongside Marcus, but he'd seen the larger-than-life man doing whatever he wanted around Chapeltown. Darren had been at Carnival when Marcus had been murdered, but in a different part of the park. He'd heard the gunshots, then run and hid with everyone else. There were always little incidents at Carnival, and even last year, there had been several stabbings, but Marcus's murder had been a planned hit. He'd since learned the internal situation and knew that Chink had planned it. He didn't know why he'd turned on Lamont, Marcus and the crew, but he was dead now because of it.

'You ever miss him?'

Sharma didn't reply straight away, his face unchanged.

'He was a cool boss. Crazy, but he always had your back if you were down with him. He put me on, paid me well, and never asked me to do anything he wasn't willing to do himself. He just let the women get to him. Some guys are just like that.'

'Nothing wrong with liking women,' replied Darren, his tone defensive.

'You can't make them your everything, especially when you're doing dirt. People will use it against you. Look at L.'

Sharma's words made sense, and Darren considered Lamont and his reaction to Jenny's death. Everyone knew Lamont loved her, and Lennox had probably targeted her because of that. He wondered if he was doing the right thing with his own girl.

'You think L shouldn't have gotten with her?'

'I can't speak for L, but this life ain't made for wives and girlfriends. With how things are at the moment, it's gonna be worse than it was a few years ago.'

'Things have calmed down, though,' replied Darren. The *OurHood* people were cooling off, confused, leaderless and arguing amongst themselves. Police were still neck-deep in Chapeltown, but they couldn't cause any further harm to Lamont's crew. K-Bar had taken the hit for that. 'All we need to do is clip Lennox and the job's done.'

Sharma smiled.

'Kid, learn to see all the angles. Lennox killed both of Delroy's sons and had the man on the ropes. He tried to take out Shorty, hit his daughter, and had Lamont's missus murdered. You think L's gonna get him easily?'

'Not easily, but he'll definitely get him. L's smarter.'

'No doubt. He's the smartest person I've ever met, but he's not perfect. He makes mistakes, and he's at the top, so those mistakes are bigger.

'Lennox is ruthless and has nothing to lose, especially with us picking away at his team and money.' Sharma pulled up outside the safe house, turning off the engine and again looking at him. 'All I'm saying is, watch your own back, think about your own moves, and don't expect your boss to sort everything out. He's hurting, and hurt people can make even more mistakes.'

LAMONT SAT INDOORS, music playing in the background. Lennox was still in the wind, and he had no idea where to find him. Akeem was right. Lennox was probably still in Leeds, but any move he made would be on his terms.

Lamont had people in place, but the surge of arrests had made them wary. K-Bar remained in prison, fighting a murder charge. He didn't know how the police had found evidence linking him to the murders of Chink's people, but it was a massive loss to the team. K-Bar was looking at a long stretch, and that affected everything.

A bottle of gin and a glass rested on the table in front of Lamont, but he hadn't touched them. He hadn't touched a drink since fighting with Shorty. He regretted their fight, but understood why it happened. It had been coming for a long time.

Rubbing his eyes, he decided to go to bed, the idea immediately erased by the vibrating of his phone. He picked it up without even checking the number.

'Yeah?' His voice was toneless. There was no pretence of being in the zone. He needed to rest.

'It's me, Charlie?'

'How are you doing?'

'Better than you, from the sounds of things. Is this a bad time?'

Lamont wanted to tell her it was always a bad time, but he liked Charlotte. He didn't want to alienate her as he had others.

'It's been a long day. Listen, I haven't forgotten what we discussed.'

'L, forget that. I heard what happened, and I'm ensuring you're okay.'

Lamont laughed, staring at the alcohol again.

'I don't have a choice. I have to be okay.'

'I'm coming to see you. Give me your address.'

'Charlie, I—'

'Now, L.'

WHEN CHARLOTTE ENTERED THE HOUSE, he was slumped on the sofa, looking at the ceiling.

'Have you eaten?' She asked.

'Earlier.'

'Earlier when? You need to eat, L.'

'I'm not hungry.'

'You're certainly thirsty.' Charlotte reached for the bottle of gin and the glass, moving them out of reach.

'I haven't even opened the bottle. Check the lid.'

Charlotte placed the bottle in the cabinet, then turned to face him. She wore a hooded top under a blue jacket, and ripped jeans, her hair tied in a basic ponytail. Lamont received the full effect of her haunting grey eyes. It was nice, especially after everything else that had transpired recently.

'Do you want me to make you some food?'

'No.'

'I'm going to anyway, so I hope there's something to cook.'

———

Soon, Lamont was playing with grilled chicken breast and crispy vegetables. Charlotte eyeballed him, waiting for him to start. Tired of the messing around, he began eating the chicken.

'How was the funeral?' Charlotte asked.

'Difficult, especially considering the fact I put her there,' said Lamont, struggling to swallow. He closed his eyes for a moment.

'She was attacked. You had nothing to do with it.'

'When someone shot at King outside your house, did you feel he had nothing to do with it?'

Charlotte paled. 'How do you know about that?'

'There wasn't much I didn't know about back then. King needed to keep guys like me sweet to even ply his trade.'

'And Justin?'

'Justin was one in a million. He had everything. He could have done anything. He just couldn't let the streets go.'

Charlotte didn't reply. Lamont felt terrible for bringing up King and Justin. Years had passed, but he couldn't imagine it was any easier for Charlotte to deal with.

'What's next?' She asked after a moment.

'Nothing that I can discuss with you.'

'Why don't you just walk away?'

'That's not an option.'

Charlotte was again silent. Lamont finished the rest of his food, then did the washing up, enjoying the mundane task. When he'd dried his hands, she waited by the kitchen door.

'Come here.'

Lamont moved to her, stiffening as she wrapped her arms around him. After a moment, he relaxed, and he tightly hugged her

TARGET PART TWO: THE TAKEDOWN

back, saying everything in the hug that he couldn't say aloud. Charlotte seemed to understand.

THE NEXT DAY, Lamont left the house with a protective cordon consisting of Akeem and several handpicked men. They climbed into a 4x4 and were about to drive away when Akeem's phone rang. He answered and handed the phone to Lamont after a few moments.

'Who is this?'

'A friend. I heard you're looking for some guys.'

'What about it?' Lamont had no time for nonsense.

'I have an address. Delete it once you've read it. You'll find something there.' With a click, the person was gone.

'Do you know who that was?' Akeem took the phone from Lamont, reading the address after the message buzzed.

'Not a clue. He said we'll find something at the address.'

'Could be a trap.' Akeem scratched his neck.

'It could be,' Lamont admitted.

'What do your instincts tell you?'

'That you and a few of your men should check out this address.'

AKEEM PARKED across the road from the address. He had two men with him. Lamont was back at home and under guard.

Signalling for his men to exit the vehicle, he checked his weapon, then followed. They kicked down the front door and surged inside. Akeem heard yells in the front room, but he was on top of the person there before they could move, driving his fist into their stomach and flinging them to the floor. His men searched each room, but found no one else.

'Get off me. You're all dead,' the man snarled. Akeem smiled grimly.

'Nice to see you, Nikkolo.'

———

Lamont hung up. Akeem had caught Nikkolo at the spot, and they had him at *The Dungeon*, where they would interrogate him.

Lamont racked his brain, thinking about the caller. He had a few suspects in mind; namely, Shorty, Akhan, or Lennox himself. He couldn't see Shorty allowing someone else to kill Nikkolo, and he didn't see Lennox trying the same trick twice, which left Akhan. The more Lamont thought about it, the less sense it made. He hadn't spoken to Akhan since the impromptu kidnapping. He would need to sit tight and see what came back.

———

Akeem came to Lamont a day later, grim-faced and unshaven.

'He's gone.'

Lamont felt nothing. He didn't care about Nikkolo's fate.

'Lennox?'

'Nikkolo knew nothing. Gave up some stash spots and safe houses. We found a lot of guns and some small-fry soldiers, but no Lennox.'

'Do you think Lennox planned this?'

Akeem shook his head. 'We completely took Nikkolo by surprise. He wasn't expecting to see us. He started speaking straight away.'

'We're back at square one then.'

'Lennox can't and won't hide forever, but if you ask me, I'd suggest letting some of the heat off. Concentrate on a few small areas, put money on his head, but let everyone else go back to work.'

'Do it.'

———

TARGET PART TWO: THE TAKEDOWN

DAYS PASSED. For the most part, Lamont's people were happy to be back at work. He spent his time hanging out by the barbers and going to the gym. He heard little titbits about the *OurHood* Initiative, but nothing major.

On the Friday, he was eating a sandwich when his phone rang. He didn't recognise the number.

'Who's this?' He asked, once he'd swallowed.

'Did you like the tip I gave you?'

'Who is this?' Lamont clutched the phone to his ear. This person was a potential link to Lennox.

'I'd like you to come and meet me. There is a warehouse near the Canal. It will say *C&C* on the building. If you come, you will receive all the answers you need.'

'I don't even know who you are. That is a lot of trust to give some voice over the phone.'

'You operate within a volatile world, Teflon. You understand the need to take measures to hide one's identity. I won't force you, but I promise that without my help, you won't succeed. Hopefully, I will see you soon.'

The person hung up. Lamont stared at the phone, trying to piece together what he remembered from the person's voice. They sounded familiar, but he couldn't pinpoint where from. It was a tremendous risk, but he didn't have any choice.

Taking a shower and throwing on some clothes, he arranged some paperwork that Levine had delivered that very morning. His will and effects had been updated, just in case. Nearly everything would be left to Marika and the kids, but there were provisions for other people. He sighed, then shrugged into his jacket and left.

LAMONT DROVE IN SILENCE. He'd chosen not to tell Akeem where he'd gone, and forbade the guards at his house from following him. He couldn't help but wonder if he'd made a misstep somewhere down the line, relating to Lennox and Akhan.

The memory of meeting Jenny for the first time planted itself in his mind, and tears prickled his eyes. He needed to focus, but it wasn't easy. Ever since Jenny's murder, he had tried so hard to bury his feelings; to work through his anguish as he had when Marcus died, but it was too hard. He wiped away the tears, blowing out a long breath.

'Get it together, you pussy,' he hissed.

The warehouse loomed in front of Lamont, and he pulled into a private car park in front. There were men milled around, two of them wearing fitted suits, the rest wearing black bomber jackets and jeans. All carried weapons, and all were glaring at him. He froze after turning off his engine, wondering again why he'd chosen to come alone. He didn't even have a weapon. For the first time, he realised he was truly alone. He had no Marcus, no Shorty, K-Bar, or any of the others who had always watched his back.

Swallowing down the fear, he climbed from the ride. Immediately the men patted him down, then they led him toward the warehouse. Lamont owned several of his own, but none that matched the scale of this one. It was enormous, and he was sure that his whole house would fit in the expansive space.

'Get in.' One of the men signalled to a buggy, similar to the ones used by golfers. Lamont did as he was told, and they drove toward an office on the other end of the room. The man who'd accompanied him, jerked his thumb toward the office, and he walked in, preparing to die.

Two men occupied the room. The first was an older Asian man whom Lamont had never seen before. The second was a more familiar face.

'Thank you for trusting me and coming, Teflon.'

CHAPTER TWENTY-ONE
TUESDAY 31 MARCH, 2015

'WHAT THE HELL IS THIS?'

Jenny's father reclined on a black leather chair. His face seemed more lined than at the funeral, and he had dark circles under his eyes as he calmly assessed Lamont. The other man said nothing.

'This is you believing in my word. I trust Nikkolo has been disposed of?"

'Where is Lennox?' Lamont asked.

'He'll be taken care of once we locate him. I can assure you my resources are extensive. This meeting pertains to a more sensitive matter, and I need you focused, not distracted like you were at the funeral. Remember, I told you to watch the angles around you.'

Lamont took a moment to reply. If Stefanos was going to ignore the third man in the room, then he would too.

'*Who* are you?'

Stefanos smiled, the Asian following suit. 'I know you're having trouble with your supplier. That should give you a small clue about the scale of things.'

'If you're in league with Akhan, then we have nothing else to say to one another.'

'Please, control your foolish stubbornness. I know of Akhan. I've done business with him over the years. Here, this is for you.'

Lamont reached for the scrap of paper Stefanos held out to him. It had an address on it.

'What's at this address?'

'One of Akhan's main warehouses. Check it out first if you don't believe me. We don't need a repeat of what went down in Cottingley. Send someone either white or Asian. Akhan and his men have a heavy distrust for blacks.'

'If Akhan is an acquaintance, then why would you give me this information?'

'You're sceptical . . . You still believe I'm trying to trap you, correct?'

He didn't reply. Stefanos grinned.

'I promise you my intentions are above board. Do as you see fit with the information, but I promise you that all will be explained soon enough.'

'CAN YOU TRUST HIM?'

It was midday, and Akeem and Lamont were in the back of the barbers. He had filled in Akeem on his conversation with Jenny's father.

'He gave us Nikkolo's address, and Lennox murdered his daughter. I can't think of a single reason why he'd work against us.'

'If he worked with Akhan, why would he suddenly switch sides?'

Lamont mulled that one over. 'He thinks we can help him more than Akhan, which means Akhan has likely overplayed his hand.'

Akeem looked at the address he'd shown him, his dark eyes absorbing the information.

'If we're going to do this, we need to move quickly. We need numbers too, in case it's a trap. We're stretched thin at present with the hunt for Lennox.'

TARGET PART TWO: THE TAKEDOWN

Lamont sipped a bottle of water, his brow furrowed.

'We need an insurance policy and some backup. I know where to get both.'

'I WAS sorry to hear about your girl.'

Lamont could only nod at Delroy's words. After a few quick conversations, they had arranged to meet at a restaurant near the city centre.

'Thank you,' he finally replied.

'I'm guessing you haven't found Lennox yet?'

'Neither have you. I'll settle up with Lennox another time. I'm here to talk business with you.'

Delroy gestured wordlessly for him to continue.

'I need your help taking down Akhan.'

Throwing his head back after a stunned second, Delroy bellowed with laughter, slapping his legs, loud guffaws resonating around the room. Lamont waited.

'Fucking hell, L . . . I haven't laughed like that in years. Go easy on me. I'm an old man.'

'I didn't make a joke.'

'L, you've worked long enough with the guy to know how deep his reach is. You can't touch him like that.'

'Have you ever known me to plan poorly, Del?'

Delroy shook his head. 'I think this thing with Lennox is the first time I've seen you make the wrong call. That and not coming to work for me.'

Lamont assessed his words, silence hanging heavily in the air.

'Believe me when I say two things; Lennox will be eliminated, and I will take down Akhan.'

'How, L? You're not talking about a rival such as Lenny or even me. You're talking about a warlord. A man with unlimited resources. Even if we combined, we couldn't match up.'

'There are powerful forces at play, Del. Together, we can win, against Akhan, then against Lennox. We both have a stake in this. He had my ex-girlfriend killed, and he took out two of your children. Not only do we have the green light to engage, but I know exactly how to damage Akhan's organisation beyond repair.'

It took Delroy only a few seconds to fully comprehend what Lamont had told him. He leaned forward.

'Tell me more.'

'Look at the size of that place . . .'

Akeem and Jamal were in a black Ford 4x4, watching Akhan's base of operations with binoculars.

They had picked carefully for the mission. Only ten highly skilled men had been selected, including them. They would work in two groups, and were already scattered around. A few of the men were Akeem's, and the rest were from Delroy's hit teams. They were all dressed in black, carrying powerful automatic weaponry. Stefanos had given them everything. He provided the layout of the base, along with blind spots, camera locations, and the details of exactly who would be in and at what time. It was no coincidence they were here in the middle of the night. Only a skeleton crew would oversee at least one hundred kilos of product.

They had staked the place out as best they could, not wanting the same problems that had befallen their attempt at storming Lennox's Cottingley base.

'Is everyone in place?' Asked Akeem. Jamal made a call on a disposable phone. He spoke for a few moments, then hung up.

'Everyone's in play.'

'Okay, let's move.'

The pair exited the ride, blending in with the night. The base was a warehouse on the outskirts of Bradford. It looked huge from the outside and had two cars parked in the small car park. The sign said something about textiles. They had learned Akhan's imports were hidden in textiles equipment, which was an effective cover.

TARGET PART TWO: THE TAKEDOWN

Sneaking around to the side of the warehouse, Akeem typed the code they had been given into the side door. There was a camera above the door, but it only turned one way. The security neglected to mention this to Akhan after a bribe, and the team were using it to their advantage.

Jamal entered the building, Akeem covering. From their studying of the blueprints, they knew there were two control rooms; one twenty yards down the hall from them, and the other at the far side. They made their way along the corridors to the control room at the far side. There was a man staring at his phone, laughing. He was the nighttime overseer, the man who gave orders to everyone else in the base during the night. Before he could blink, Akeem and Jamal had their weapons trained on him. He glared, but didn't move.

'On the floor. Now,' Jamal growled, the weapon pointing at the overseer's chest. He didn't look afraid, but slowly complied, lying face down on the floor. Akeem covered Jamal whilst he secured the man, tying up his arms and legs, then stuffing a rag in his mouth. They used his system to turn off the cameras. They saw four more people on the premises, bagging large quantities of cocaine in a room.

'Right, you guys can come in now. Go straight to Room B.' Akeem hurried from the room with Jamal at his tail. They heard yelling and movements, but no gunshots. They secured the other rooms, finding no resistance, then headed to Room B.

Akeem and Delroy's teams had secured the workers. Jamal's legs shook at the sight in front of him. He was no stranger to drug spots in his time. This was on another scale. There were bricks and bricks of product, all sealed and lined up. Some of it was already boxed up, the boxes hosting the same Textile insignia on the outside of the building.

'Are the trucks ready?' Akeem asked one of his men. The soldier nodded.

'Get all of this loaded up. You and you stay here and make sure this lot try nothing. No one will get hurt if they don't resist.'

Lamont was in his office drinking a cup of coffee when he got the call he had been waiting for. He paused a few beats, before answering the PGP phone.

'Hello?'

'Where is it?'

Lamont took another sip.

'I'm sorry, who is this?'

'Teflon, I beg of you not to play games with me. My compound was attacked. Well-trained men made off with a tremendous amount of product. I want this back immediately. If I get it, there will be no further conflict.'

Lamont again waited. Akhan was on the back foot for once, and he relished it. The move on the warehouse had been a success. As per the arrangement, the drugs were being guarded by Lamont's people, with Delroy's men in reserve. They didn't have a final count, but there were well over one hundred kilos, and that was just the cocaine.

He grinned, realising this was the first time Akhan had made his own phone call.

'You're presuming that I know what you're talking about.'

'Teflon, I politely asked you not to play games. I want the product back. If I have to, I will tear apart Chapeltown and the surrounding areas to find it.'

'No, you won't.'

'Excuse me?'

'Let's cut the shit and act like two men who know all about this business. Now, you want the consignment. I understand that. I'm willing to deal with you.'

'There will be no deals. I have told you what I want.'

'Are you sure? If I hang up on you now, I won't pick up the phone again.'

There was an ugly silence on the other end. Lamont wanted to smile, but stayed in the moment.

'What do you want?'

'The same thing I always wanted. To walk away, free of all retribution. I also want the name of the person who betrayed me, along with all material relating to that situation. If I get all of this, then you will get your product back.'

'Done. We will meet in twenty-four hours and exchange information. My men will have the videos and paperwork pertaining to your personal situation. You will verify that these are original, undoctored copies. You will bring the product to the location, and we will both send our respective teams on their way. Is this a deal?'

'Yes. Now, who was it who told you what transpired with me last summer?'

There was a long silence, and then Akhan uttered one name.

'Chink.'

Lamont clenched his fists as Akhan continued.

'He approached me in an official capacity, wanting me to work with him. He proposed a great deal of money upfront, and as a sweetener, he gave me information about you, and what you had done.'

It all made sense now. Chink was excellent at staying under the radar. It was his kind of move, and it might have worked, had he not been murdered.

'Are you still there, Teflon?'

'Yes.'

'Twenty-four hours, and we will end this for good. One last thing, in turn for the information that I have provided you with . . .'

Lamont finished his coffee. 'Name it.'

'Who told you where my drugs were kept? Very few people knew this information.'

'Lennox Thompson.'

'Nonsense. He is a bandit. There is no way he could have found out that information.'

'He's resourceful. He can find things when he needs to. He gave me the information before we became enemies. I held off until I needed to.'

'I see.' Lamont heard the anger in Akhan's tone, maintaining an indifference that he knew added credibility to his story.

'I would never try to tell you your business, but I would be careful going after him. He's a dangerous man.'

'We will speak again in twenty-four hours.' With a click, Akhan was gone.

Lamont placed his phone on the desk, a wide smile encompassing his face. He was almost finished. He was so close to the finish line, and this time, there would be no stumbles. He hoped that Jenny was looking down, and that she saw the lengths he was going to in order to be free. He stared into space a while longer, then he rose to his feet.

There was still work to be done.

———

DARREN FROWNED AT HIS PHONE, sipping the bottle of Lucozade clutched in his hand. He was with Maka and Terry. They had been told that business was back to normal. There had been whisperings of things going on in the background, Delroy's men being seen with theirs, which he didn't understand.

'Guys, am I missing something?'

Terry glanced at Maka, then to Darren.

'About what?'

'Everything. We're smacking around Lenny's men, then we're not. Then we're back to business, now Delroy's people are around. I don't get it.'

Maka sniggered.

'Lennox made the biggest mistake of his life when he went at Tef's girl. Tef will murder him. That's a given.'

'It's mad, though. We're warring because Tef's ex got killed?' Darren held up a hand before Maka could reply. 'I know, fam. He's the boss, and he calls the shots. He's done a lot for all of us, but we're talking about war. We could die or get locked up tomorrow. I guess I just wanna make sure I'm doing it for the right reasons.'

TARGET PART TWO: THE TAKEDOWN

Sharma's words to Darren had made him delve deeper into the situation, looking past the money and responsibility. There was a price to be paid for his new success, and he was terrified about paying it.

'Don't worry, just be careful, because we've all got targets on our backs. I trust Tef, and whatever he's doing, I know it's gonna be good for us,' said Maka. Before Darren could respond, one of Akeem's men entered.

'You two are needed outside,' he said, pointing to Maka and Darren.

'What about me?' Terry asked. A look from Akeem's man had him glancing at the floor. Darren and Maka followed the man, who signalled to a black 4x4 vehicle. They climbed in the back. Akeem waited, dressed for combat, openly wearing a bullet-proof vest over a dark sweater. Darren felt his hands tremble as the reality of the situation started to sink in.

'Everything good?' He asked.

'Yeah, the lines are smooth. Pure dodgy things going on, though. What the hell's up with Delroy's people?'

'That will be explained soon enough. For now, Teflon needs you to front an important deal.'

'What's the deal for?' Maka asked. Darren remained quiet, his heart pounding.

'You'll see. Meet me out here this evening at seven. You won't need anything. I'll speak to you then.'

'What was that all about?' Darren asked. Maka didn't reply, his jaw clenched as they watched Akeem drive away, wondering what would transpire next.

LAMONT LOOKED around Stefanos's garden. It was practically a field, seeming to stretch on as far as his eye could see. He kept his hands jammed in his pockets, his fleece coat and boots doing an excellent job of keeping out the cold. He wished he'd opted for a scarf.

He'd always hated the cold with a passion. Jenny had liked winter, he remembered. It struck him that they hadn't spent much of one together. Their first winter together had been fraught with his recovery. He didn't even remember what he had done last Christmas, but he was sure it was done under the haze of painkillers.

'L.'

Lamont whirled around, shocked that Stefanos had managed to sneak up on him. He wore a jumper, fleece trousers, and shoes, a broad smile on his bushy face.

'I called out to you several times, but you were in your own world.'

'Sorry about that. I was just thinking.'

'About what, if you don't mind me prying?'

'Jen. I was remembering that she used to love winter, and I always hated it. The cold reminded me.'

Stefanos met his eyes, smiling sadly.

'She used to write long letters to Santa when she was younger, detailing exactly how good she had been, and why she deserved presents. Halloween, Bonfire Night and Christmas. She loved them all.'

'I never got to spend much of a winter with her . . . My recovery was long.'

'I heard. We will talk about my daughter in greater detail soon enough, but I have more information to relay to you. It relates to Akhan.'

Lamont straightened.

'What is it?'

'He will come for you. Regardless of how the exchange goes down later.'

'Let him,' said Lamont. He and Delroy's partnership would need to contend with Akhan's shooters.

'Akhan has a tremendous amount of resource.' Stefanos had a shrewd expression on his face.

'I won't be subjugated, and I won't back down. I faced death once before, and I'm still here. Let him come.'

Stefanos was silent, looking out at the darkening sky.

'Come inside, please.'

Lamont followed him. Akeem knew where he was, but if this was an ambush, he wouldn't be able to reach Lamont in time. His heart hammered, but he controlled his emotions, looking for potential escape points.

'Take off your shoes in the hallway, please.'

Lamont unlaced his boots, expecting to feel a gun being pressed to the back of his head. No such action came.

'Would you like to take your jacket off?'

Lamont shrugged out of his jacket, and Stefanos hung it up for him.

'Follow me.'

He followed Stefanos down the hallway. They entered a room. It contained a small sofa, an office desk and a computer. In the corner was a roaring fire, and on the sofa, a man sat. He was brown-skinned, with cropped hair and a tailored beard. He wore a black shirt, trousers, and had his shoes on. He stared at Lamont with fathomless dark eyes, a small smile on his ratty face. Lamont remembered seeing him at the warehouse with Stefanos.

'Lamont, this is Jakkar. He is a friend of our friend Akhan.'

Lamont shook his hand. His grip wasn't as firm as Stefanos's, but he still felt the strength of him.

'Nice to meet you, Lamont.'

'Tell me about Akhan.'

Jakkar's smile widened.

'You work with him, correct?'

Lamont nodded.

'How do you find him?'

Lamont considered this for a moment.

'Resourceful.'

It was Jakkar who nodded now.

'Akhan was bred for this life. I knew him growing up. He was skinny, frail, a magnet for the bullies. Like many smart people, he learned to use his weaknesses to his advantage. He was hungry and willing to do what needed to be done. These traits brought him to the attention of The Council.'

'Tell me about this council.' Lamont had never heard of them.

'One thing at a time. Akhan began working for the council. He was in place as a lackey, but he waited, and he listened. He rose through the ranks until he was given control of the drugs at a local scale. He took this to England and worked to make it stick. Others were in play in different areas doing the same, but Akhan started showing the council a lot of return for their investment. They gave him more drugs. He was loyal, or so it seemed.'

'What do you mean?'

'In 1989, Akhan asked for permission to leave. He promised to pay a five percent tax for life, but wanted to work for himself. The council vetoed his request, and he attempted to go rogue. Fourteen of his men, both here and in the Middle East, were slaughtered. He returned to the fold, but he wasn't beaten.'

Lamont's heart hammered as he processed everything he was being told.

'When Akhan returned, he was seemingly loyal. But, he was moving money around and making his own connections. He invested in local housing in areas such as Chapeltown, where drugs and crime were rife. He sat on these properties and, in the early 2000s, sold them and made a ton of money. His own money.'

Lamont saw where this was going. 'He was trying to establish his independence.'

'Akhan saw his way out as a purely financial one. He wanted to amass his own wealth so he could gain his freedom from the council. He began working many schemes, ensuring the council was paid, but lining his own pockets at the same time. When funds were low, he blamed it on recession and promised to get things working.'

'He was skimming.'

'Millions of pounds, over a nearly twenty-year period. He bribed many of the council's emissaries. Finally, they sent me.'

'Why finally?'

'I wanted to be the one to end this little reign. Akhan has run unchecked. I warned the council of his ambition and advised them to restrain him. Finally, they are listening to me.'

Lamont watched Jakkar. His eyes were hard as he talked of Akhan. He thought of Chink. Chink, too, had ambition. Even when they were dirt poor, he always planned to be rich. He wondered what Chink would have become if he hadn't befriended him.

'So, it's your turn now. Why?'

'You'll have to be more specific.'

'Why do you want to bring down Akhan? You've become profitable under his charge.'

'I was profitable long before I met Akhan. He forced me into a servitude that I didn't want.'

'So it's freedom you desire . . .?'

'Always.'

CHAPTER TWENTY-TWO
SATURDAY 4 APRIL, 2015

DARREN SWALLOWED DOWN HIS FEAR.

Akeem had briefed him and Maka. He knew the meeting involved their supplier, but that was all. They were outside a building, five of them in all. Maka was near a wall, staring at the ground. Darren had tried speaking with him about the situation, but he wasn't talking. Darren motioned to the surrounding men to drop the bags on the floor. It was a simple drop-off. They had driven the consignment in a white transit van emblazoned with the name of a haulage company. If anyone was diligent enough to Google the company, it would bounce back with nothing.

He checked the time. The supplier's men had let them in. They seemed unfriendly, but hadn't been hostile so far.

Darren was shocked at the size of the building. It had various doors and sections, almost like an office building. He noted a camera pointing down at them, but noticed there was no blinking red light. He felt the hairs on his arms stand on end, his palm itching. There was a whirring noise as the metal gate by the entrance slowly rose.

A black panel van coasted into the main room, followed by a 4x4 vehicle. Men descended from both vehicles, eight in all, all

TARGET PART TWO: THE TAKEDOWN

armed to the teeth. Darren didn't look to Maka or the other men, but sensed their anxiety. They were outnumbered.

'Good of you to join us,' a man said, climbing from the passenger seat of the 4x4. Darren froze. He'd been briefed on Saj and knew he reported to Akhan.

'There's the stuff. We'll be on our way.' Darren motioned to the men with the bags. Saj smirked.

'There has been a change of plan.' Saj raised an arm, and his men pointed their weapons at the group. 'Call Teflon. Tell him to come to this warehouse. If he does not come, or is delayed, then you will die.'

'What the hell—'

'There is a time for wondering, and there is a time for action. Make the call to your boss immediately, or die.'

Darren tensed, slowly reaching for his phone. He located the number with shaking hands and pressed the call button.

'Tef?' he said after a moment, looking at Saj to confirm Lamont had answered. 'I'm here now. Listen, Saj is here. Yes.' Darren grinned. 'They acted exactly as you predicted.'

Before Saj could react, he and the others hit the floor as doors all around the warehouse opened. Men armed with automatic rifles opened fire on Saj's crew. They tried turning their guns onto the invaders, but were too slow. They were cut down before they could let off a shot.

When the gunfire subsided, Darren motioned to the shooters to finish any survivors. As he and Maka left the building, they heard a few bursts of gunfire, then silence. They changed into spare clothing hidden in the back of the van, placing the worn clothing into a single black sports bag. Once done, they climbed back into the van and drove away, leaving Akeem's hired killers to take care of the clean-up.

Lamont sat in his office with Akeem, waiting for the confirmation to come through. He'd suspected a double-cross. The first flag had been the need to wait twenty-four hours. It was too long for a man of Akhan's calibre. He moved quickly, reaching out to Stefanos about more locations of Akhan's. Stefanos reported back with the best locations, and his men spread themselves, trying to find the right one. When they'd seen Akhan's team setting up a few hours ago, they'd sprung the trap.

'You should have set the warehouse on fire with the bodies inside,' said Akeem.

'I wanted him to know that he couldn't beat me.'

'You're not thinking about the bigger picture. You are already becoming more of a target with the police. This display will only further propel your name out there.'

'Akhan has plenty of enemies. There's no reason my name should be the one people hear.'

'And, if he works against you with the police?'

Lamont rubbed his eyes. Akeem was giving him food for thought. He'd never contemplated the possibility of Akhan choosing to work with the police.

'We'll cross that bridge when we get to it.'

The pair sat in silence until Lamont's phone rang. He checked the number and put the phone on speaker.

'Yes?'

'It's done.'

Darren hung up. Lamont grinned at Akeem.

'How long do you think it will take for Akhan to ring?'

'I'm guessing ten minutes.'

Three minutes later, his phone rang.

'Nice to hear from you, Akhan.'

'That was a mistake, Teflon. I'm sorry to say you won't live long enough to regret making it.'

'Remember, you started this. All I did was retaliate.'

'You really think you can win against me?'

Lamont hung up. Akeem calmly assessed him, waiting for instruction.

'Put everyone on alert.'

LAMONT HAD A FITFUL SLEEP, tossing and turning, drifting off after three in the morning. He was up by seven, showering and shovelling down some breakfast. He'd spoken with Delroy. They had all bases covered, waiting for Akhan's fist to come down. Lamont hoped he hadn't overextended himself.

Lennox was still a ghost, as was Shorty. He didn't know if he would ever see Shorty again, and now that the anger had abated, that feeling hurt. He rubbed his eyes. There was no time for sentiment. There were too many things going on. When everything died down, he would locate Shorty, and they would talk.

Lamont checked in with Akeem, who was on the frontline, organising both their soldiers and Delroy's. They hadn't decided how to distribute the drugs without upsetting the flow, so they were being kept in storage for now. The split would be fifty/fifty, and profits would be huge. Lamont was considering the idea of moving them out of town, but it wasn't his top priority. He'd started to doze off when his phone began ringing, startling him. He wiped his eyes and answered.

'Yes?'

'We need to see you.'

THEY WERE at Stefanos's home again. Lamont noted that he hadn't seen Jenny's mother either time he had visited, but shrugged it off. Jakkar waited in the study. He greeted Lamont with a smile and a handshake. Stefanos offered drinks, but they declined.

'Excellently done, Lamont. You played Akhan beautifully, but he will come for you with all his force now. He'll attack your men, your drug spots, your family. This is a dangerous path you've undertaken,' said Jakkar.

Lamont shook his head. 'I know what he's capable of, but I'm the wrong person to back into a corner. He underestimated me, and it's cost him both money and men. My team are ready, no matter what direction he wants to take it.'

'Are you truly prepared to take it to the wire?' Stefanos spoke now.

Lamont already had his answer ready.

'Your daughter was my reason to leave. Akhan prevented that for his own ends, manipulating me into a position that meant I couldn't stop her murder. No matter what happens, he doesn't survive, nor does Lennox.'

'This will help you,' Stefanos fished into his pocket and removed a piece of paper. He looked at Jakkar before handing it to Lamont. Lamont glanced at the scribbled address. He looked up at both men, who were gauging his reaction.

'What's this for?'

'That's Akhan's home address.'

LAMONT CLUTCHED THE ADDRESS TIGHTLY. His men had worked overtime trying to collate this information in the streets, bribing people and threatening others. Nothing had worked. Now, Stefanos had pulled this out of nowhere.

'Where did you get this?'

'It wasn't hard,' Jakkar spoke up again. 'It's sensible to keep a close eye on a dangerous subordinate.'

'And now you want me to do your dirty work for you,' replied Lamont, letting the pair know he was hip to the attempted manipulation.

'You stated you won't allow him to survive. We're simply helping.'

'This has to benefit you in some way.' He studied the pair,

concentrating on their body language, looking for the slightest slip. They were composed, almost amused by his attempts.

'It's up to you if you choose to do it. If you don't, this will be the last we speak of it.' Jakkar slid to his feet. Stefanos followed suit, glancing at Lamont, who recognised it was time to leave. He shook hands with both men as Stefanos walked them to the exit. Jakkar lingered, smiling at him.

'It was nice to meet you, Teflon. I hope this isn't the last time.'

'I'm confident it won't be,' said Lamont, as he left, the piece of paper with Akhan's address in his pocket.

———

LAMONT HEADED HOME, staring at the address. He had in his hands the power to change his whole life. He couldn't comprehend Stefanos's motives, but Akhan had outlived his usefulness with them, and they were willing to let him die. There were questions he needed to be answered, but for now, he had to do it. He had to go to Akhan.

———

AKEEM DROVE. It had started raining earlier in the afternoon, and the roads were slick. Lamont played with the leather gloves he wore, trying to imagine how Shorty, Marcus and the rest had done this so often. He thought back to his earlier days, when he'd gone on a job with Marcus, and how terrified he had been. He remembered fighting Ricky Reagan for his life. That murder had stained him, but it was necessary. What happened tonight would also be necessary.

Akeem was armed. Lamont was too. He couldn't remember the last time he'd held a gun, but the 9mm felt comfortable, and he wasn't sure how to feel about that. Akeem pulled to a stop fifty yards from Akhan's house, turning to him.

'Are you sure about this?'

'Yes.'

They were shocked at the location. Akhan lived in a simple semi-detached house in Bradford. There were no signs of wealth. A Mercedes was parked outside, but looked several years old. There was a single light on downstairs.

'Follow me. Keep the weapon down until you need to use it. He doesn't look to have any security measures in place, but if he does, I'll disable them,' said Akeem.

Lamont expected sophisticated, state-of-the-art security, or at least guards patrolling. He saw the move for what it was: arrogance. Akhan had never considered the idea that anyone would get close to him, and now he would pay for it.

Lamont blew out a breath, trying to calm down. His senses were on overdrive, sure that every sound was something harmful. Akeem disappeared around the side of the house as he crouched in the garden, hoping he was well-hidden. He heard a sound to his left, and his heart leapt in his chest as he raised his gun, but it was just a cat. In any other situation, he would have laughed.

Akeem materialised next to Lamont after another minute.

'I've double-checked the perimeter. There might be an alarm when I break in, so move quickly toward the room with the light. If it looks bad, shoot first, ask questions later.'

Lamont nodded. Akeem took a tool from his pocket, and started fiddling with the back door. It opened, and they slipped through. There was no sound, but he crept into the house, listening to the rain tapping relentlessly against the roof and windows.

Soft piano music came from one of the rooms. Other than that, there were no sounds. No one else seemed to be in the house. Lamont moved along the hallway, looking at the classical paintings on the wall, illuminated by the soft lighting, dotted along like an exhibit in a museum. He followed the music, his heart hammering, hoping he wasn't walking into a trap. He paused outside the lit room, able to hear the music clearly now. It was *Mozart's Requiem*. He pushed gently at the door, then entered.

The room was larger than it appeared from the outside. It was full of books, a large desk, and two regal leather chairs. It reminded Lamont of his own study. The music blared from an old CD player against the wall—a Hitachi. The room had large, Georgian-style windows. At these windows, Akhan stood, looking out at the rain, and giving no indication he'd heard the door opening.

Lamont stood and watched him, and for a few moments, neither man spoke.

'Are you going to do it then?'

Akhan's voice startled him. The elderly man faced him now. He wore an impressively white shirt, grey trousers and matching grey tie. His expression was impassive.

'I have to.'

'I know,' said Akhan. 'Everything is in order. I worked out what was going on when Stefanos stopped returning my calls. He had you do his dirty work.'

'No, he didn't.'

'You don't think so?'

'You forced this, when you forced my hand. You made me stay in this life and cost me everything. For what? So you could make more money? How's that going to help you now?'

'This is your destiny.' Akhan ignored his questions. His hands rested by his sides. Lamont raised the pistol. The cleaning team was already on standby. He wanted to talk more. He wanted to question Akhan, but it had gone beyond that. Both men knew it.

'Remember. One day, you'll be where I am, and you'll be staring down the gun. When you pull the trigger, you will never be free.'

Lamont nodded at Akhan's final words.

'Freedom is a myth. Thank you for teaching me the lesson.'

Then, he fired.

CHAPTER TWENTY-THREE
MONDAY 6 APRIL, 2015

LAMONT AWOKE THE NEXT DAY, feeling strangely light. The spectre of Akhan was removed. The cleaners had done their job, but he had several alibis just in case. As he used the bathroom and washed his hands, his only regret was that Jenny wasn't there to enjoy it with him. Sadly, her murder had been the catalyst to force him to take action. Lennox was next.

Lamont spent a long time in the shower, then picked out a khaki polo shirt and black jeans. His phone rang as he was forcing breakfast down his throat. Akeem was outside. Grabbing his wallet and dumping the remains of the cereal, he left.

'Stefanos wants to see you,' was all Akeem said, as Lamont buckled himself into the passenger seat, then busied himself looking out the window at the fractured streets. Chapeltown was capable of so much more. With Lamont at the helm, spearheading the change, pumping money into the community, it could reach its full potential.

Akeem stopped outside a small office building. They climbed out, and they were shown inside by a dumpy, grey-haired woman with olive skin and a sweet smile. Stefanos rose from his seat when he saw them. Pumping Lamont's hand, then Akeem's, he signalled for both men to take a seat.

'Can I get you gentlemen anything to drink?'

They both shook their heads.

'That will be everything, Agatha,' Stefanos said to the elderly woman. She left with a swift nod.

'How are you feeling?' Stefanos asked.

'Well-rested.'

'I heard from Jakkar early this morning. He spoke of a home invasion. I have people in the local press who will write up that story. The killers will never be found. Akhan's family will bury him back home, and likely stay there. There is panic among the people who worked for him. They are worried about where the next meal will come from.'

'I'm sure Jakkar will plug the gap.'

Stefanos smiled slowly.

'He has a way of doing this. You.'

A flush of adrenaline tingled through Lamont's body.

'What do you mean?'

'Jakkar wants you to take Akhan's place. He wants you to run the entire Yorkshire distribution for the council.'

'That's ridiculous. I'm not even Asian,' spluttered Lamont. Stefanos allowed himself a wider grin.

'It's a brave new world, predicated on trust far more than bloodlines. You have done them a service, and they recognise your worth.'

Lamont shared a look with Akeem, his bodyguard's face blank. He'd always thought himself a decent poker player, but he was sure Akeem would best him if they ever played.

'Is this an offer, or a demand?'

A chill descended over the office. Every man in the room knew precisely where Lamont was going with the question, and Stefanos wasted no time answering.

'The days of you being forced to do anything against your will are over. There will be no attempt at blackmail. This is an opportunity for you to assume control of your destiny.'

'By answering to someone else.'

Stefanos shook his head, looking almost disappointed.

'Everyone answers to someone. But, this life we live is all about power. It's about ascending, so we hold dominion over more and look up to fewer. You take this position, and you will experience true power.'

'Like Akhan did?'

'Akhan was greedy. He sought to overthrow the council, and they took necessary action. I have more faith in you.'

'You believe I should take it then?'

'I do.'

'Why?'

'Because I need my daughter's death to mean something.'

Lamont's stomach lurched, and for a moment, he was back cradling Jenny's cold body against his. He would never be rid of the images that plagued his thoughts. She shouldn't have died. Lamont still believed this with every fibre that remained of his heart.

'My daughter was touched by greatness. She hadn't even begun to utilise her gifts. I don't want you to waste your potential.'

'I wouldn't. I have money and investments in place. There's no risk of going to prison.'

Stefanos shot him a look. 'If you don't want to go to prison, then don't. You put together a formidable team on the streets. Everyone played their roles, and you all made money. This is the opportunity to do that on a larger scale.'

Lamont was quiet for a moment.

'I promised your daughter that I would walk away.'

Stefanos's eyes were gentle. 'I believe you meant it when you said it, Lamont, but you were forced to break that promise. You want to honour my daughter's memory? Do it by wielding power from the seat you earned.'

TARGET PART TWO: THE TAKEDOWN

'I'm . . . filled with so much guilt,' Lamont admitted, feeling the lump in his throat as the words tumbled from his mouth.

'About my daughter?' Stefanos hadn't taken his eyes from him.

'About many things. My parents had high hopes for me, yet I picked a life that keeps me at the bottom. I pedal misery.'

'That's life. You may not be working a nine-to-five for *The Man*, but it's up to you how you affect your community. If you want to be a force for good, do it from a position of power.' Stefanos paused, his eyes alight with the passion of his words. 'It's all about power,' he repeated.

Lamont took a few moments to consider.

'I'll do it.'

Stefanos grinned. 'I hoped you would. I'll be in touch. We have much to discuss.'

LAMONT LEFT the meeting with a spring in his step. He would speak with Delroy about the situation later. For now, he had some other issues to resolve. As Akeem drove, he dialled a number.

'Hey, L. How are you feeling?'

'Will you go for dinner with me?'

Lamont heard her breath catch. He waited.

'You want to go on a date?'

'Yes.'

'Why?'

'Because we get along.'

Charlotte didn't speak for a moment. He could almost hear the conflict churning within, but he wasn't worried.

'Okay. I'll let you arrange everything.'

'I'll be in touch.'

Putting his phone away, he again thought about Jenny. He needed to let her go. He'd made his decision about the life, and he needed to be stronger than he'd been before. Charlotte had experienced the crime life with both Justin and King. He didn't know if things with them would go anywhere, but they could help each other.

Akeem drove to a spot in Moortown. Darren sat in the living room playing on a PlayStation. He hopped to his feet when he saw Lamont, dropping the pad.

'Teflon? What are you doing here? I mean, shit, is everything good?'

Lamont smiled at his nervousness.

'I wanted to personally thank you for your recent work. You stepped up when I needed you to, and I want to reward that.'

Darren started protesting, but stopped speaking when Akeem gave him an envelope. His mouth widened at the array of notes.

'Akeem said you preferred cash to direct transfer. I'm different, but to each his own.'

'Thank you, man. I mean, there's thousands here.'

'Plenty more where that came from. A lot of change is coming, and our money will go through the roof. I want you to work with Maka and recruit. Don't rush it. We want capable men. Can you handle that?'

'Yeah, course I can, boss. Thank you.'

Lamont grinned.

'I know you were worried about how things would go. That's fine. I'd be more concerned if you weren't. Focus on your task, and when the time is right, we'll discuss more.'

WHEN LAMONT LEFT, Darren pumped his fist.

'Yes!'

His heartbeat raced. The rumours of an alliance between Delroy and Lamont were true, the team was on the rise, and he would be right there when it all happened. He dialled Clarissa, tapping his foot and waiting for her to pick up.

'Daz, what's up?'

'Book a holiday. Anywhere you like. First-class even.'

TARGET PART TWO: THE TAKEDOWN

'Oh my God, babe! Are you serious?'

'Deadly serious. Look, I'm gonna come and see you soon, but get looking. We're gonna do it big!'

LAMONT STOPPED AT MARIKA'S. He'd called ahead and arranged it after realising he didn't know where now she lived. The house was off Roundhay road and appeared comfortable.

The gate squeaked as he entered the garden, and the door swung open. Marika looked more like their mother every time Lamont saw her, and it made his heart ache. He wasn't sure about greetings, but when she flung her arms around him, he clutched her tightly. Minutes passed before they let go, neither looking the other in the eye, embarrassed over the show of vulnerability.

'Are you okay?'

He nodded.

'Day by day. How are the kids?'

'Getting older. They want to do their own thing more, but still.'

'I'm glad you're doing well, sis. Sorry I haven't contacted you. I've been dealing with some shit.'

'I know. I saw how you were at the funeral. I really am sorry about Jenny. She was right for you.'

Lamont nodded, remembering his thoughts earlier.

'Thank you.'

'Have you heard from K-Bar?'

'My solicitors are working on his case as we speak. Why?'

Marika let out a deep breath.

'We're involved, okay?'

Lamont couldn't help it; he laughed. Marika glared, hand on her hip.

'Why are you laughing?'

'You just love the thugs, don't you?'

She grinned. 'K-Bar's not a thug. He just does bad things sometimes. I thought you'd be angry.'

'I don't have the right. I've made too many mistakes lately to judge anyone, sis. If you want to be with K-Bar, I have no problem with that. I'll get him out, no matter the cost.'

Marika squeezed his hand, and he smiled.

'Come with me. I want to take you to see someone.'

———

LAMONT, Marika, and Akeem walked along the hospital corridors until they found the correct room.

Amy sat by Grace's bed, watching her daughter, still hooked up to complex machines. Lamont's heart lurched when he thought of the proud, wilful little girl who always made him take her to the shop. The little girl he viewed as a niece; same as Bianca. Amy looked at him, but didn't move. He kissed her on the cheek, noting how cold she felt.

'How is she?'

'She's still fighting, but she's not in the clear yet.'

'Is there anything I can do?'

She shook her head.

'I took a leave of absence from work. They understand the situation, and there's no pressure to get me back.'

'Do you need money?'

'I'm fine, L. Even if I wasn't, your boy took care of that.'

'You've heard from Shorty?'

Amy hesitated, then shook her head. Ignoring the strange gesture, Lamont glanced at Marika, remembering she was unaware of the fallout between him and Shorty. He would check with Stacey to see if she too had received any money from Shorty. If possible, he would use it to track down his friend.

'I'll come back and see you soon, Ames. Please ring me if anything changes.'

———

TARGET PART TWO: THE TAKEDOWN

THAT AFTERNOON, Lamont and Akeem were at his home. They'd been planning strategy for several hours, and both were yawning from fatigue. It had been a trying period. Lamont was ready to leave Akeem in charge and take a break, but he needed things to be solidified.

'Lennox must have family; some connection keeping him in Leeds other than revenge. Between ourselves and Delroy, we'll find it. For now, Darren and Maka will handle recruitment. You'll oversee them. My legal team are working with K-Bar. When we understand the new scope of the operation, we'll get into that aspect of it. My thinking is—'

Lamont's phone vibrated, and he snatched it up, annoyed.

'Who is this?' His eyes widened, and he stumbled towards the door, Akeem watching him in alarm.

'L?'

'We need to go. Someone blew up the barbers.'

AKEEM'S RIDE sped through the streets as Lamont made more phone calls, trying to find someone who could confirm if Trinidad was okay. He'd tried calling his direct number, but couldn't get through. Panic gnawed at his insides. Trinidad wasn't involved in this. He wondered if it was Lennox, or if Akhan had orchestrated something before his murder.

There was a crowd already gathered. They pushed through them, but it was futile. Lamont saw the firefighters nearby, trying to put out the blaze. His building, the first one he ever owned. Akeem moved forward, asking about survivors, but Lamont knew it was too late. Trinidad would have been working. He never took days off.

With a lurch, he thought about the only other thing he valued; his father's chessboard. Someone would pay for this, he decided, clenching his fists. Akeem headed back over.

'I spoke with the fireman, he said—'

There were two sharp cracks from a gun, and Akeem toppled to the floor, unmoving. The shooter, a skinny teenage kid, looked at Lamont, grinned, then disappeared into the crowd.

People screamed, running to get away as Lamont stared dumbly down at his bleeding bodyguard, his building burning in the background.

EPILOGUE

RIGBY WAS in his office catching up on paperwork when Murphy bounded over.

'Rig, you're not going to believe this.'

'Can it wait? I've got a lot of paperwork to do.'

Murphy turned Rigby's chair, so his colleague faced him.

'What the bloody hell is wrong with you? I just said that I've got work to do.'

'Trust me; you want to hear this. K-Bar's solicitor is trying to reach us.'

Rigby forgot about his paperwork in an instant. They had charged K-Bar, but he hadn't received a court date yet. All attempts to speak with him had been stonewalled, and an expensive and tricky legal team were fighting his corner.

'Why?'

Murphy's yellow-toothed grin was full of gleeful malice.

'K-Bar wants to talk.'

DID YOU ENJOY THE READ?

Thank you for reading book 3 in the Target series!

I wrote the first scene for Takedown back in 2009, and it was an exhaustive process to get it right.

I go into more detail on my blog, but Takedown showed me I could truly fulfil my dream of finishing the Target series in a satisfying manner.

Please take a minute or two to help me by leaving a review – even if it's just a few lines. Reviews help massively with getting my books in front of new readers. I personally read every review and take all feedback on board.

To support me, please click the relevant link below:

UK: http://www.amazon.co.uk/review/create-review?&asin=B081PC6N96

US: http://www.amazon.com/review/create-review?&asin=B081PC6N96

I'll see you at Book 4 for the conclusion of Lamont's journey!

TARGET PART 3 PREVIEW

Check out the first chapter of Target Part 2, The fourth and final book in the Target series

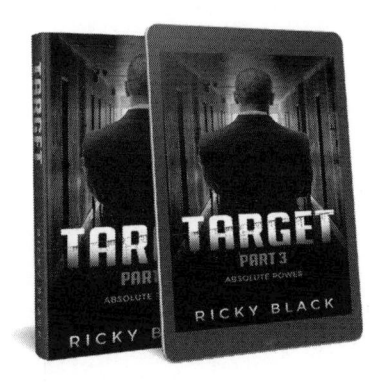

CHAPTER 24
CHAPTER ONE
MONDAY 6 APRIL, 2015

BEING a multimillionaire criminal engendered little community sympathy, yet as Lamont Jones stood on the tough streets of Chapeltown, he silently prayed for help. His eyes flitted from the bleeding man at his feet, to his burning building, as he tried desperately to think of a plan. He could hear the loud shouts of the firefighters and the screams of the people still brave enough to be standing there. The acrid stench of gunpowder stung his nostrils. Never in his life had Lamont felt more vulnerable. He didn't know if the shooter was still in the vicinity, or if there was more than one.

The gunman had given him a smile after pumping bullets into his bodyguard, Akeem. He couldn't take it. He was sick of all of it. As unnerved as he was, part of him wondered what that sweet release would feel like. He closed his eyes, ready for it to be over.

A second later, he opened them, feeling foolish. He needed to be strong. Now more than ever. Lamont pulled out his phone, and with only a split-second to decide between calling an ambulance or calling for backup, he made his choice.

'L, what's happening?' Asked Manson, one of his lieutenants, when he answered.

'There's a situation. The office got blown up. Trinidad is dead,

TARGET PART TWO: THE TAKEDOWN

Akeem got shot. I need people sweeping the Hood, looking for the shooter. He's skinny, short hair, light-skinned, wearing a black jacket and trackies. Question anyone you don't recognise. I need you to do this now.'

'Got it. Catch me up when I get there. I'll have people en route.'

Lamont hung up, again glancing down at Akeem before finally calling an ambulance, only to learn the firefighters had already called through. Akeem was unmoving, the pool of blood surrounding him growing by the second. He knelt down, trying to stem the bleeding. He didn't know what he was doing, or if he was making a difference, but he needed to try something. Marcus Daniels had died in his arms in a similar fashion two years ago, and he hoped history wasn't repeating itself. Giving the ambulance five minutes to arrive, Lamont called again, stressing that they needed to hurry.

He sensed the crowd growing closer and instinctively concealed his emotions. The idea the shooter could be watching meshed with the rage he felt. Lennox had caught him off-guard, and given Lamont yet another reason to hunt him down.

'You're going to make it,' he said quietly to Akeem, his hands warm with the man's blood. The wet body armour had done nothing to stop the bullets. The crowd's murmuring grew louder. A man had his phone out, recording. A glance from Lamont, and he put the phone away, mumbling an apology.

'Let me help you,' a woman he didn't recognise pushed her way through the crowd. 'I have medical training.'

He stepped away, overcome with dizziness. Nothing about the situation seemed real, but it was. This was life for him.

The sounds of screeching tyres announced Lamont's people arriving in two cars. Manson jumped out, along with half a dozen other men. They hurried over, most of the crowd dispersing when they noticed.

'I've got people sweeping the Hood now. Which direction did he run in?'

'He ran toward Nassau Place,' said Lamont. Manson shouted

instructions, and four men peeled off, hurrying back to the car and driving away. Manson looked from Lamont to Akeem, his face solemn.

'We need to get you out of here.'

'I'm not leaving him,' said Lamont immediately. He didn't know if the woman was helping, but she was checking airways, keeping one hand pressed to the bleeding area. She certainly seemed more composed than he was. Manson gripped his shoulder, stealing his attention.

'You're too exposed out here. Trust me, you need to go.'

Still dazed, Lamont was bundled into the remaining car and driven away.

―――

AT HOME, Lamont waited for news about Akeem. Several hours had elapsed. Manson had checked in, saying they still hadn't found the shooter, and he was racking his brain trying to work out who it was. Lamont had been right in his sights, and the shooter had left him alone. He couldn't work out what Lennox was thinking. The conflict that had escalated between them could have ended right there.

Was he toying with him?

The thought filled him with both dread and frustration. It struck him that he knew little about Lennox's organisation. Even his assault on Nikkolo had only been possible because of the information Stefanos's contacts gave him. It was something he would need to rectify.

A shooting in public would need an immediate police response and investigation. There was nothing in the building or on records that would negatively link Lamont to the business. The business he had helped Trinidad grow. Trinidad was dead, and it was all his fault. Nausea swam over him, and he took several deep breaths, trying to control himself. Trinidad had died for his stupidity. He should have warned him of the danger, rather than leaving him to suffer.

Lamont paced the room, his temples throbbing. Trinidad had a family, and someone would need to contact them. The phone rang, and he scrambled to answer it.

'Lamont?'

It was his solicitor, Levine.

'Yes?'

'I don't know all the details of what you're involved in, but the police want to ask you some questions in connection with two murders.'

Lamont's stomach plummeted. He knew he had heard correctly, but still needed to check.

'*Two* murders?'

'A second man died on Chapeltown Road, and witnesses placed you at the scene. I want you to come to my office, and we will draft a statement together.'

Lamont didn't respond. Akeem was dead, and it hurt to hear. He closed his eyes, his shoulders slumping.

'Lamont. Are you listening?'

'I heard you. I will come to your office tomorrow.'

'Time is of the essence here. The police aren't looking to arrest you at this stage, but if I'm going to protect you, I need to know the facts.'

'I said, I will come tomorrow. Or did you forget you work for me and not the other way around?'

The coldness of Lamont's tone reminded Levine who he was dealing with.

'Tomorrow will be fine. I'll be in the office from ten.'

Lamont hung up without responding. There was no reason for him to react to Levine like that, yet he couldn't help it. The police wanting to speak to him was nothing important. He wouldn't be giving them any information that would help.

Sitting back down, he rubbed his temples and closed his eyes.

What the hell was Lennox thinking?

LENNOX THOMPSON WAITED for news of his attack with no emotion. He had prepared his message with care. Teflon had located one of his hidden spots. He didn't know how, but it had rattled him, and needed answering in kind. The plan was simple. He would destroy Teflon's business. Everyone knew he owned the barber shop, and that Trinidad ran it for him. It would send a clear-cut sign that war wasn't a good idea. If he showed, his shooter, Sinclair, was to kill whoever was with him. He wanted Teflon to know he could get him whenever he wanted.

The spot Lennox was in was on Well House Drive, off Roundhay Road. He had several spots dotted all around, and after Teflon had located one, he had instantly moved. It was spartan, with a television, a lumpy grey sofa, and a simple table in the middle of the living room.

Soon, two booming knocks at the door alerted him. He slid into a seat and waited for a worker to let them in.

The pair traipsed into the living room. One was stocky, with straight brown hair, steely blue eyes, and rugged features. The other, Sinclair, looked like a kid. He was twenty-four years old, but had the build and features of a teenager. Lennox signalled for both men to sit.

'Is it done?'

'Yes,' said the stocky man. He was Mark Patrick, and had been elevated by Lennox after Nikkolo's demise. He had served time in the army and had connections and experience with explosives. 'The owner bit it too.'

Lennox straightened in his seat. 'You killed Trinidad?'

'By the time we realised he was in there, it was too late.'

Lennox glared at him. 'You messed up.' He wasn't pulling punches.

'You wanted a message sent, and I sent it. He was an old man, and he was down with Teflon.'

TARGET PART TWO: THE TAKEDOWN

'He was a civilian.' Lennox continued to stare Mark down. 'Watch how you speak to me.'

'You should have let me drop Teflon too,' Sinclair added, bored with the conversation. 'His bodyguard went down easy. Never even saw it coming.'

Lennox ignored the boasting. 'We have a primary target in place. What happened today was payback, and Teflon will realise that.'

'Do you know how they found Nikkolo yet?' asked Mark. Lennox shook his head.

'I spoke with everyone connected with that hideout, and no one gave anything away. No one stands out either. It's possible they just got lucky, but I doubt it.'

'What's the next step then? Teflon and his people are gonna be gunning for you.'

'Set up a meeting with Nicky Derrigan.'

Mark and Sinclair exchanged looks. They knew Derrigan by reputation, and it wasn't a move they expected Lennox to make.

'Are you sure you want to go there?'

Lennox's stare only intensified, and Mark looked away.

'I'll make the call.'

DETECTIVE RIGBY WAITED in an interview room as K-Bar was shown in. His solicitor was with him, and they both took seats opposite Rigby. K-Bar appeared well for a man on remand. His expression remained as guarded as it had during the initial interview. He brushed a stray dreadlock from his face, not taking his eyes from Rigby, waiting for him to speak.

'You wanted to talk,' said Rigby after a long moment. He hadn't started recording. The conversation was informal at this stage, but for anything to be agreed, they would need to have it on record.

'I want to know what's on offer.'

'Do you have something to trade?'

K-Bar evaded the question. 'What do I get if I did?'

'What do you want?'

K-Bar smiled. It was the first bit of emotion he'd shown since entering the room.

'I'm innocent. I want to be released.'

'If you were innocent, you wouldn't be behind bars, would you?'

K-Bar's smile widened. 'Wouldn't be the first time you lot got it wrong. You don't have a clue what's really going on out there.'

Ignoring the jab, Rigby pressed on.

'You're looking at serious time, Keiron. If you want to spend your time dicking around, I'm sure you would be more comfortable doing that from your cell. You killed people — men and women — to further your interests. You're not innocent, and your hands are not clean. So, you can help yourself, or you can go back.'

'Innocent until proven guilty.' K-Bar remained unruffled, though his smile had vanished.

'We have nothing but time. Time, and some key witnesses.'

'That saw me kill people? Can't be the case if I'm innocent, can it?'

Rigby shook his head. His temper crept up, and he couldn't stop it.

'Innocent? You've no shame, have you? You take away somebodies daughter, a lifelong friend . . . a life. Then you sit here giving it *innocent until proven guilty*. You'll see what we have when you're in court fighting for your freedom.'

Rigby was unsure how he expected K-Bar to react, but he hadn't expected his eyes to light up. A moment later, he was back to normal.

'I think I made a mistake. I changed my mind, and I don't wanna talk anymore. You're never gonna get what you want. That's a promise.'

'What do you mean by that?'

Shaking his head, K-Bar rose to his feet. His solicitor, who had remained silent throughout the exchange, followed suit. After directing an officer to take him away, Rigby headed back to his desk. Murphy immediately came over.

'What did he have to say then?'

'Nothing. He was fishing to see what he could find out.'

Murphy frowned. 'That's a shame. I'd have liked to stuff Teflon in the cell next to him.'

'We'll let K-Bar stew a while, then go for him again. He is the key to bringing down the whole crew.'

———

AFTER RIGBY LEFT, K-Bar asked to speak with his solicitor. The officer was hesitant, but allowed it after a glance over his shoulder to see who was around.

'What was the point of that, Mr Barrett?' the solicitor started. 'You overplayed your hand with the officers, which didn't help our position.'

K-Bar grinned.

'There was never a deal to be made. I just wanted to confirm something.'

'What could you have possibly confirmed from that interaction?' The solicitor frowned. K-Bar's grin only widened.

'We don't have long, but I need you to pass on a message for me.'

ALSO BY RICKY BLACK

The Target Series:

Origins: The Road To Power

Target

Target Part 2: The Takedown

Target Part 3: Absolute Power

The Complete Target Collection

The Deeds Family Series:

Blood & Business

Good Deed, Bad Deeds

Deeds to the City

READ BLOOD AND BUSINESS

Tyrone Dunn wants to take over Leeds, and he is willing to battle anyone who gets in his way.

Even family.

Will it be settled by blood . . . or business?

Order now, and find out.

ABOUT RICKY BLACK

Ricky Black was born and raised in Chapeltown, Leeds. He began writing seriously in 2004, working on mainly crime pieces.

In 2016, he published the first of his crime series, Target, and has published seven more books since.

Visit https://rickyblackbooks.com for information regarding new releases and special offers and promotions.

For MyMy.

It's all for you.

© Ricky Black 2019. All rights reserved worldwide. No part of this book may be reproduced or copied without the expressed written permission of the Author.

This book is a work of fiction. Characters and events in this novel are the product of the author's imagination. Any similarity to persons living or dead is purely coincidental.

Printed in Great Britain
by Amazon